# bad machinery

## THE CASE OF THE FIRE INSIDE

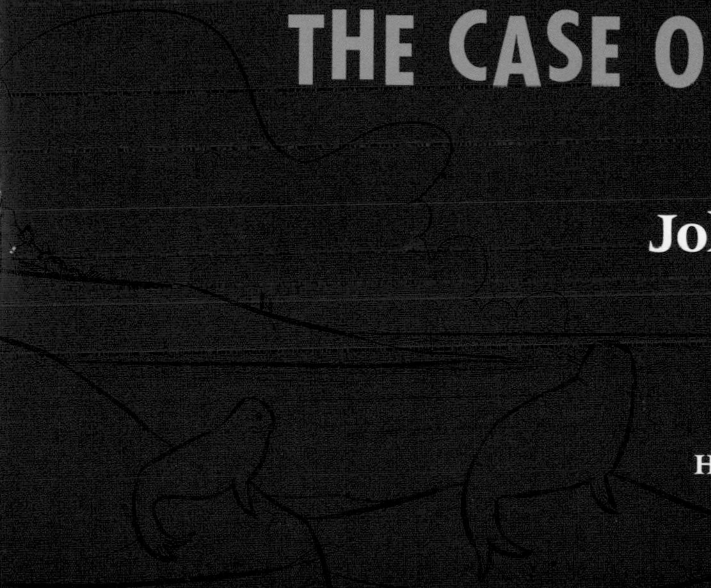

by
**John Allison**

Edited by
**Ari Yarwood**

Designed by
**Hilary Thompson**

**PUBLISHED BY ONI PRESS INC.**
*founder & chief financial officer,* **Joe Nozemack**
*publisher,* **James Lucas Jones**
*v.p. of creative & business development,* **Charlie Chu**
*director of operations,* **Brad Rooks**
*marketing manager,* **Rachel Reed**
*director of publicity,* **Melissa Meszaros**
*director of sales,* **Margot Wood**
*director of design & production,* **Troy Look**
*senior graphic designer,* **Hilary Thompson**
*junior graphic designer,* **Kate Z. Stone**
*junior graphic designer,* **Sonja Synak**
*digital prepress lead,* **Angie Knowles**
*executive editor,* **Ari Yarwood**
*senior editor,* **Robin Herrera**
*associate editor,* **Desiree Wilson**
*administrative assistant,* **Alissa Sallah**
*logistics associate,* **Jung Lee**

onipress.com
facebook.com/onipress
twitter.com/onipress
onipress.tumblr.com
instagram.com/onipress

First Edition: April 2016
Pocket Edition: June 2018

ISBN 978-1-62010-504-7
eISBN 978-1-62010-298-5

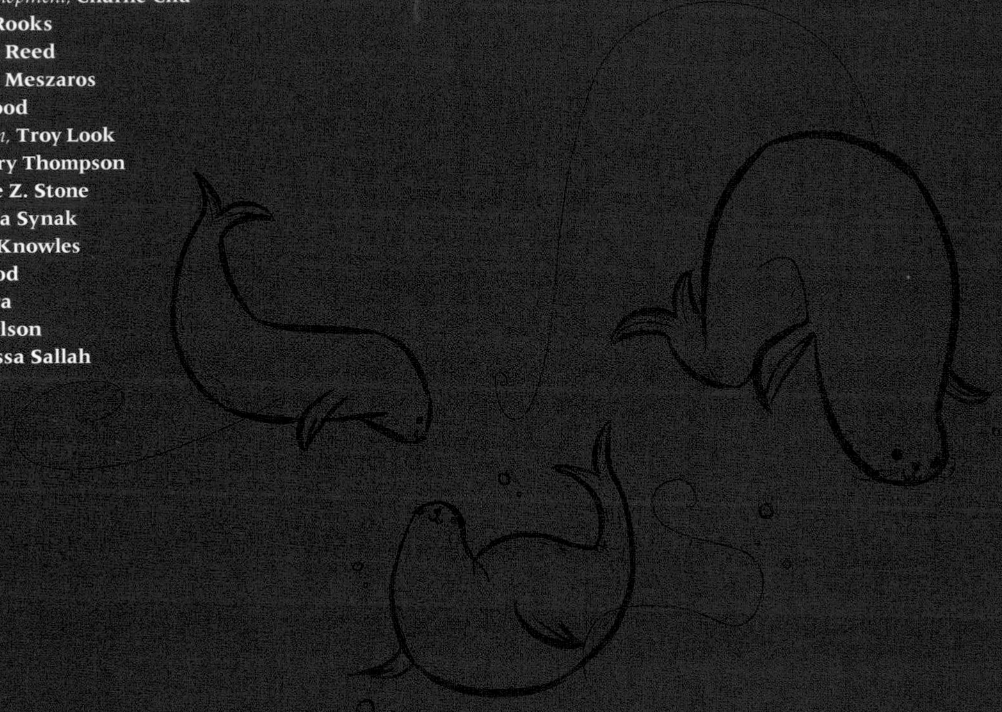



Printed in China.

Library of Congress Control Number: 2017959236

1 2 3 4 5 6 7 8 9 10

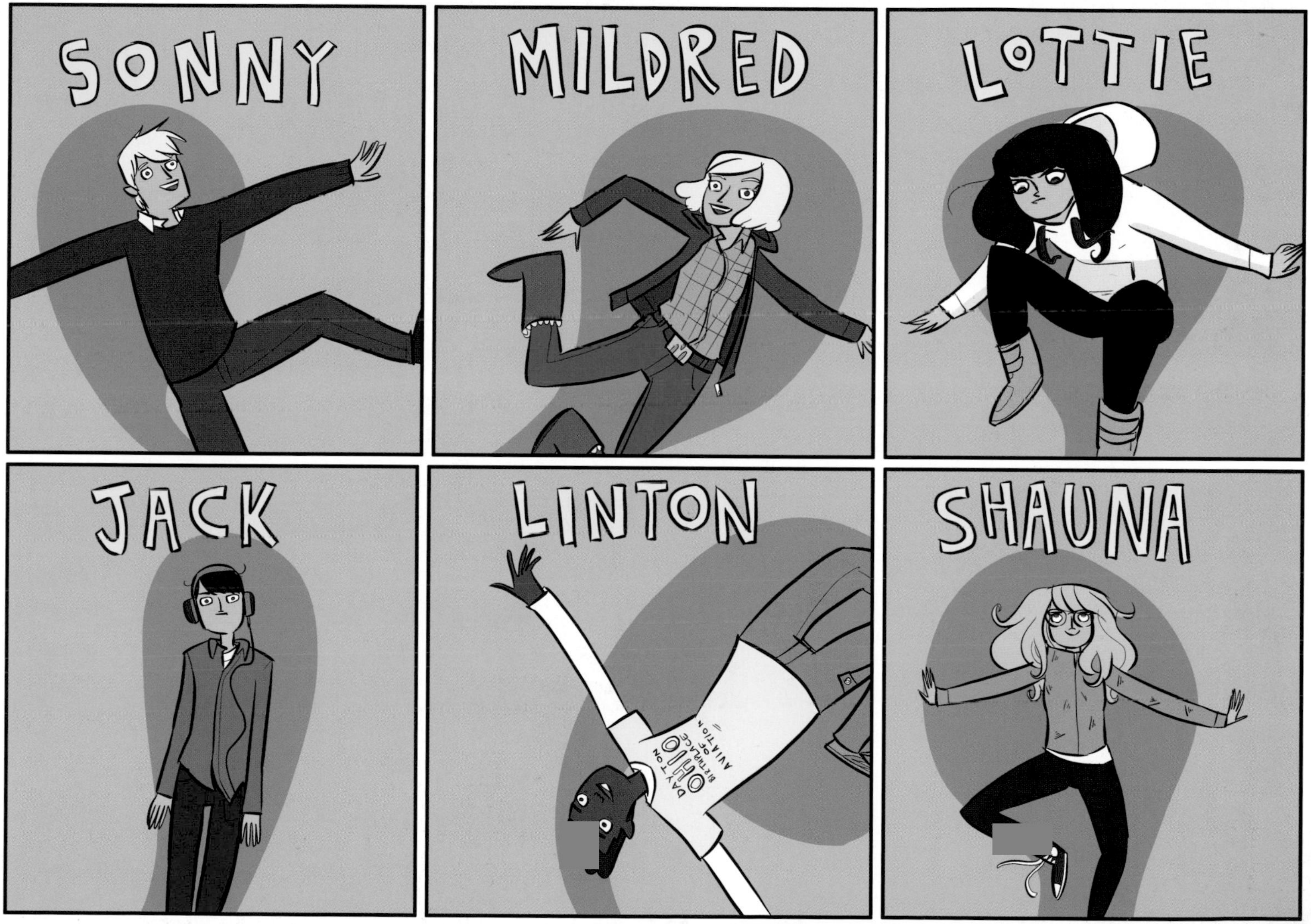
SONNY
MILDRED
LOTTIE
JACK
LINTON
DAYTON OHIO BIRTHPLACE OF AVIATION
SHAUNA

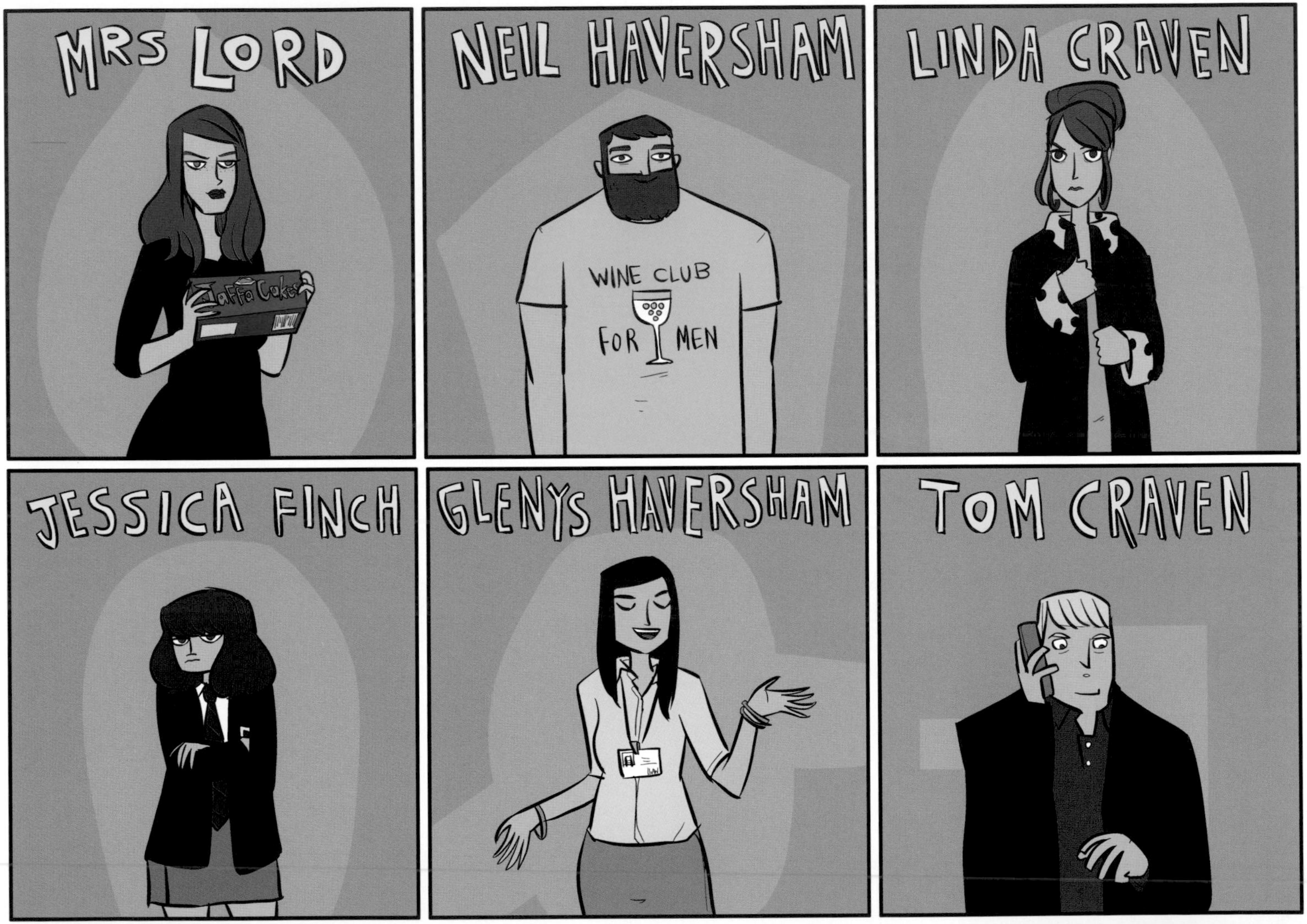
MRS LORD
Jaffa Cakes
NEIL HAVERSHAM
WINE CLUB FOR MEN
LINDA CRAVEN
JESSICA FINCH
GLENYS HAVERSHAM
TOM CRAVEN

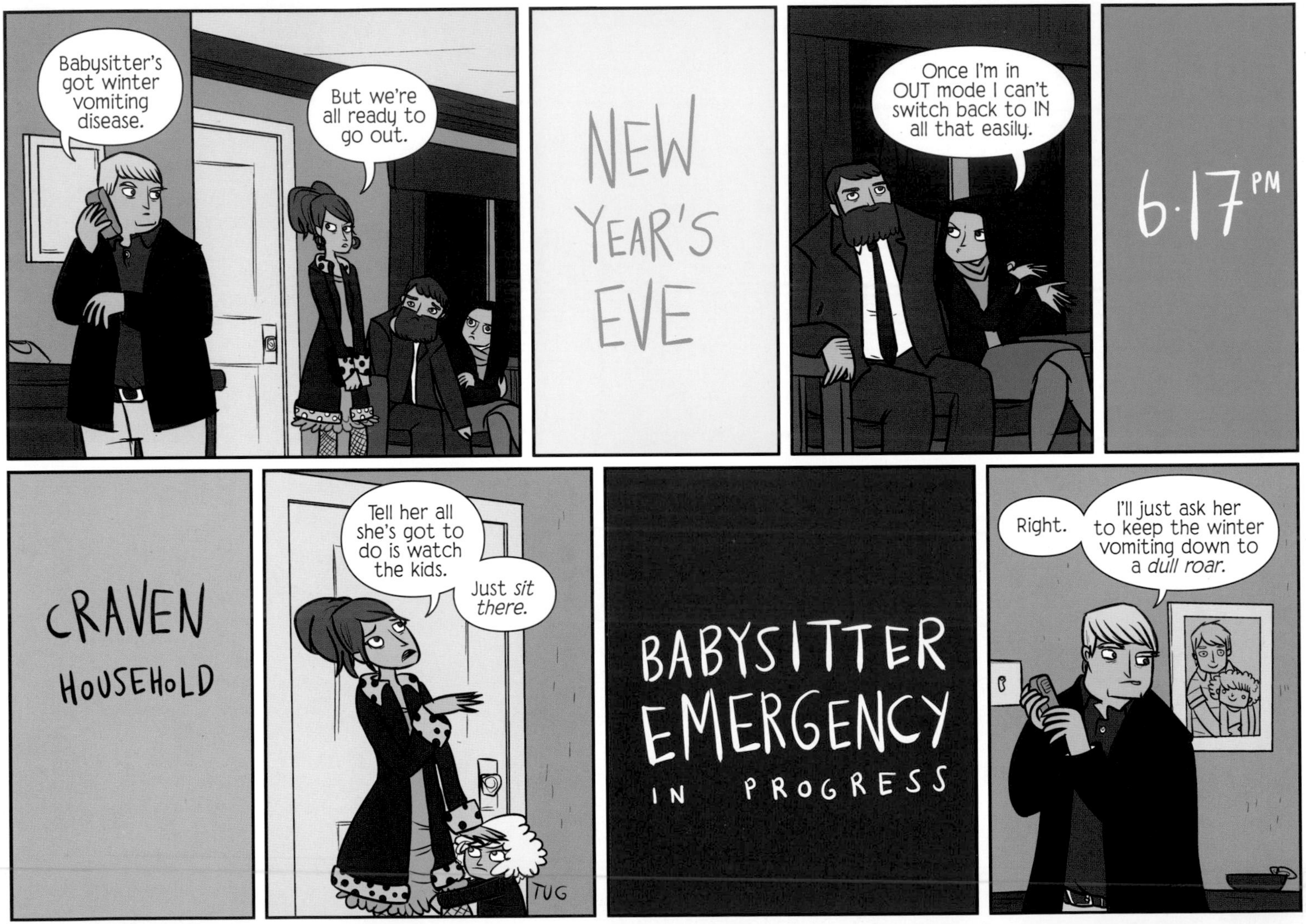
Babysitter's got winter vomiting disease.
But we're all ready to go out.
NEW YEAR'S EVE
Once I'm in OUT mode I can't switch back to IN all that easily.
6·17 PM
CRAVEN HOUSEHOLD
Tell her all she's got to do is watch the kids.
Just *sit there.*
TUG
BABYSITTER EMERGENCY IN PROGRESS
Right.
I'll just ask her to keep the winter vomiting down to a *dull roar.*

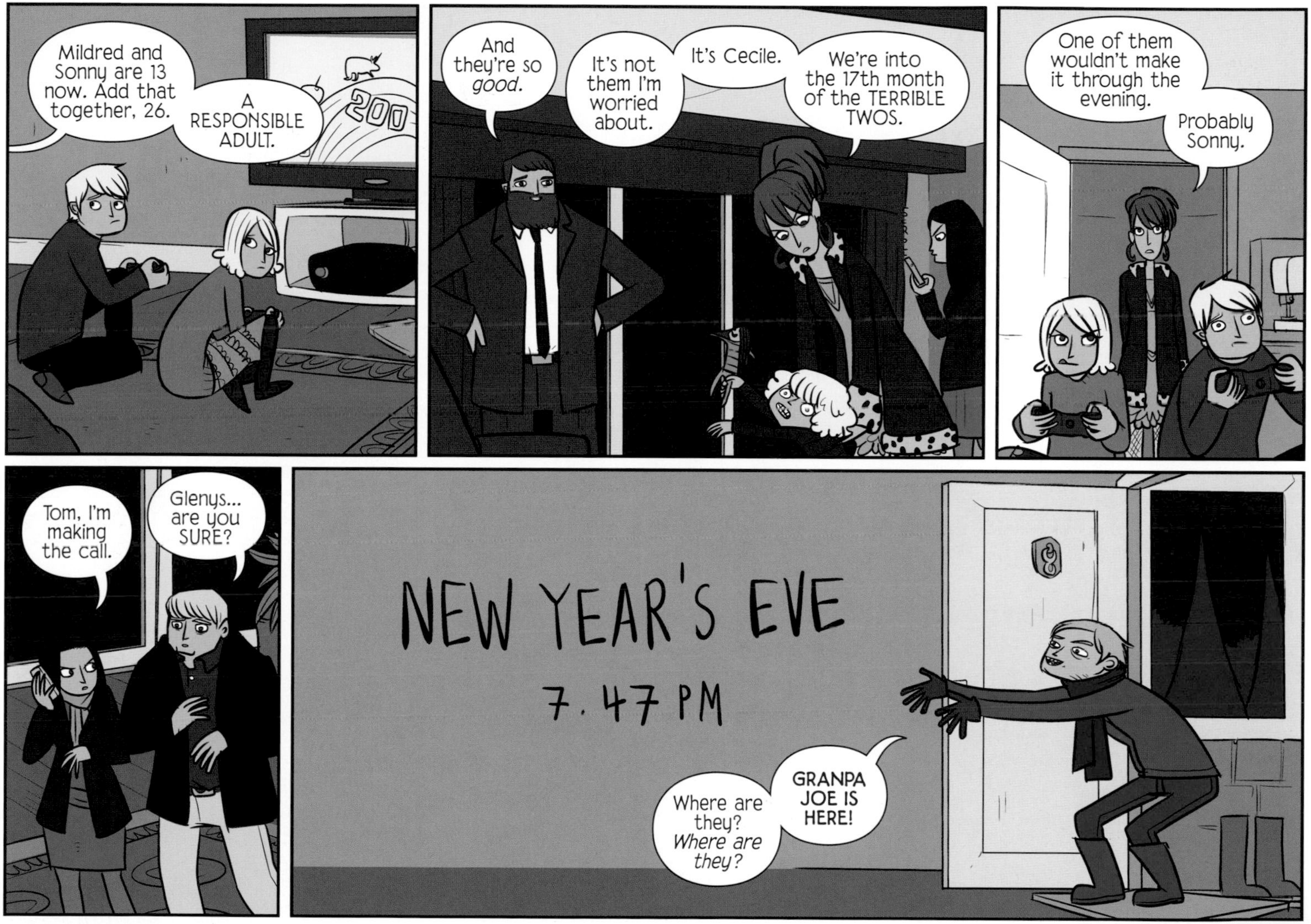
Mildred and Sonny are 13 now. Add that together, 26.
A RESPONSIBLE ADULT.
200
And they're so *good*.
It's not them I'm worried about.
It's Cecile.
We're into the 17th month of the TERRIBLE TWOS.
One of them wouldn't make it through the evening.
Probably Sonny.
Tom, I'm making the call.
Glenys... are you SURE?
NEW YEAR'S EVE
7.47 PM
GRANPA JOE IS HERE!
Where are they? *Where are they?*

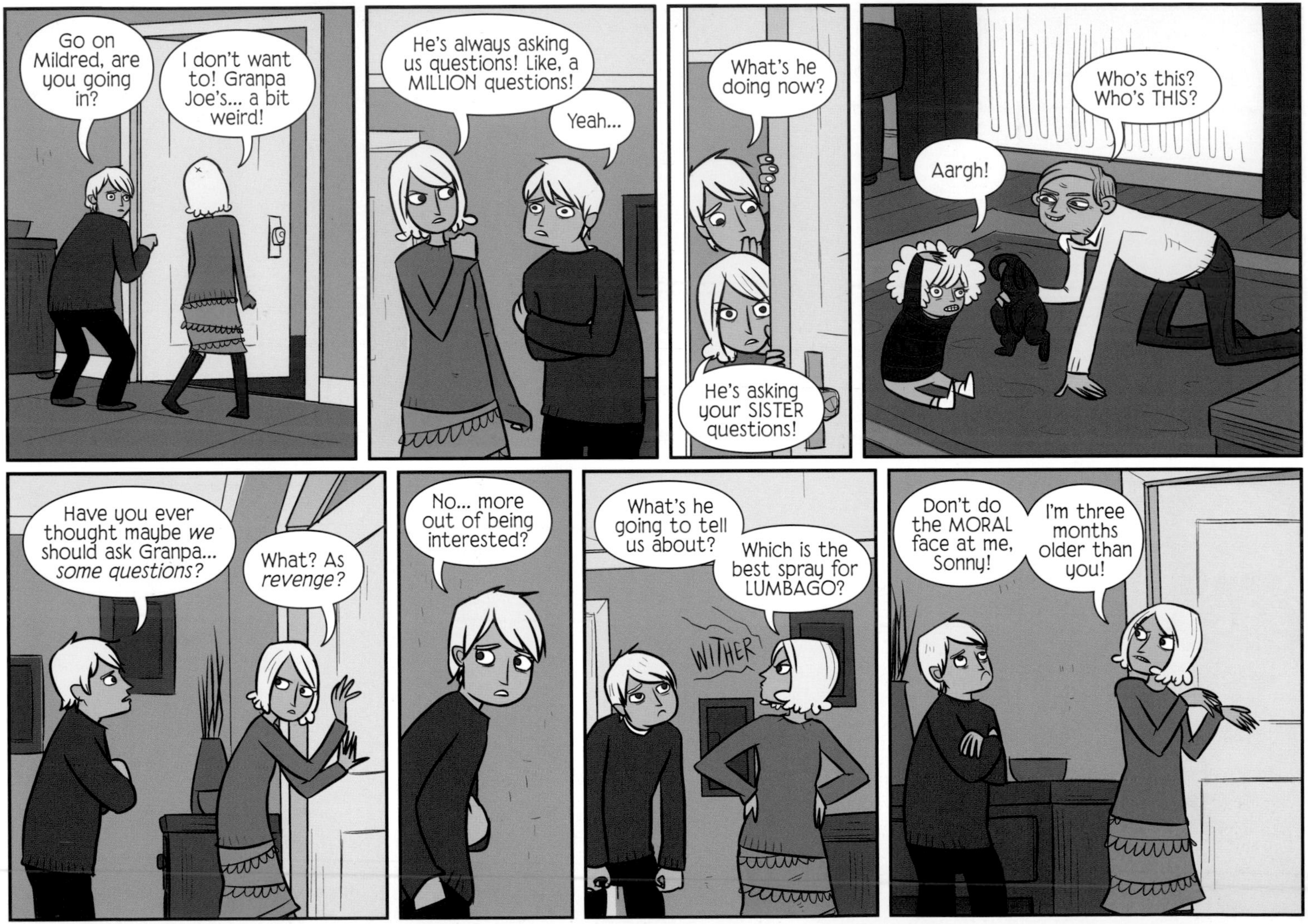
Go on Mildred, are you going in?
I don't want to! Granpa Joe's... a bit weird!
He's always asking us questions! Like, a MILLION questions!
Yeah...
What's he doing now?
He's asking your SISTER questions!
Who's this? Who's THIS?
Aargh!
Have you ever thought maybe *we* should ask Granpa... *some questions*?
What? As *revenge*?
No... more out of being interested?
What's he going to tell us about?
Which is the best spray for LUMBAGO?
WITHER
Don't do the MORAL face at me, Sonny!
I'm three months older than you!

The Case of the Fire Inside

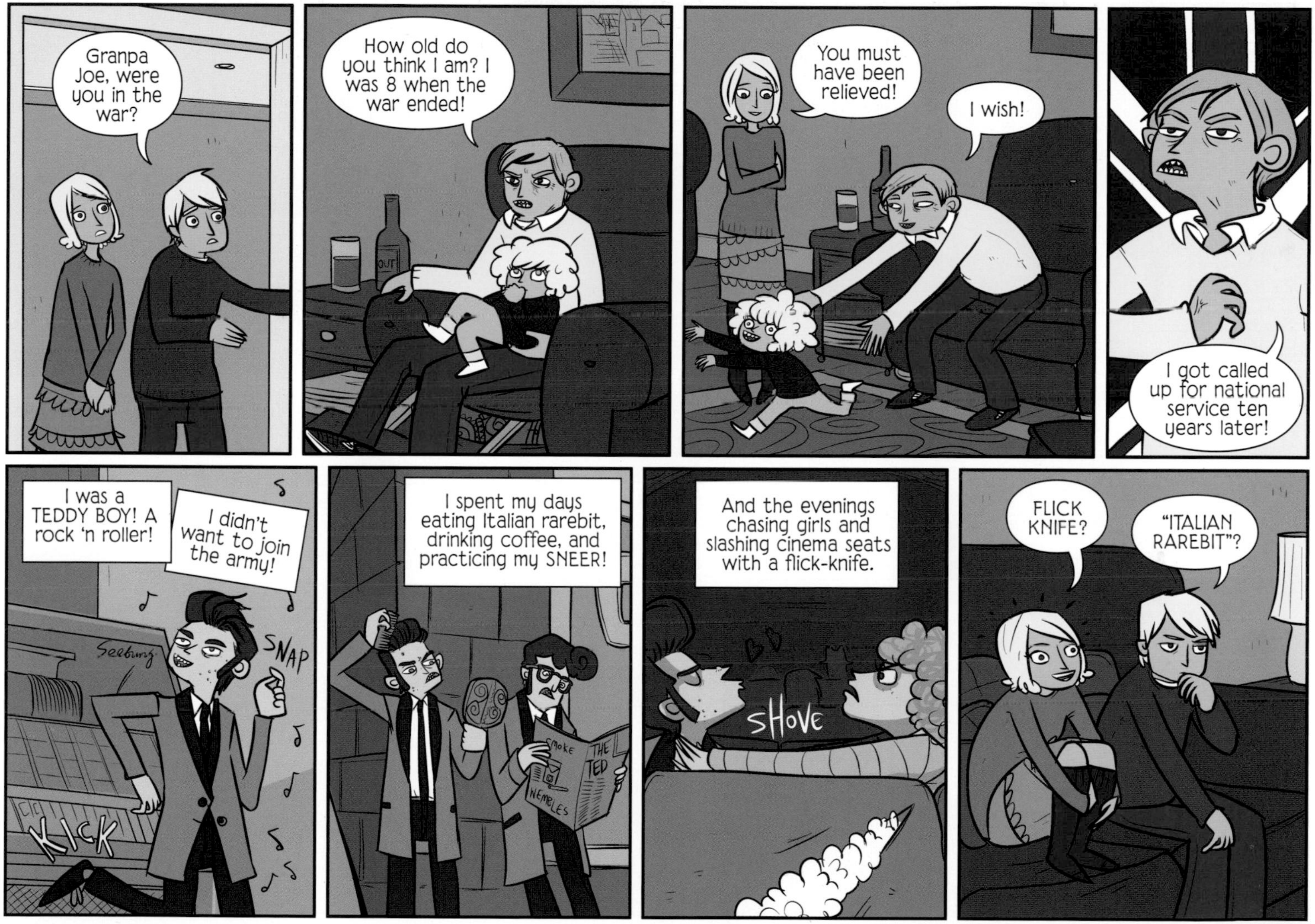

Granpa Joe, were you in the war?
How old do you think I am? I was 8 when the war ended!
OUT
You must have been relieved!
I wish!
I got called up for national service ten years later!
I was a TEDDY BOY! A rock 'n roller!
I didn't want to join the army!
Seeburg
SNAP
KICK
I spent my days eating Italian rarebit, drinking coffee, and practicing my SNEER!
SMOKE
THE TED
NEMPLES
And the evenings chasing girls and slashing cinema seats with a flick-knife.
SHOVE
FLICK KNIFE?
"ITALIAN RAREBIT"?

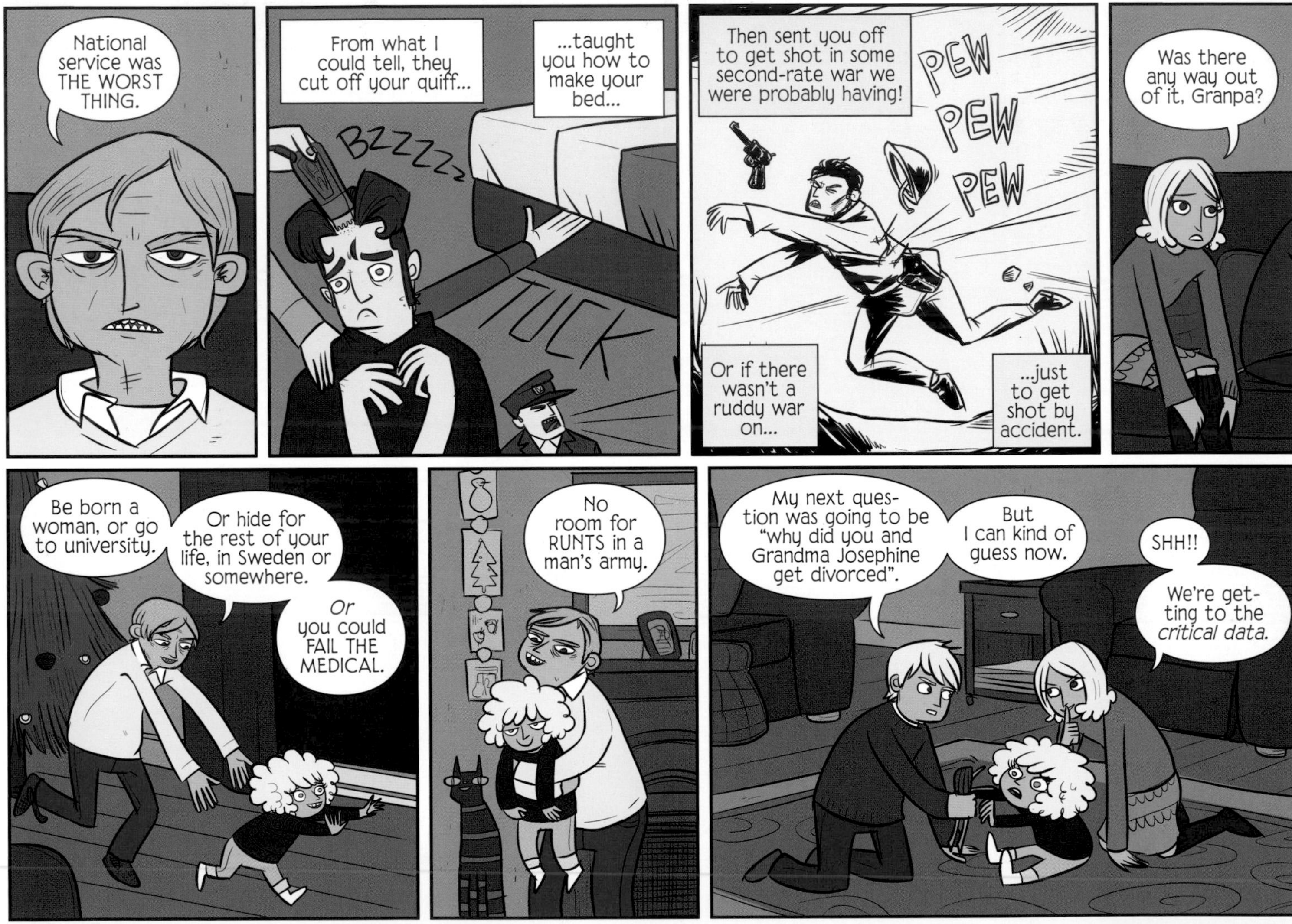
National service was THE WORST THING.
From what I could tell, they cut off your quiff...
...taught you how to make your bed...
BZZZZZZ
TUCK
Then sent you off to get shot in some second-rate war we were probably having!
PEW
PEW
PEW
Or if there wasn't a ruddy war on...
...just to get shot by accident.
Was there any way out of it, Granpa?
Be born a woman, or go to university.
Or hide for the rest of your life, in Sweden or somewhere.
*Or* you could FAIL THE MEDICAL.
No room for RUNTS in a man's army.
My next question was going to be "why did you and Grandma Josephine get divorced".
But I can kind of guess now.
SHH!!
We're getting to the *critical data.*

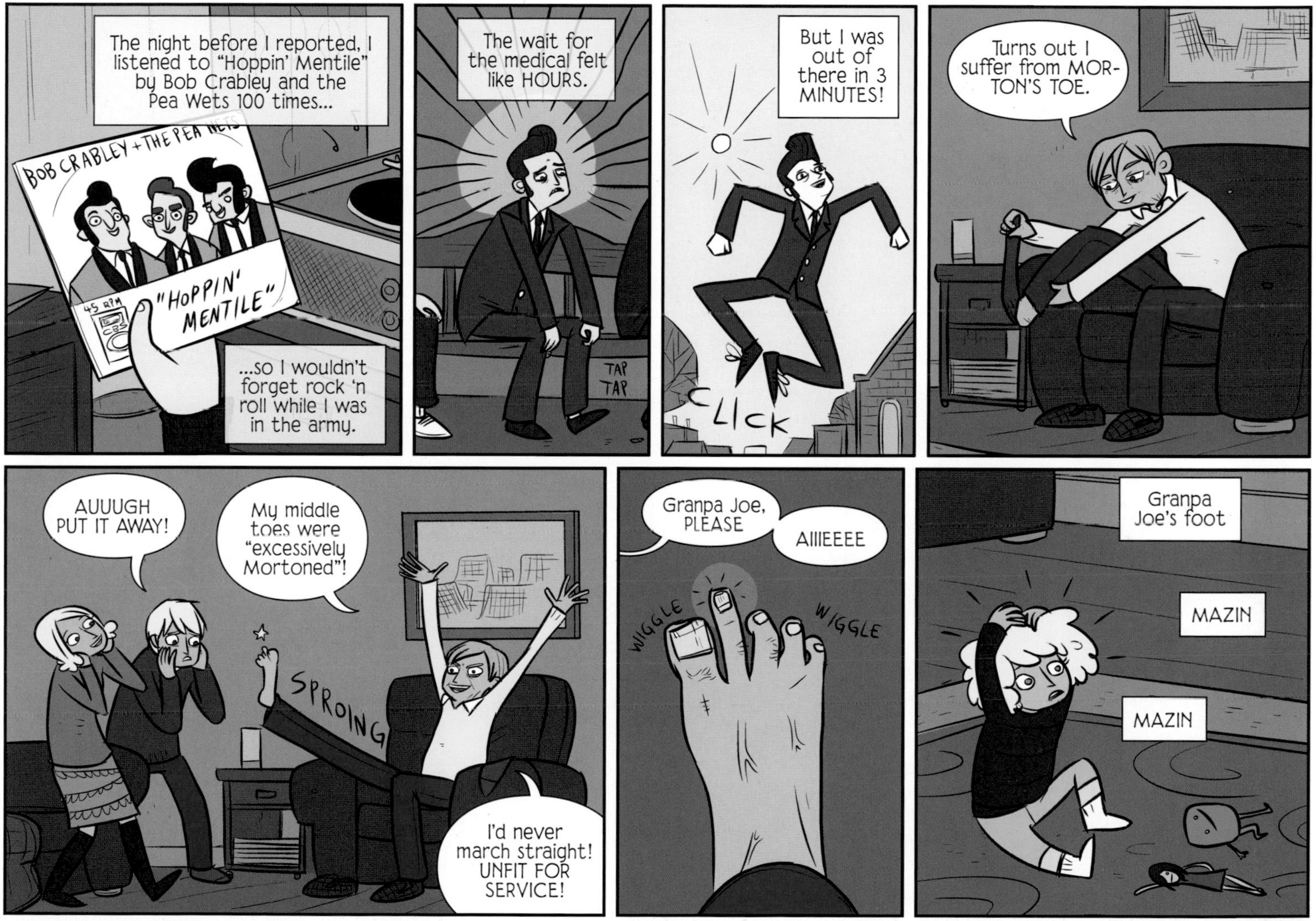
The night before I reported, I listened to "Hoppin' Mentile" by Bob Crabley and the Pea Wets 100 times...
BOB CRABLEY + THE PEA WETS
"HOPPIN' MENTILE"
45 RPM
...so I wouldn't forget rock 'n roll while I was in the army.
The wait for the medical felt like HOURS.
TAP TAP
But I was out of there in 3 MINUTES!
CLICK
Turns out I suffer from MORTON'S TOE.
AUUUGH PUT IT AWAY!
My middle toes were "excessively Mortoned"!
SPROING
I'd never march straight! UNFIT FOR SERVICE!
Granpa Joe, PLEASE
AIIIEEEE
WIGGLE
WIGGLE
Granpa Joe's foot
MAZIN
MAZIN

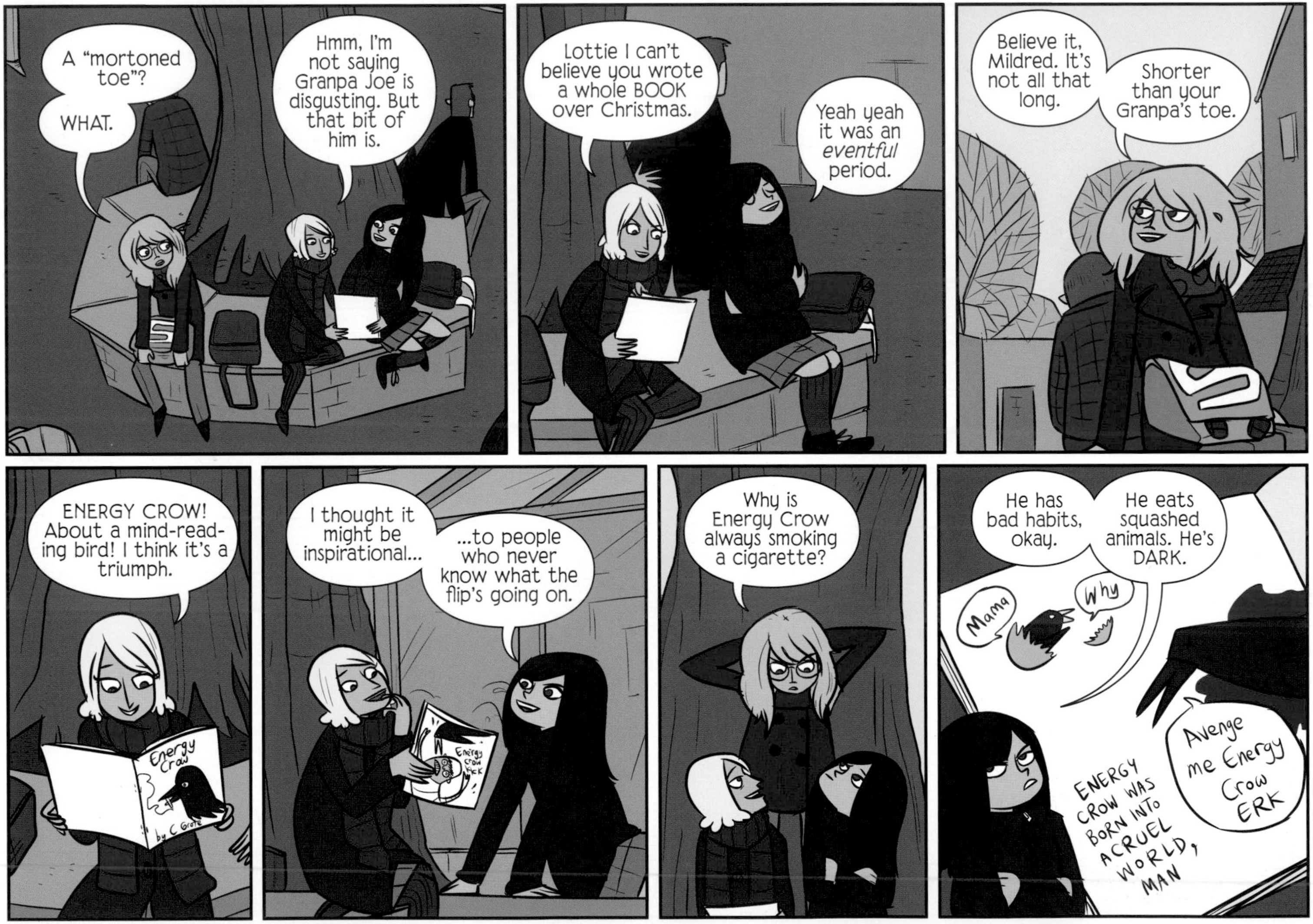
A "mortoned toe"?
WHAT.
Hmm, I'm not saying Granpa Joe is disgusting. But that bit of him is.
Lottie I can't believe you wrote a whole BOOK over Christmas.
Yeah yeah it was an *eventful* period.
Believe it, Mildred. It's not all that long.
Shorter than your Granpa's toe.
ENERGY CROW! About a mind-reading bird! I think it's a triumph.
Energy Crow
by C Grote
I thought it might be inspirational...
...to people who never know what the flip's going on.
Why is Energy Crow always smoking a cigarette?
He has bad habits, okay.
He eats squashed animals. He's DARK.
Mama
Why
ENERGY CROW WAS BORN INTO A CRUEL WORLD, MAN
Avenge me Energy Crow ERK

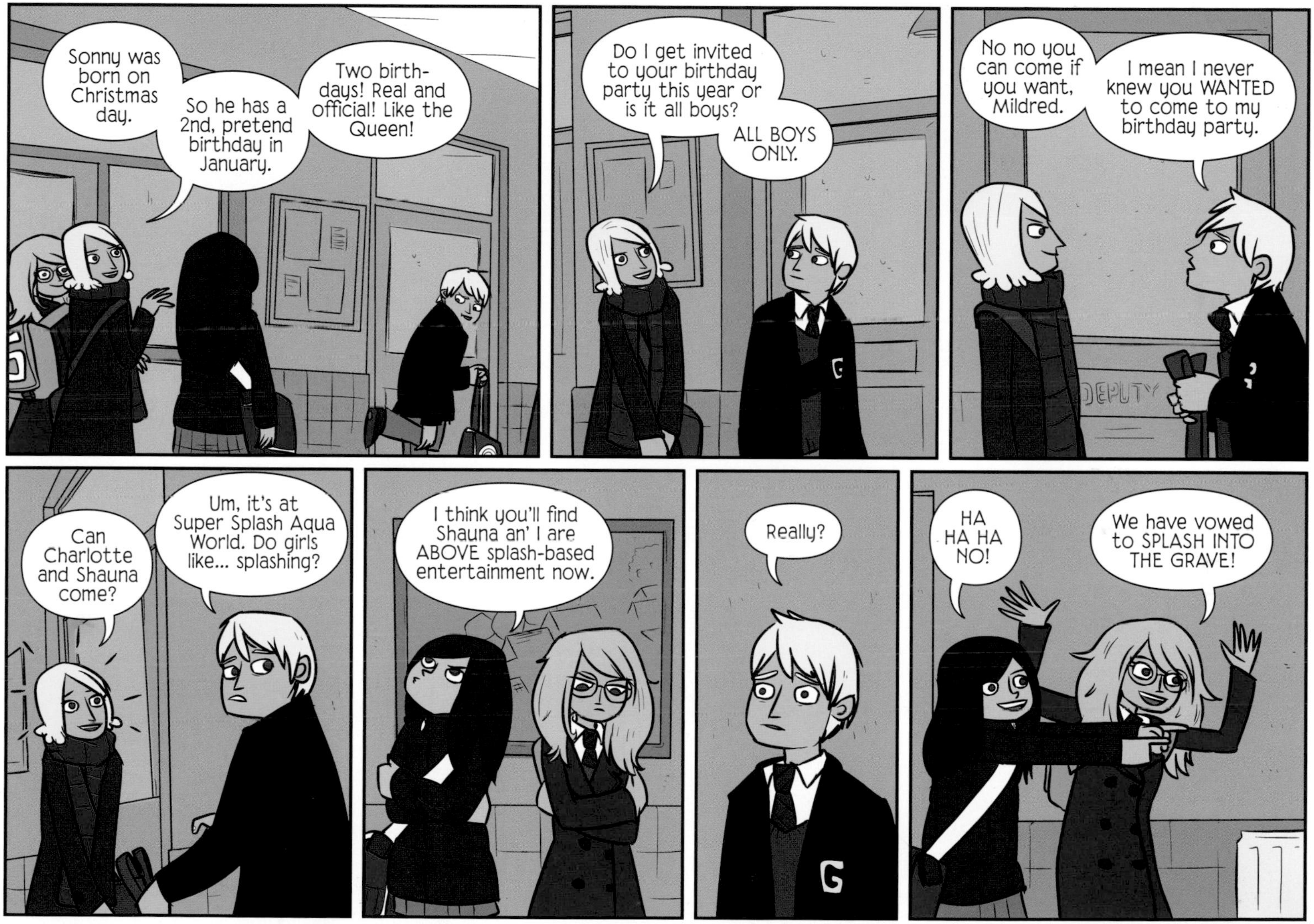
Sonny was born on Christmas day.
So he has a 2nd, pretend birthday in January.
Two birth-days! Real and official! Like the Queen!
Do I get invited to your birthday party this year or is it all boys?
ALL BOYS ONLY.
No no you can come if you want, Mildred.
I mean I never knew you WANTED to come to my birthday party.
DEPUTY
Can Charlotte and Shauna come?
Um, it's at Super Splash Aqua World. Do girls like... splashing?
I think you'll find Shauna an' I are ABOVE splash-based entertainment now.
Really?
HA HA HA NO!
We have vowed to SPLASH INTO THE GRAVE!

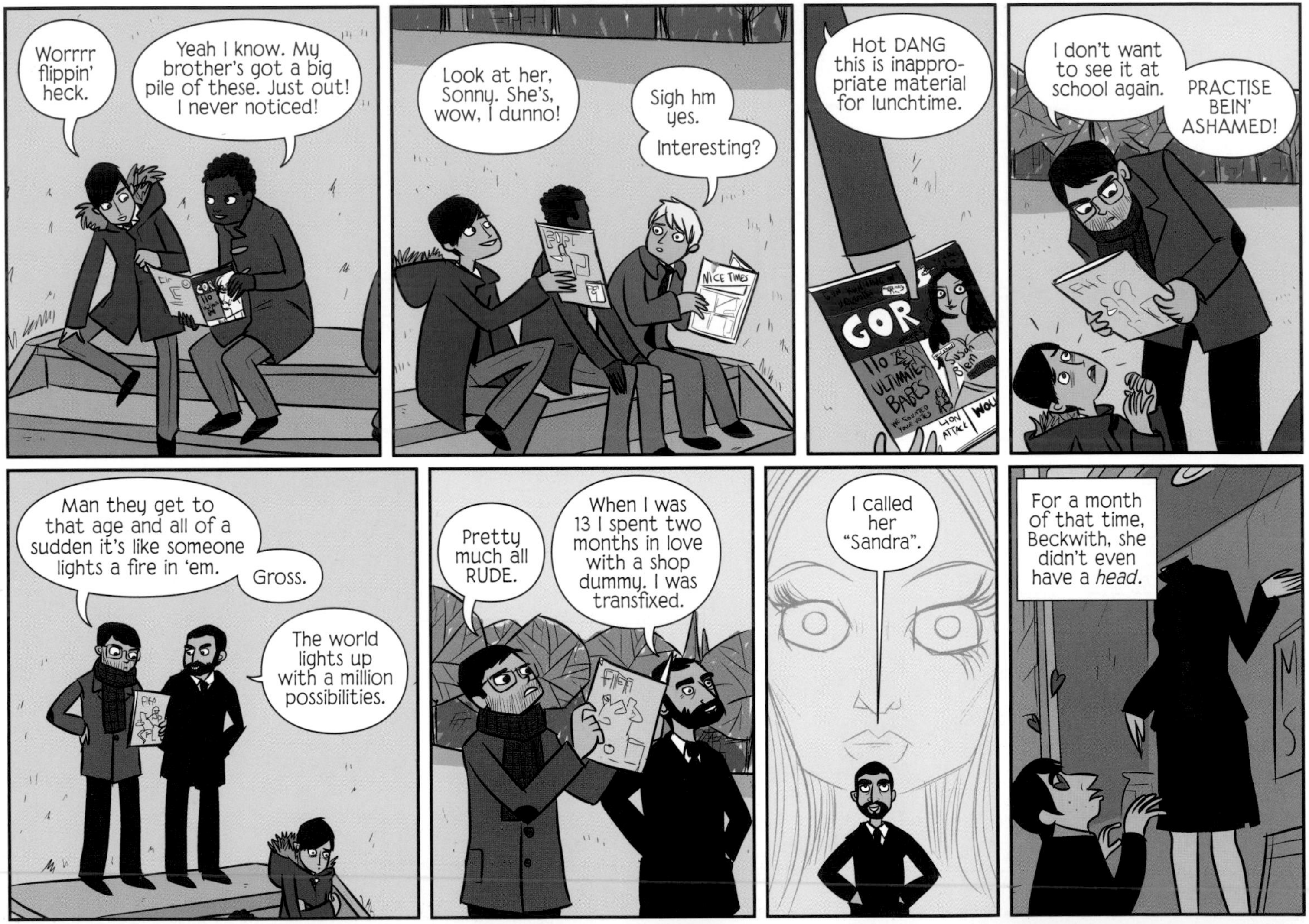
Worrrr flippin' heck.
Yeah I know. My brother's got a big pile of these. Just out! I never noticed!
Look at her, Sonny. She's, wow, I dunno!
Sigh hm yes.
Interesting?
NICE TIMES
Hot DANG this is inappropriate material for lunchtime.
GOR
110 ULTIMATE BABES
LION ATTACK
I don't want to see it at school again.
PRACTISE BEIN' ASHAMED!
Man they get to that age and all of a sudden it's like someone lights a fire in 'em.
Gross.
The world lights up with a million possibilities.
Pretty much all RUDE.
When I was 13 I spent two months in love with a shop dummy. I was transfixed.
I called her "Sandra".
For a month of that time, Beckwith, she didn't even have a *head*.

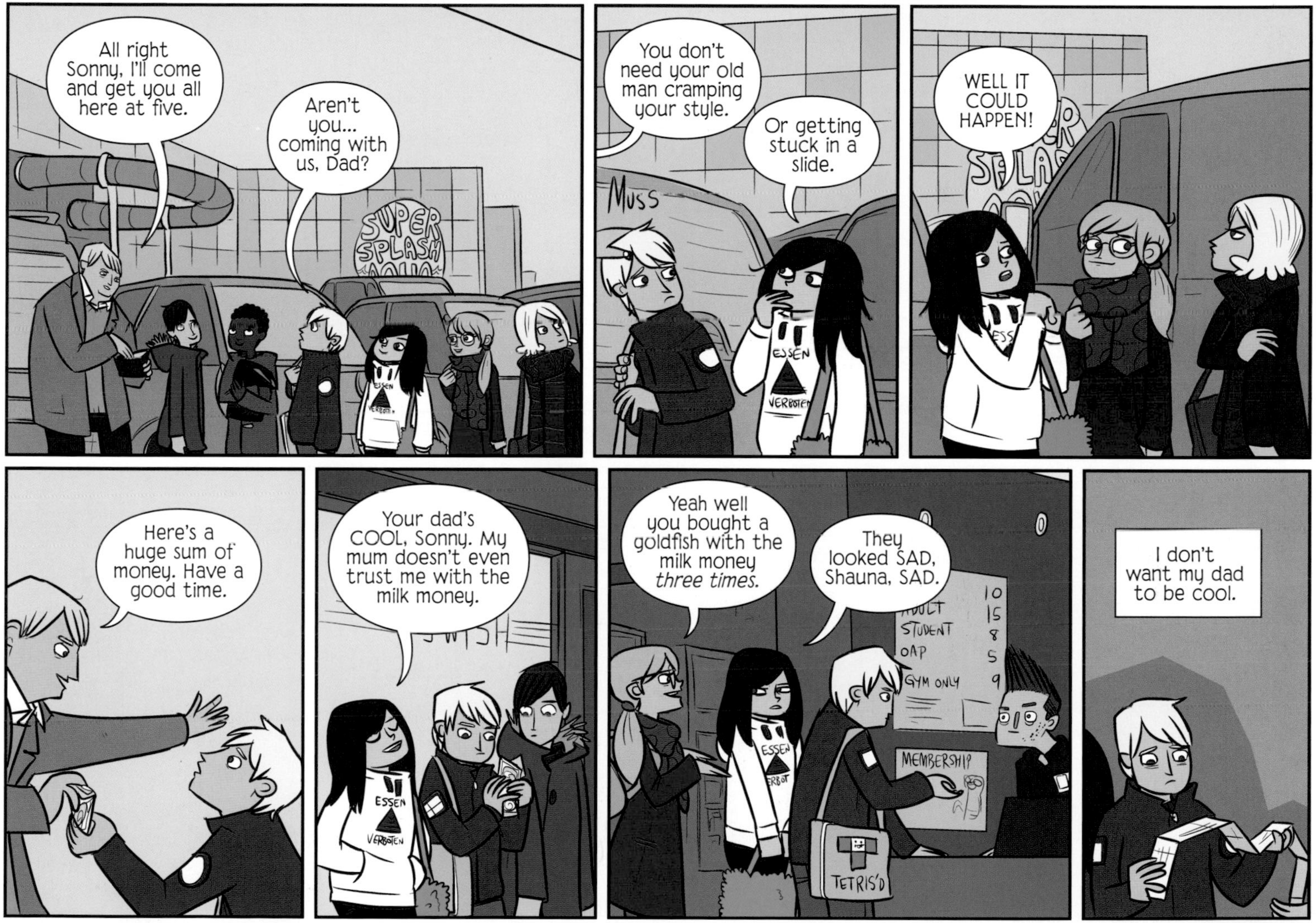
All right Sonny, I'll come and get you all here at five.
Aren't you... coming with us, Dad?
SUPER SPLASH
You don't need your old man cramping your style.
Or getting stuck in a slide.
MUSS
ESSEN
VERBOTEN
WELL IT COULD HAPPEN!
Here's a huge sum of money. Have a good time.
Your dad's COOL, Sonny. My mum doesn't even trust me with the milk money.
ESSEN
VERBOTEN
Yeah well you bought a goldfish with the milk money *three times.*
They looked SAD, Shauna, SAD.
STUDENT 8
OAP 5
GYM ONLY 9
MEMBERSHIP
TETRIS'D
I don't want my dad to be cool.

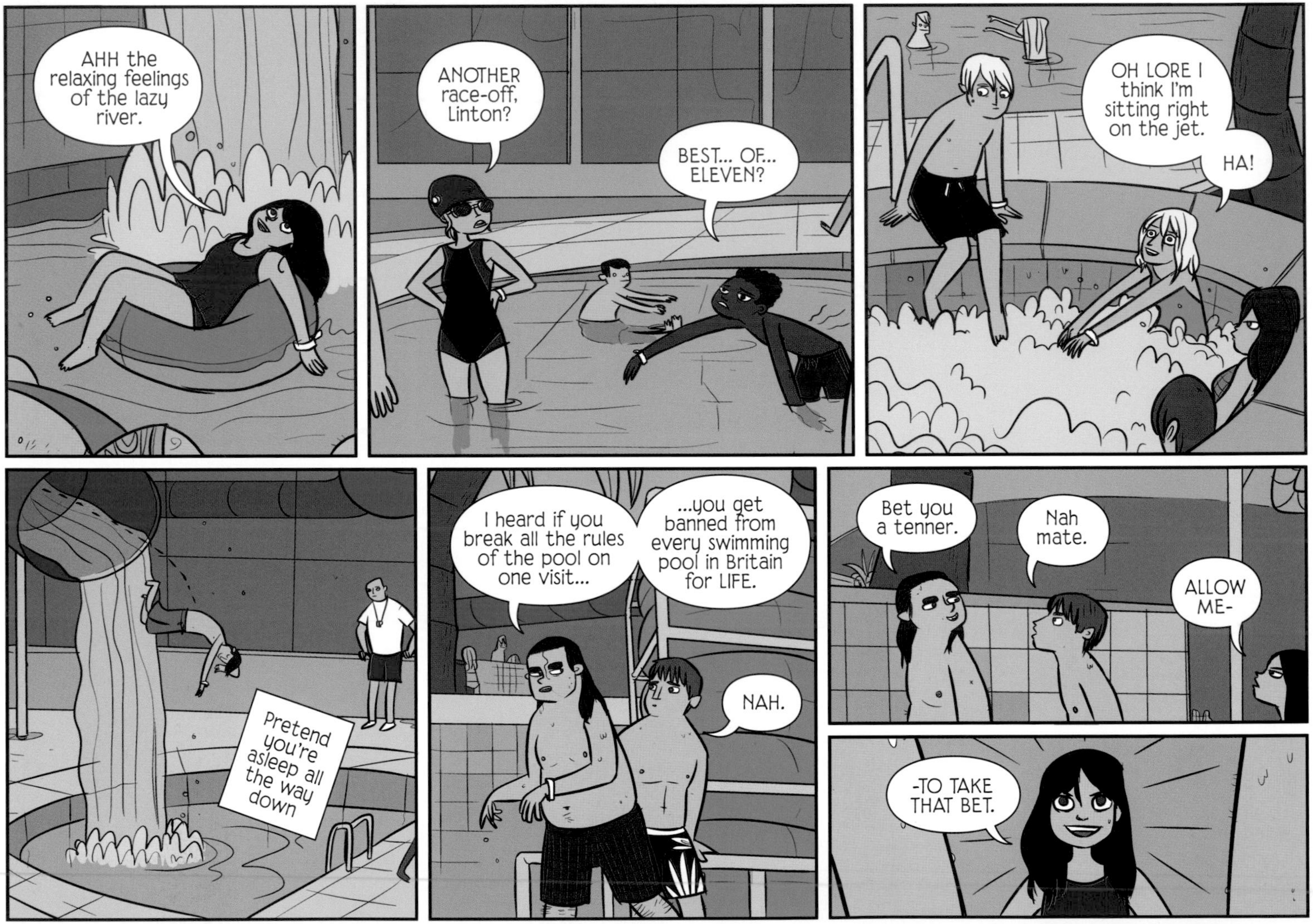
AHH the relaxing feelings of the lazy river.
ANOTHER race-off, Linton?
BEST... OF... ELEVEN?
OH LORE I think I'm sitting right on the jet.
HA!
Pretend you're asleep all the way down
I heard if you break all the rules of the pool on one visit...
...you get banned from every swimming pool in Britain for LIFE.
NAH.
Bet you a tenner.
Nah mate.
ALLOW ME-
-TO TAKE THAT BET.

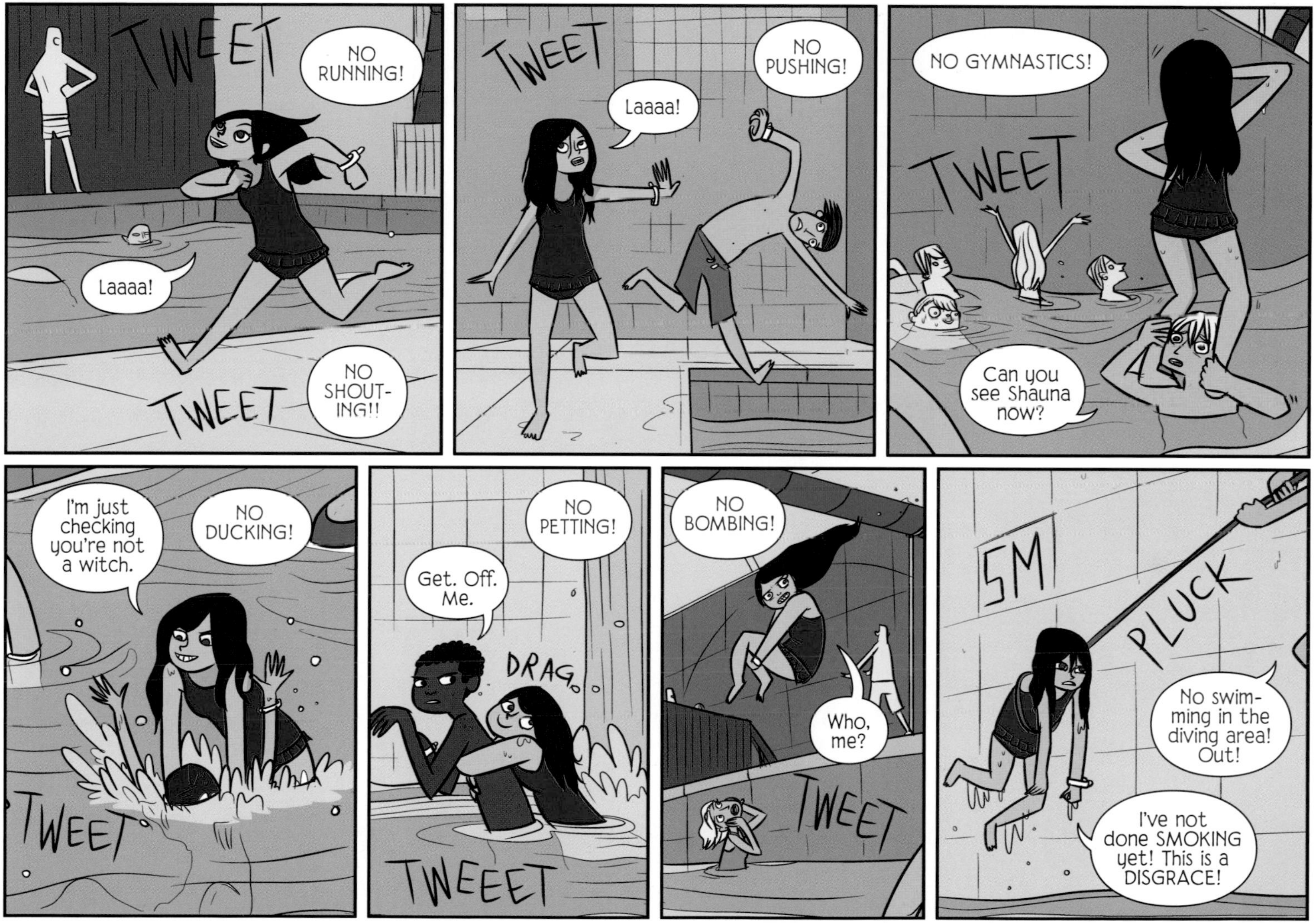
TWEET
NO RUNNING!
Laaaa!
TWEET
NO SHOUTING!!
TWEET
NO PUSHING!
Laaaa!
NO GYMNASTICS!
TWEET
Can you see Shauna now?
I'm just checking you're not a witch.
NO DUCKING!
TWEET
NO PETTING!
Get. Off. Me.
DRAG
TWEEET
NO BOMBING!
Who, me?
TWEET
5M
PLUCK
No swimming in the diving area! Out!
I've not done SMOKING yet! This is a DISGRACE!

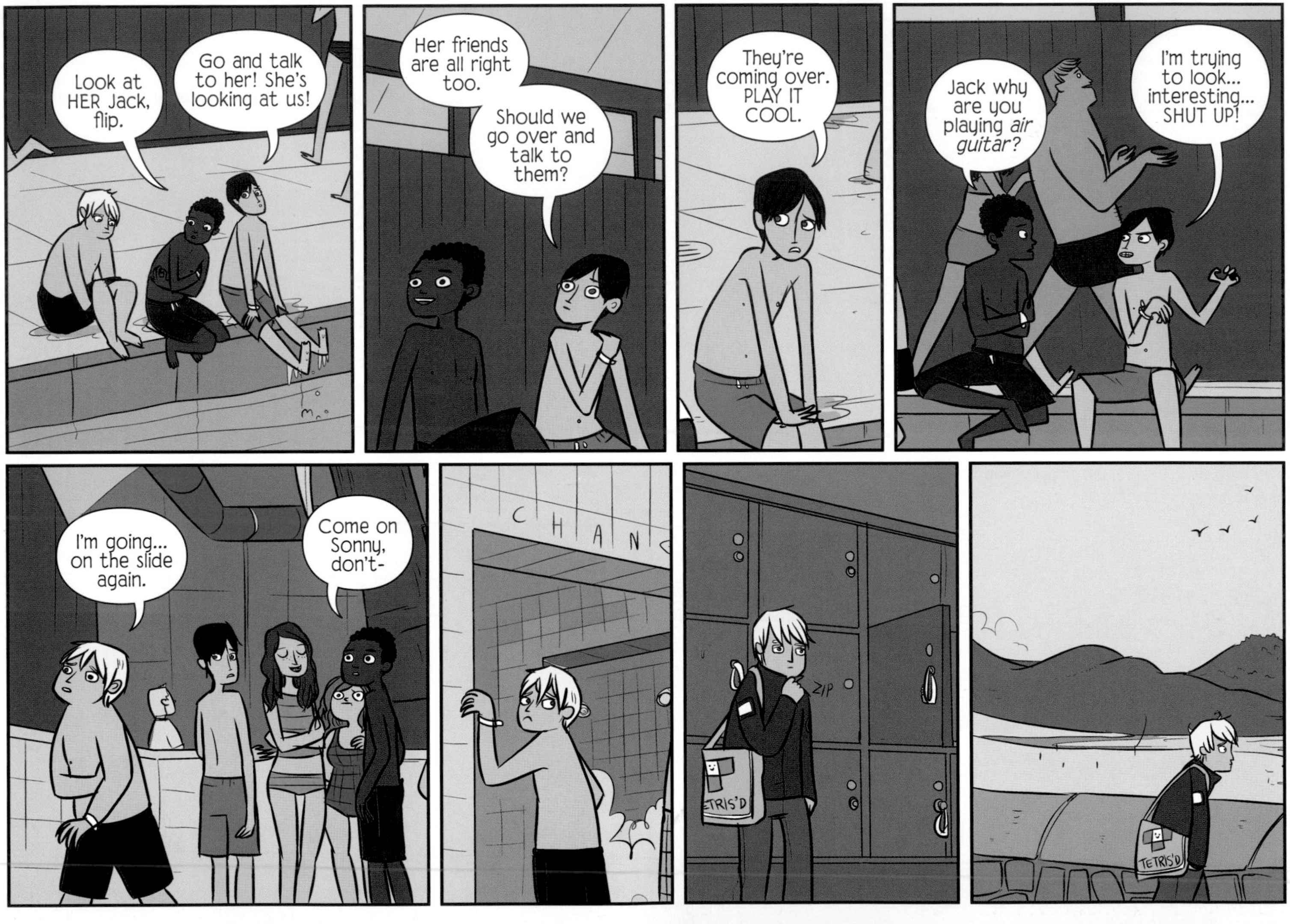
Look at HER Jack, flip.
Go and talk to her! She's looking at us!
Her friends are all right too.
Should we go over and talk to them?
They're coming over. PLAY IT COOL.
Jack why are you playing *air guitar*?
I'm trying to look... interesting... SHUT UP!
I'm going... on the slide again.
Come on Sonny, don't-
CHAN
ZIP
TETRIS'D
TETRIS'D

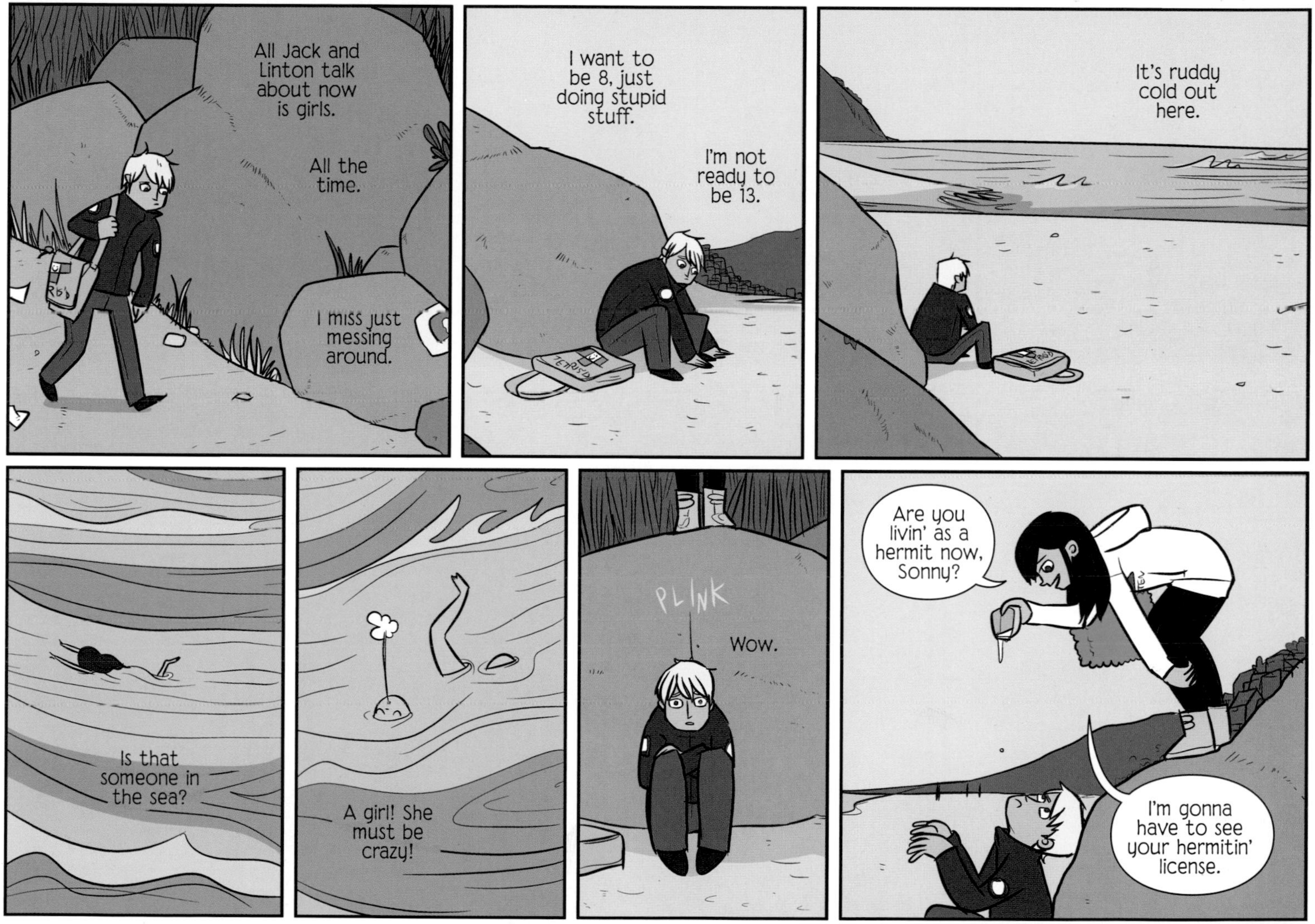
All Jack and Linton talk about now is girls.
All the time.
I miss just messing around.
I want to be 8, just doing stupid stuff.
I'm not ready to be 13.
It's ruddy cold out here.
Is that someone in the sea?
A girl! She must be crazy!
PLINK
Wow.
Are you livin' as a hermit now, Sonny?
I'm gonna have to see your hermitin' license.

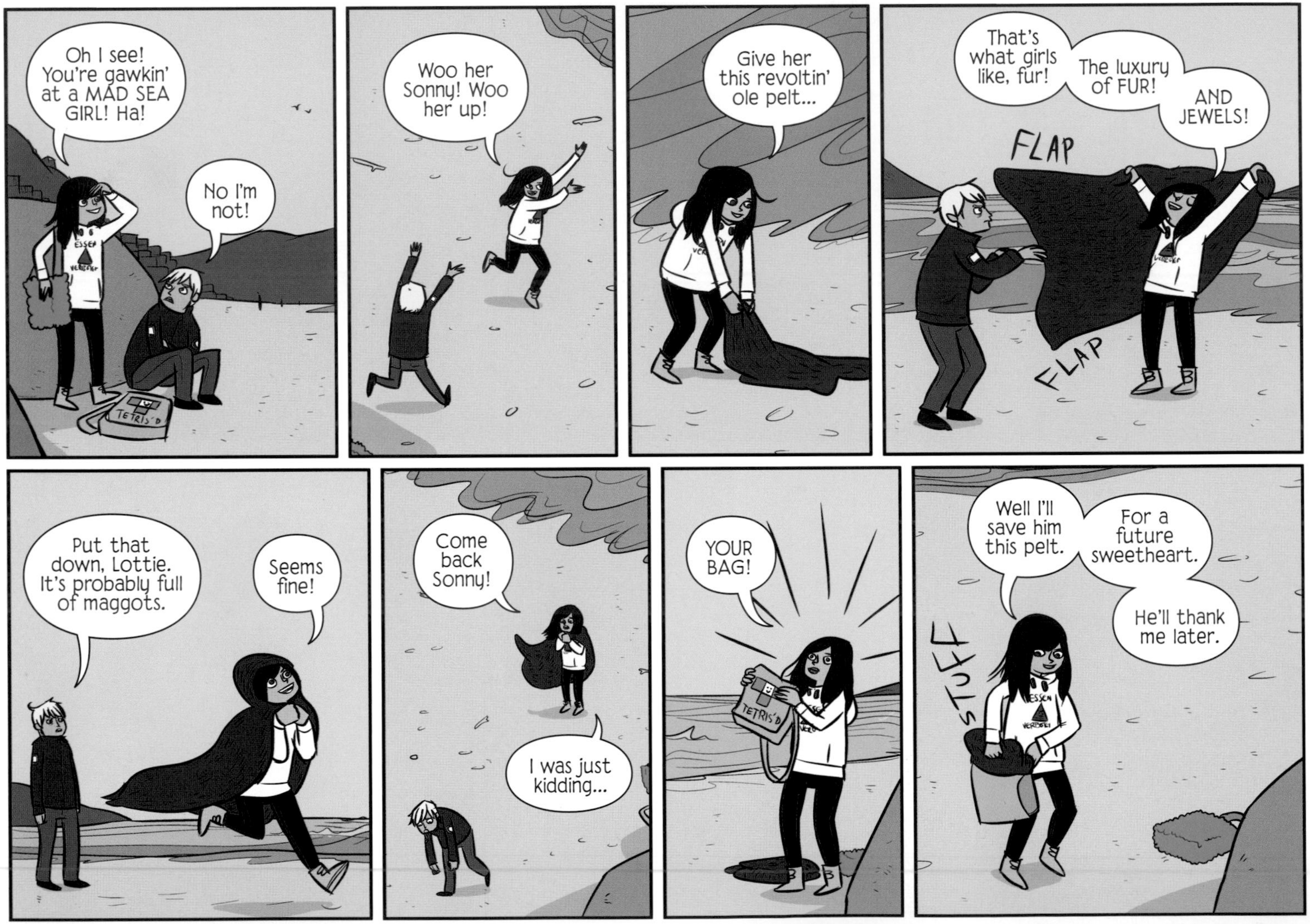
Oh I see! You're gawkin' at a MAD SEA GIRL! Ha!
No I'm not!
TETRIS'D
Woo her Sonny! Woo her up!
Give her this revoltin' ole pelt...
FLAP
That's what girls like, fur!
The luxury of FUR!
AND JEWELS!
FLAP
Put that down, Lottie. It's probably full of maggots.
Seems fine!
Come back Sonny!
I was just kidding...
YOUR BAG!
TETRIS'D
STUFF
Well I'll save him this pelt.
For a future sweetheart.
He'll thank me later.

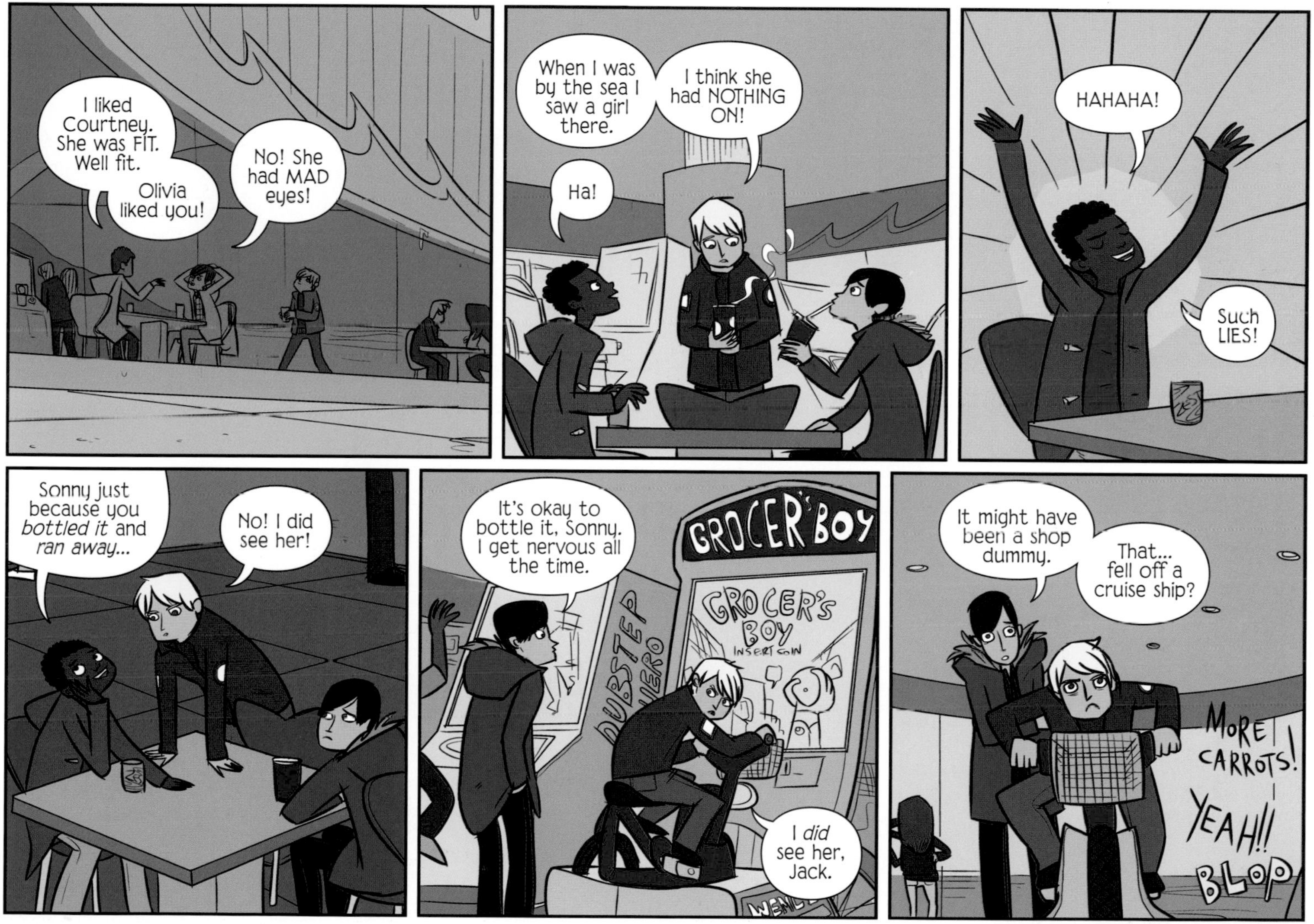

I liked Courtney. She was FIT. Well fit.
Olivia liked you!
No! She had MAD eyes!
When I was by the sea I saw a girl there.
I think she had NOTHING ON!
Ha!
HAHAHA!
Such LIES!
Sonny just because you *bottled it* and *ran away*...
No! I did see her!
It's okay to bottle it, Sonny. I get nervous all the time.
GROCER'S BOY
DUBSTEP
GROCER'S BOY
INSERT COIN
I *did* see her, Jack.
It might have been a shop dummy.
That... fell off a cruise ship?
MORE CARROTS!
YEAH!!
BLOP

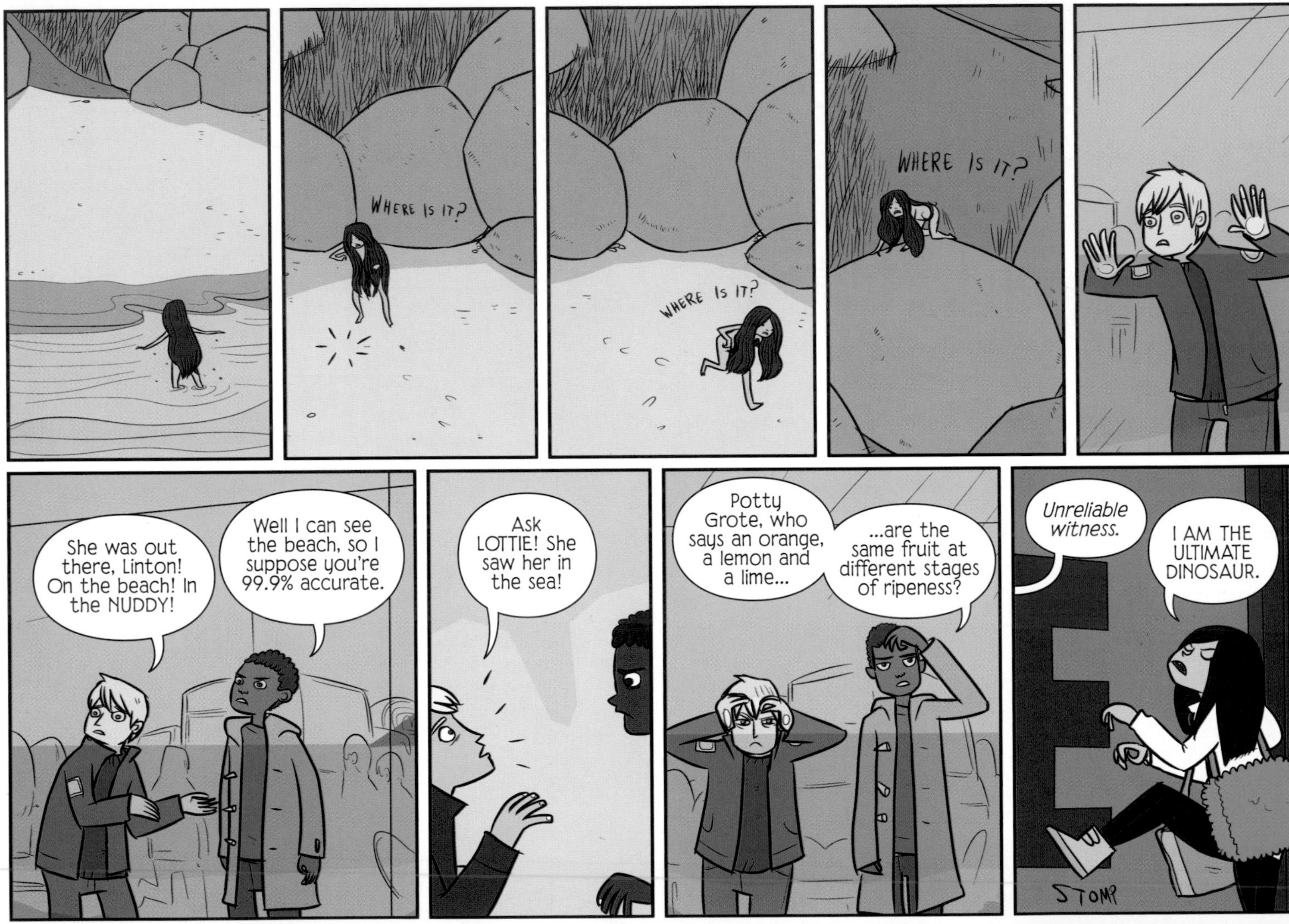
WHERE IS IT?
WHERE IS IT?
WHERE IS IT?
She was out there, Linton! On the beach! In the NUDDY!
Well I can see the beach, so I suppose you're 99.9% accurate.
Ask LOTTIE! She saw her in the sea!
Potty Grote, who says an orange, a lemon and a lime...
...are the same fruit at different stages of ripeness?
*Unreliable witness.*
I AM THE ULTIMATE DINOSAUR.
STOMP

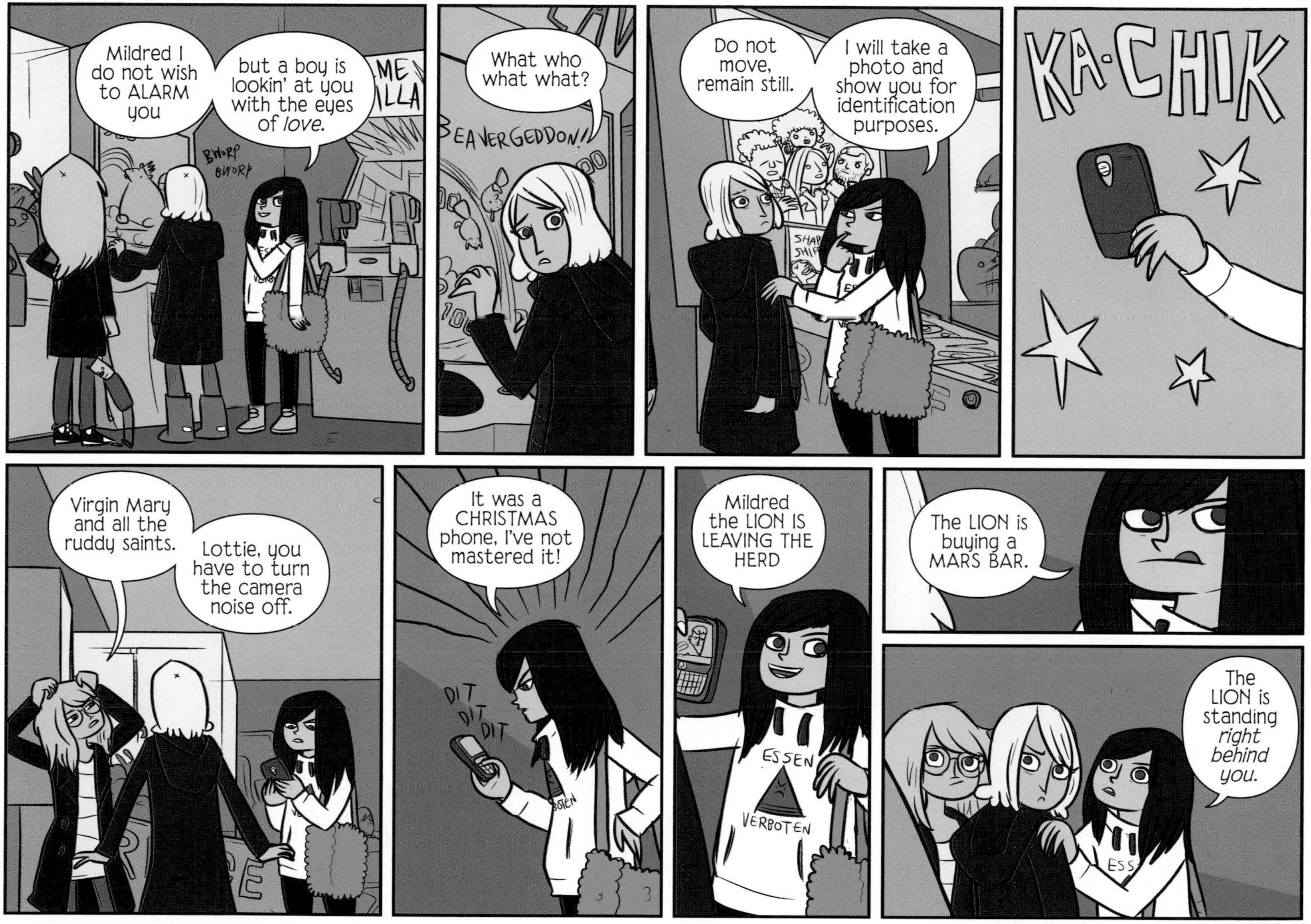
Mildred I do not wish to ALARM you
but a boy is lookin' at you with the eyes of *love.*
BWORP BWORP
What who what what?
BEAVERGEDDON!
Do not move, remain still.
I will take a photo and show you for identification purposes.
KA-CHIK
Virgin Mary and all the ruddy saints.
Lottie, you have to turn the camera noise off.
It was a CHRISTMAS phone, I've not mastered it!
DIT DIT DIT
Mildred the LION IS LEAVING THE HERD
ESSEN
VERBOTEN
The LION is buying a MARS BAR.
The LION is standing *right behind you.*

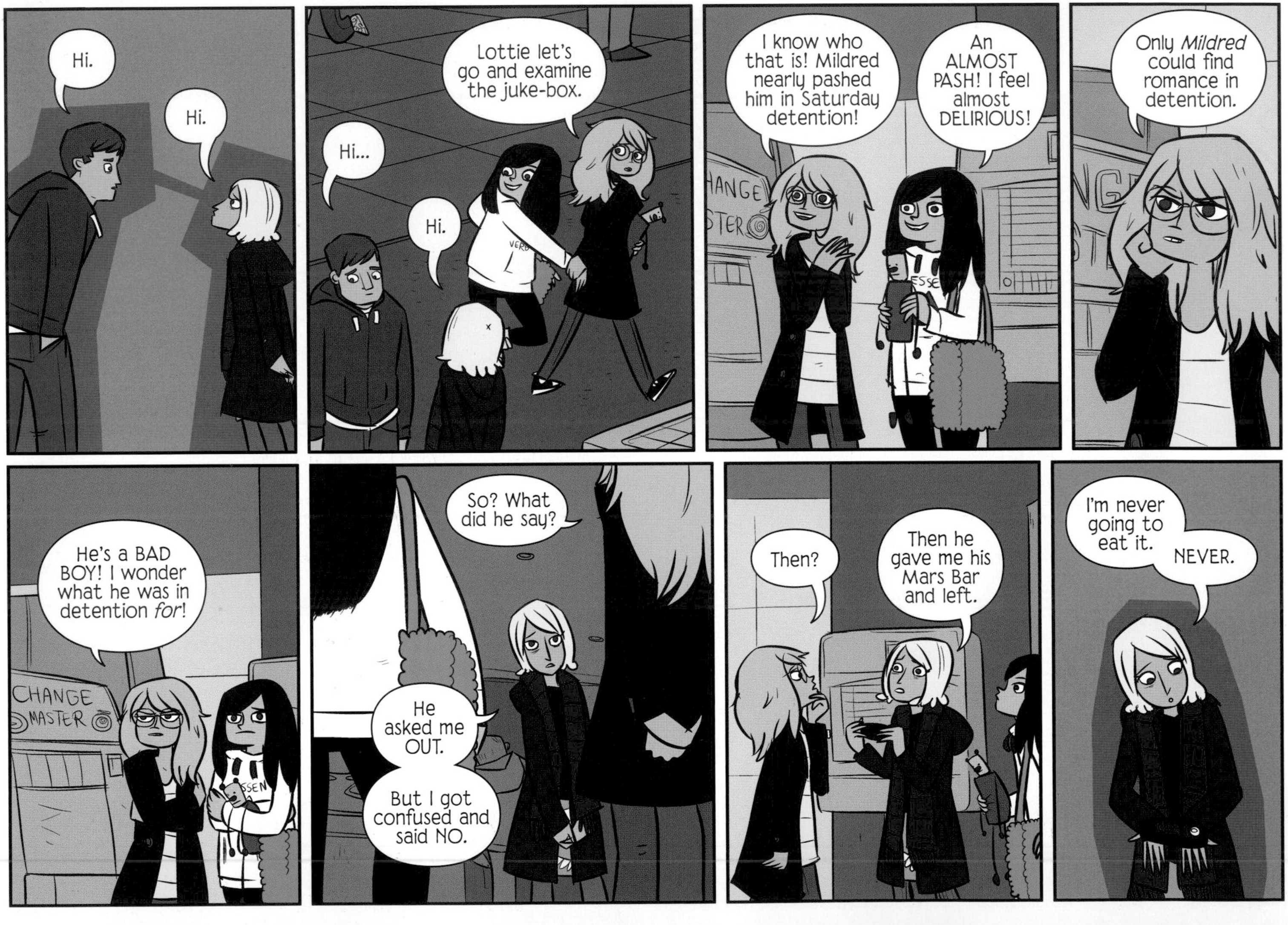

Hi.
Hi.
Lottie let's go and examine the juke-box.
Hi...
Hi.
I know who that is! Mildred nearly pashed him in Saturday detention!
An ALMOST PASH! I feel almost DELIRIOUS!
Only *Mildred* could find romance in detention.
He's a BAD BOY! I wonder what he was in detention *for*!
CHANGE MASTER
So? What did he say?
He asked me OUT.
But I got confused and said NO.
Then?
Then he gave me his Mars Bar and left.
I'm never going to eat it.
NEVER.


The Case of the Fire Inside

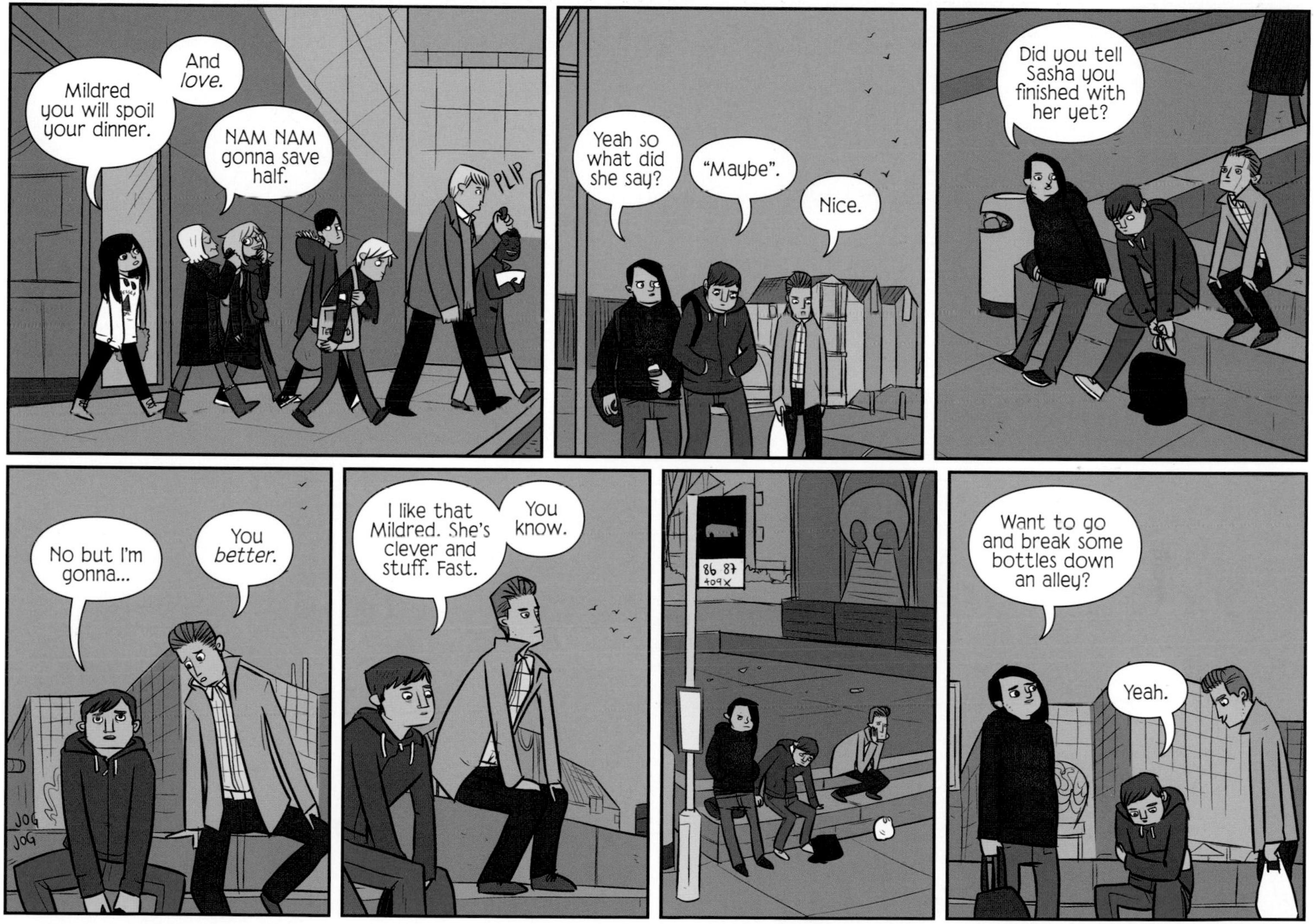
Mildred you will spoil your dinner.
And *love.*
NAM NAM gonna save half.
PLIP
Yeah so what did she say?
"Maybe".
Nice.
Did you tell Sasha you finished with her yet?
No but I'm gonna...
You *better.*
JOG JOG
I like that Mildred. She's clever and stuff. Fast.
You know.
86 87 409X
Want to go and break some bottles down an alley?
Yeah.

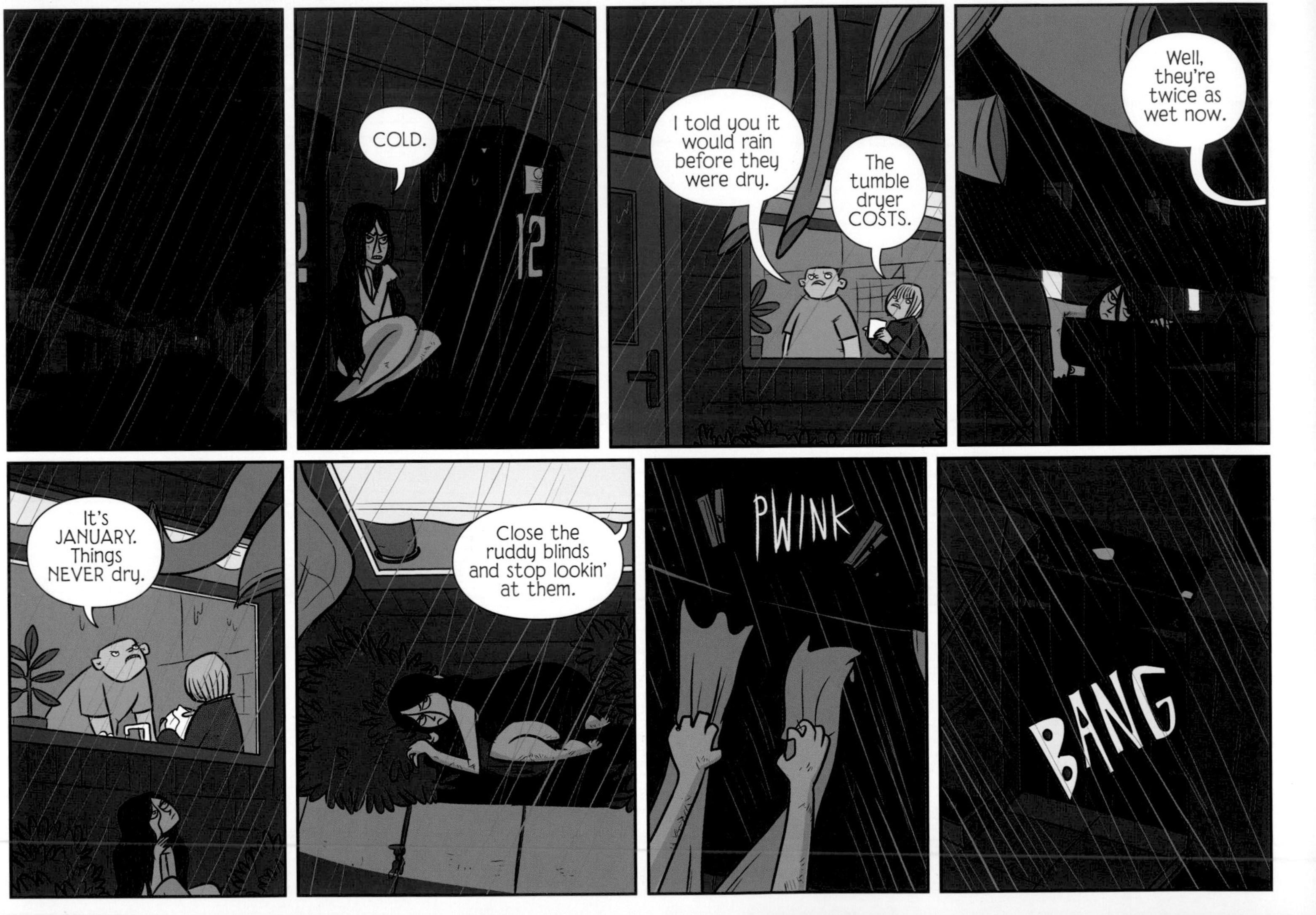

COLD.
I told you it would rain before they were dry.
The tumble dryer COSTS.
Well, they're twice as wet now.
It's JANUARY. Things NEVER dry.
Close the ruddy blinds and stop lookin' at them.
PWINK
BANG

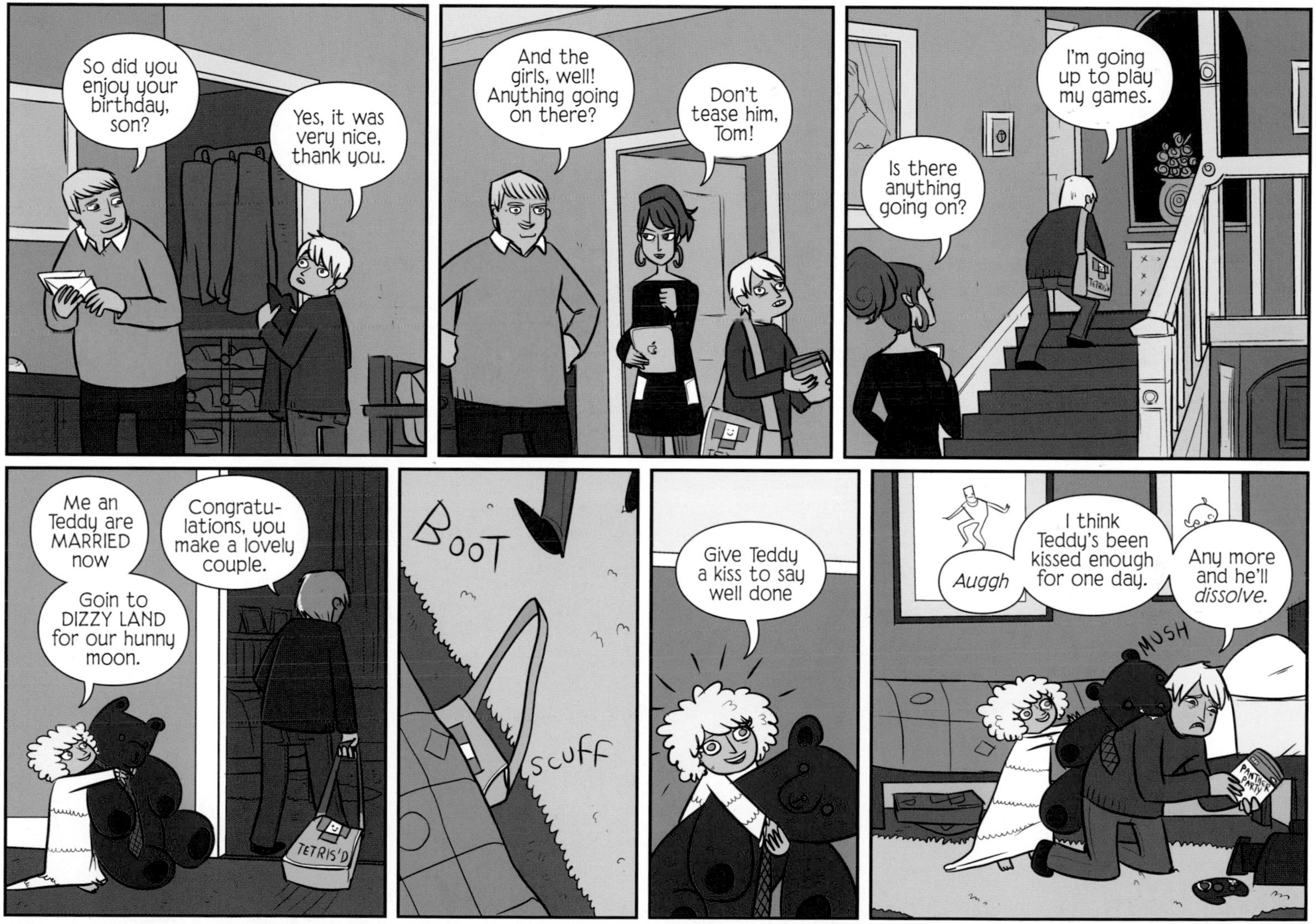
So did you enjoy your birthday, son?
Yes, it was very nice, thank you.
And the girls, well! Anything going on there?
Don't tease him, Tom!
I'm going up to play my games.
Is there anything going on?
TETRIS
Me an Teddy are MARRIED now
Goin to DIZZY LAND for our hunny moon.
Congratu-lations, you make a lovely couple.
TETRIS'D
BOOT
SCUFF
Give Teddy a kiss to say well done
Auggh
I think Teddy's been kissed enough for one day.
Any more and he'll *dissolve.*
MUSH
PANTHER PARTY

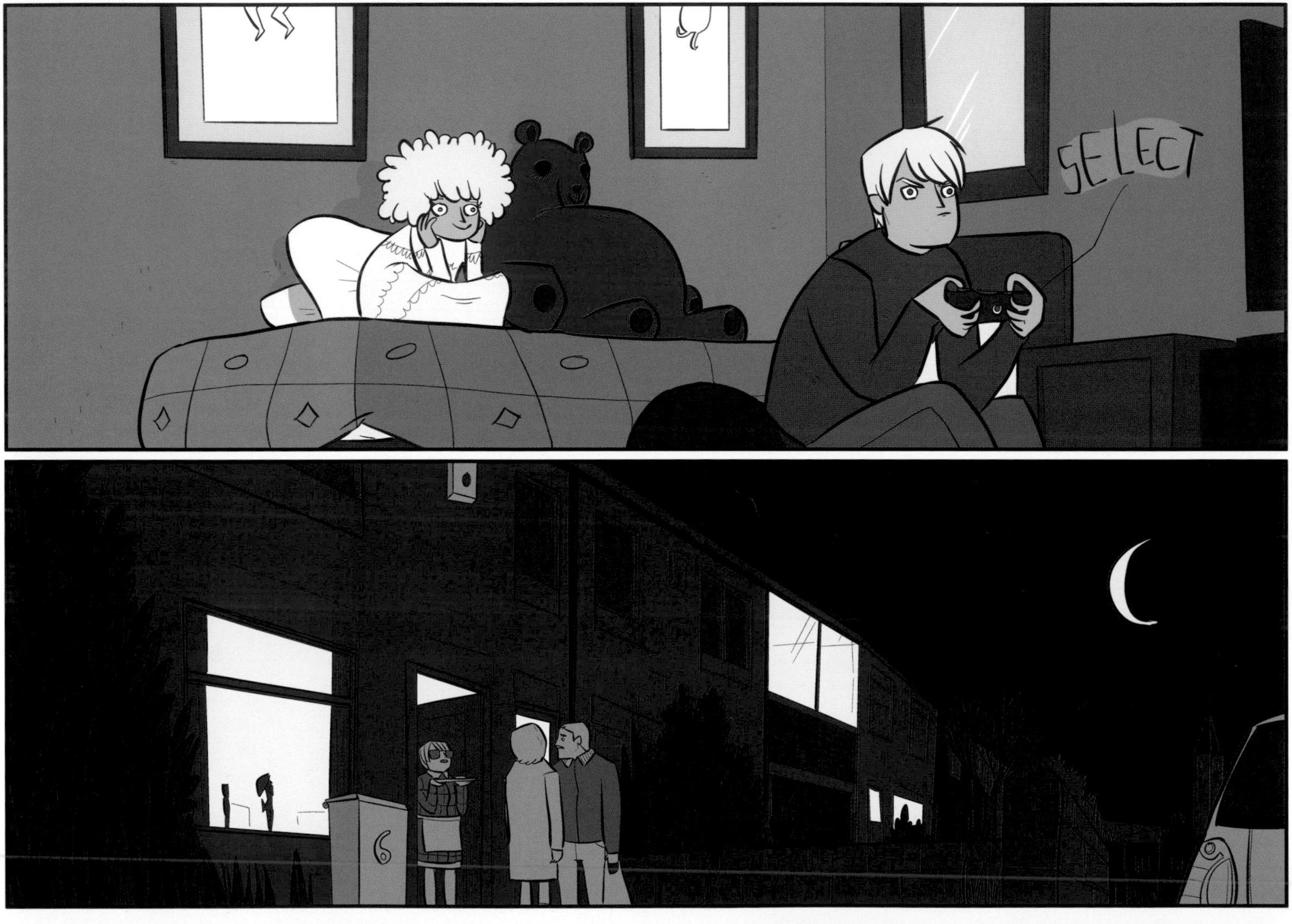
SELECT
6

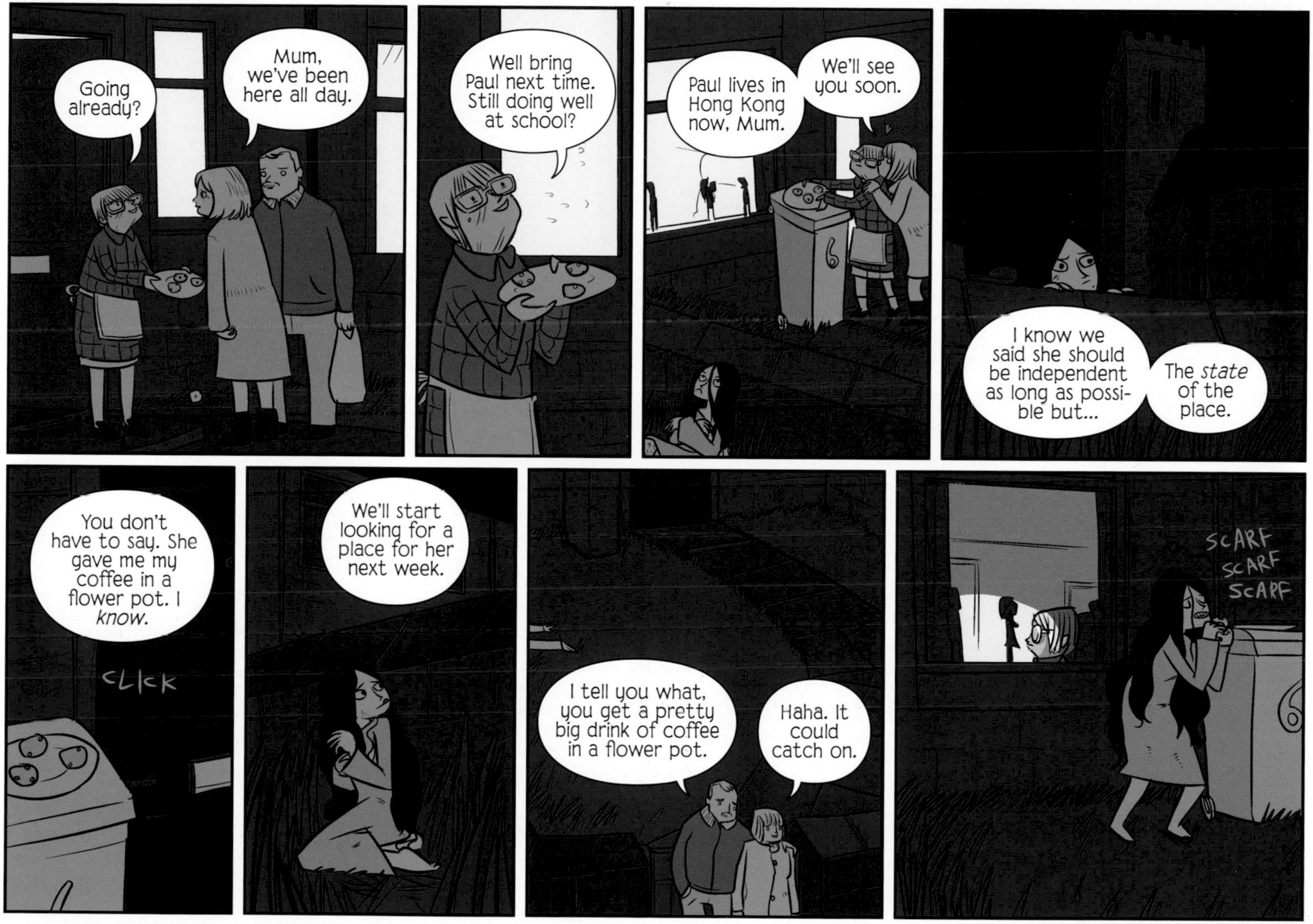
Going already?
Mum, we've been here all day.
Well bring Paul next time. Still doing well at school?
Paul lives in Hong Kong now, Mum.
We'll see you soon.
I know we said she should be independent as long as possible but...
The *state* of the place.
You don't have to say. She gave me my coffee in a flower pot. I *know*.
CLICK
We'll start looking for a place for her next week.
I tell you what, you get a pretty big drink of coffee in a flower pot.
Haha. It could catch on.
SCARF SCARF SCARF

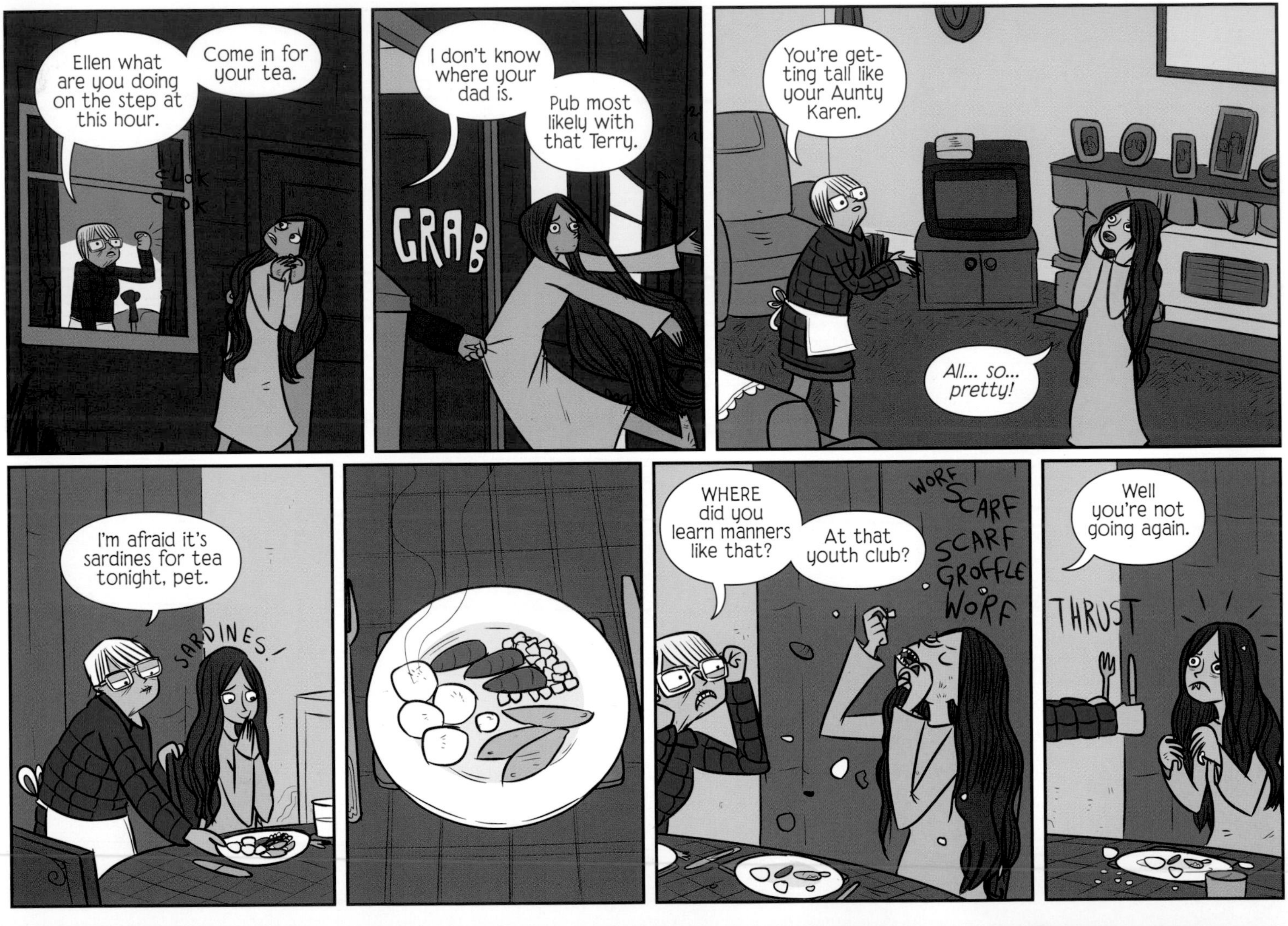
Ellen what are you doing on the step at this hour.
Come in for your tea.
CLOK CLOK
I don't know where your dad is.
Pub most likely with that Terry.
GRAB
You're getting tall like your Aunty Karen.
All... so... pretty!
I'm afraid it's sardines for tea tonight, pet.
SARDINES!
WHERE did you learn manners like that?
At that youth club?
WORF SCARF SCARF GROFFLE WORF
Well you're not going again.
THRUST

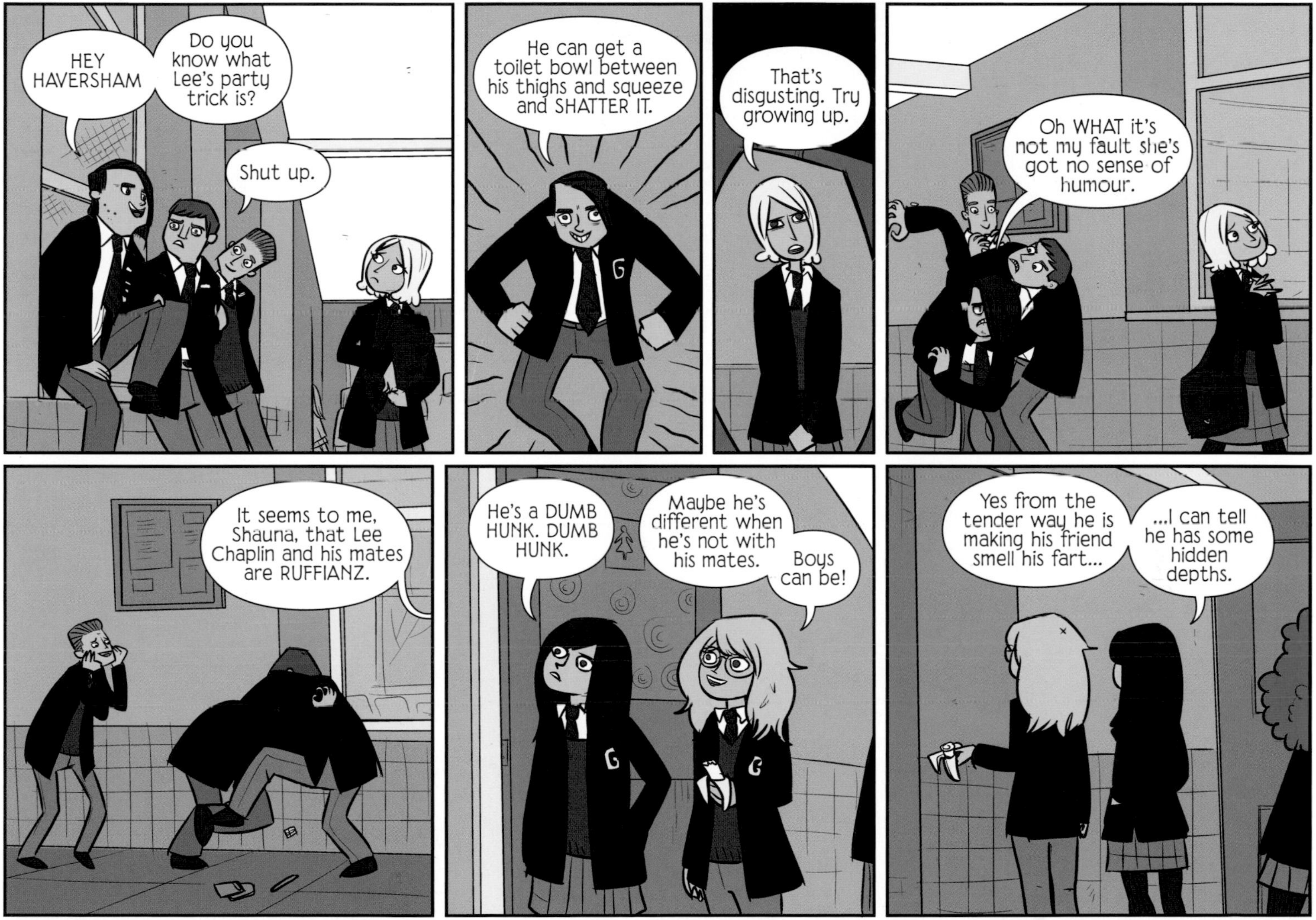
HEY HAVERSHAM
Do you know what Lee's party trick is?
Shut up.
He can get a toilet bowl between his thighs and squeeze and SHATTER IT.
That's disgusting. Try growing up.
Oh WHAT it's not my fault she's got no sense of humour.
It seems to me, Shauna, that Lee Chaplin and his mates are RUFFIANZ.
He's a DUMB HUNK. DUMB HUNK.
Maybe he's different when he's not with his mates.
Boys can be!
Yes from the tender way he is making his friend smell his fart...
...I can tell he has some hidden depths.

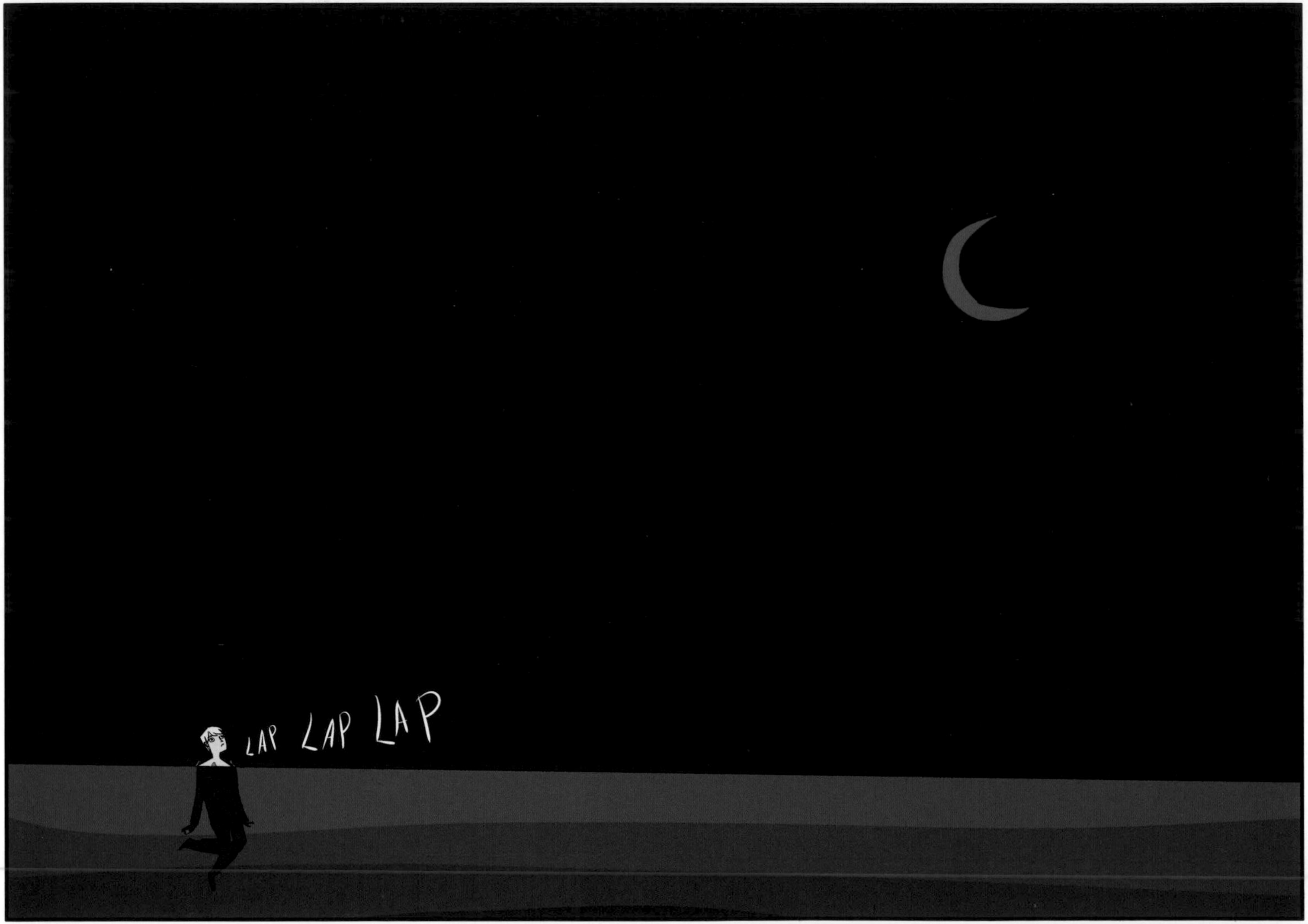
LAP LAP LAP

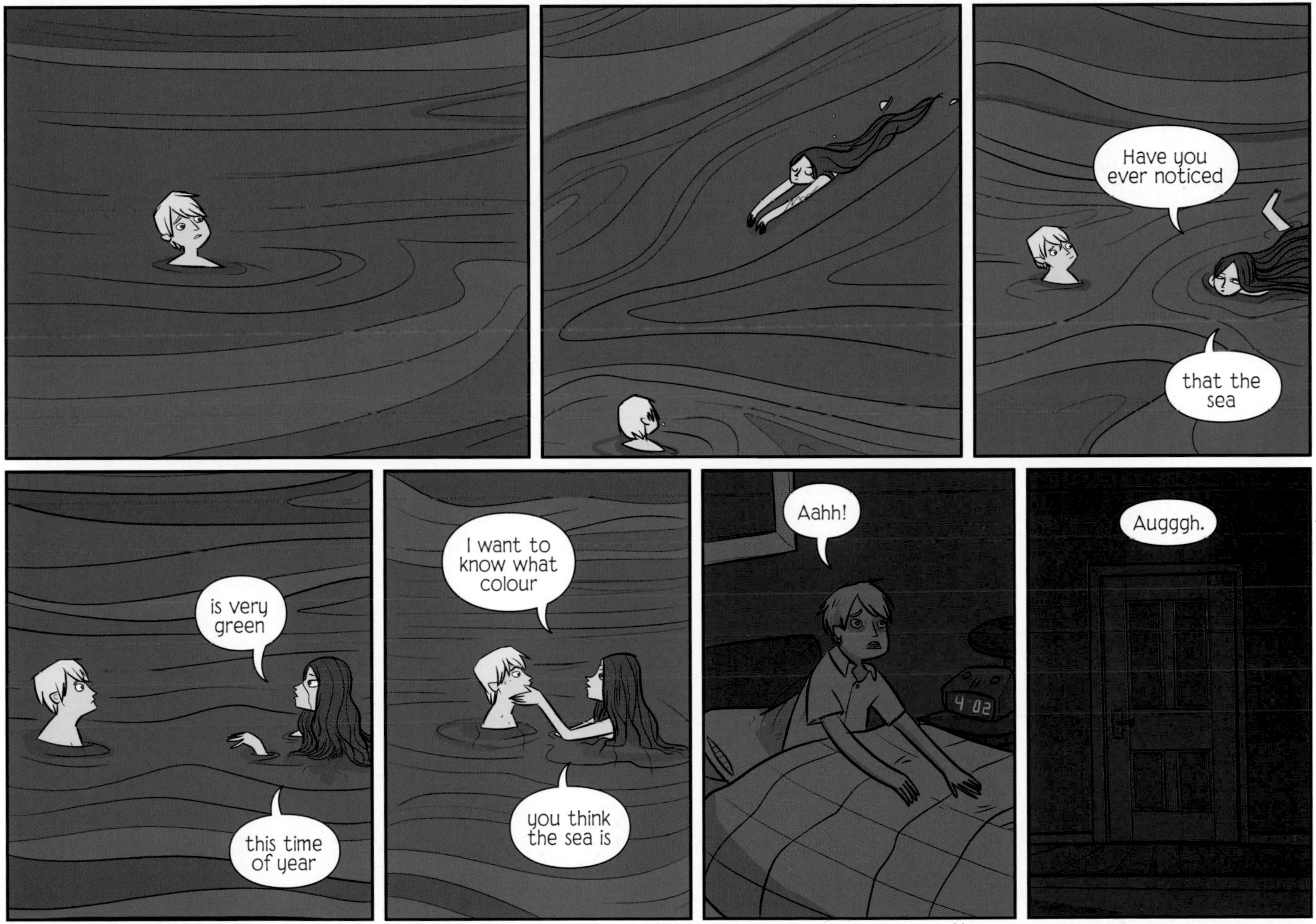
Have you ever noticed
that the sea
is very green
this time of year
I want to know what colour
you think the sea is
Aahh!
4:02
Augggh.

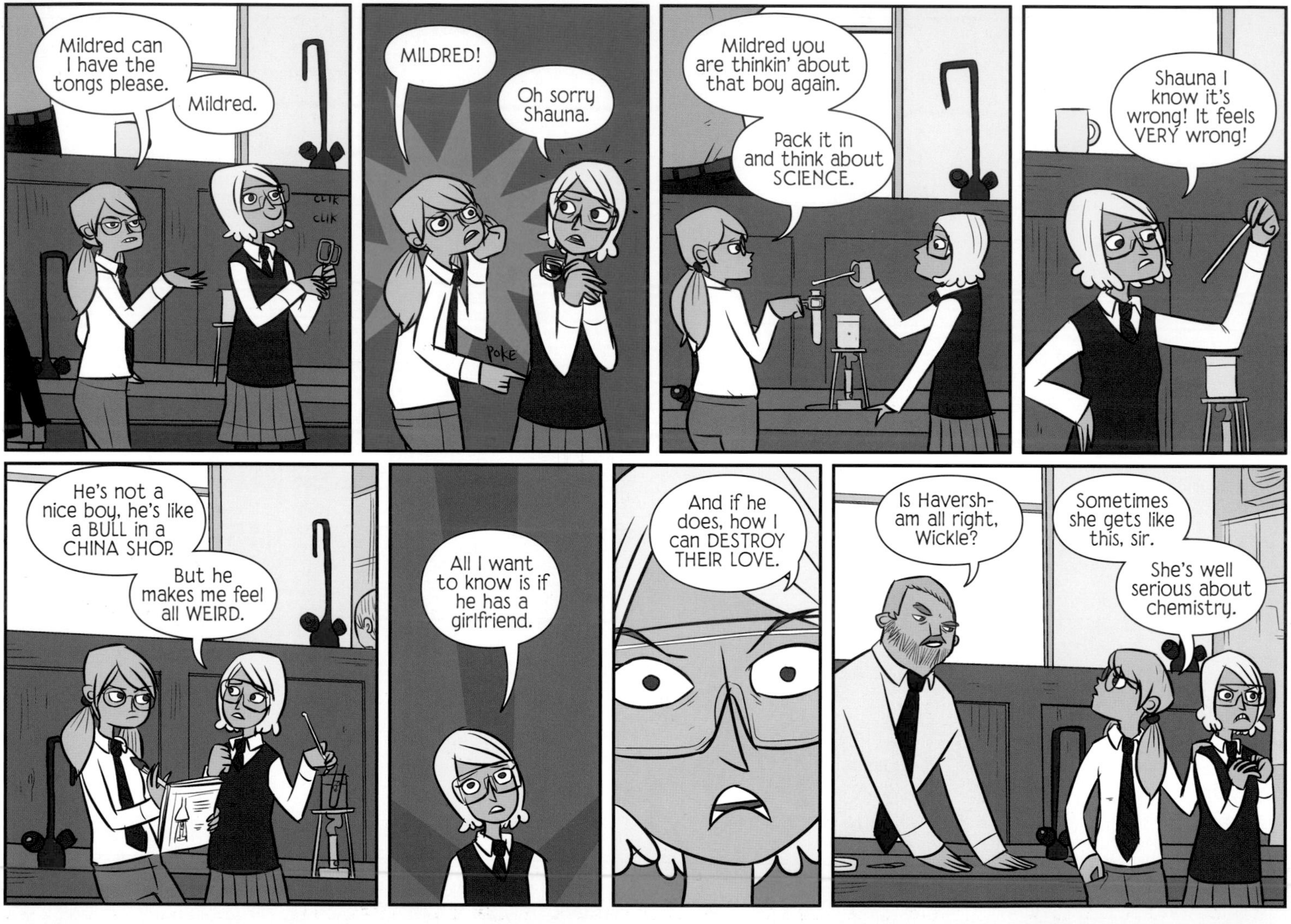
Mildred can I have the tongs please.
Mildred.
CLIK CLIK
MILDRED!
Oh sorry Shauna.
POKE
Mildred you are thinkin' about that boy again.
Pack it in and think about SCIENCE.
Shauna I know it's wrong! It feels VERY wrong!
He's not a nice boy, he's like a BULL in a CHINA SHOP.
But he makes me feel all WEIRD.
All I want to know is if he has a girlfriend.
And if he does, how I can DESTROY THEIR LOVE.
Is Haversh-am all right, Wickle?
Sometimes she gets like this, sir.
She's well serious about chemistry.

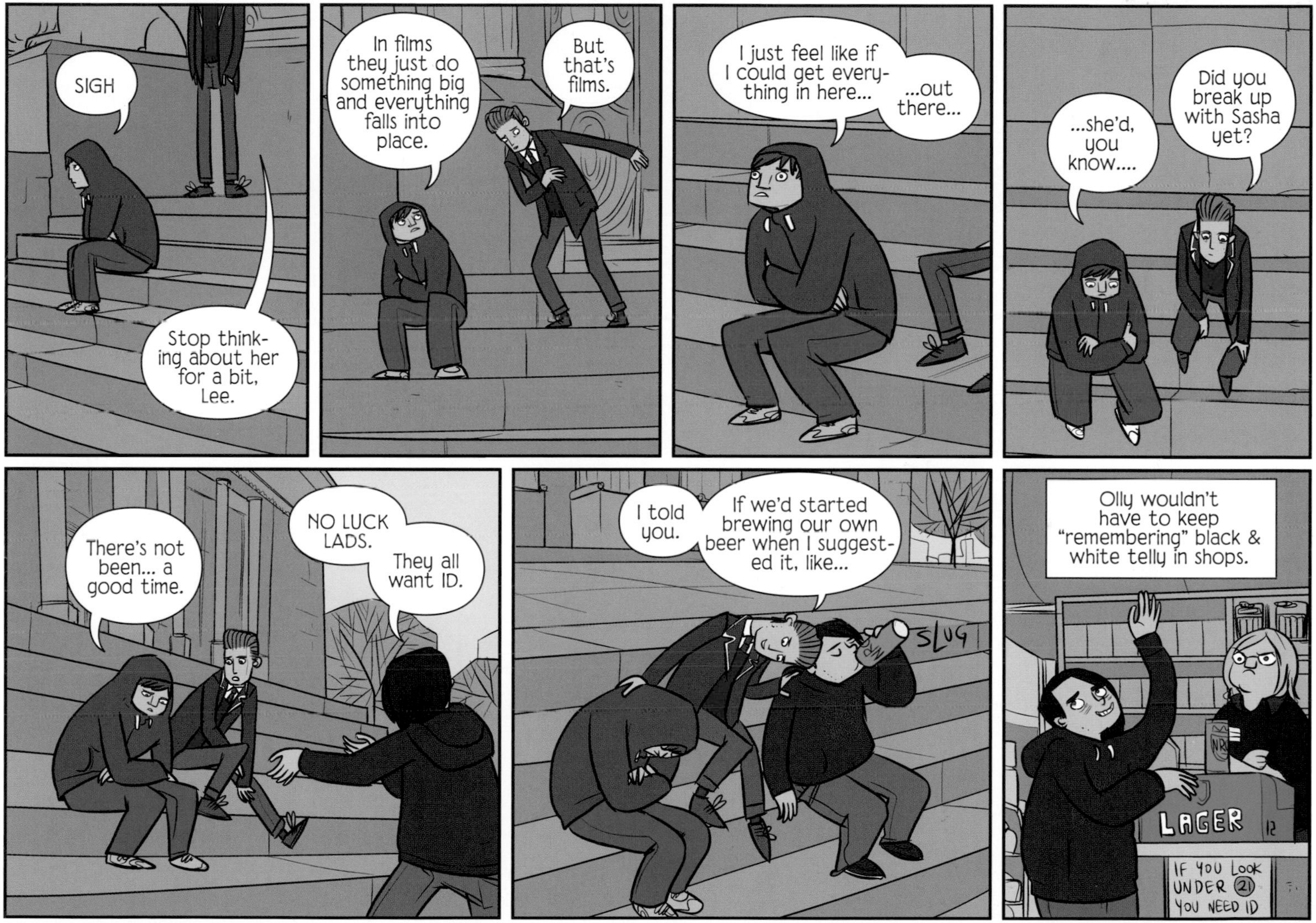
SIGH
Stop thinking about her for a bit, Lee.
In films they just do something big and everything falls into place.
But that's films.
I just feel like if I could get everything in here...
...out there...
...she'd, you know....
Did you break up with Sasha yet?
There's not been... a good time.
NO LUCK LADS.
They all want ID.
I told you.
If we'd started brewing our own beer when I suggested it, like...
SLUG
Olly wouldn't have to keep "remembering" black & white telly in shops.
LAGER
IF YOU LOOK UNDER 21 YOU NEED ID

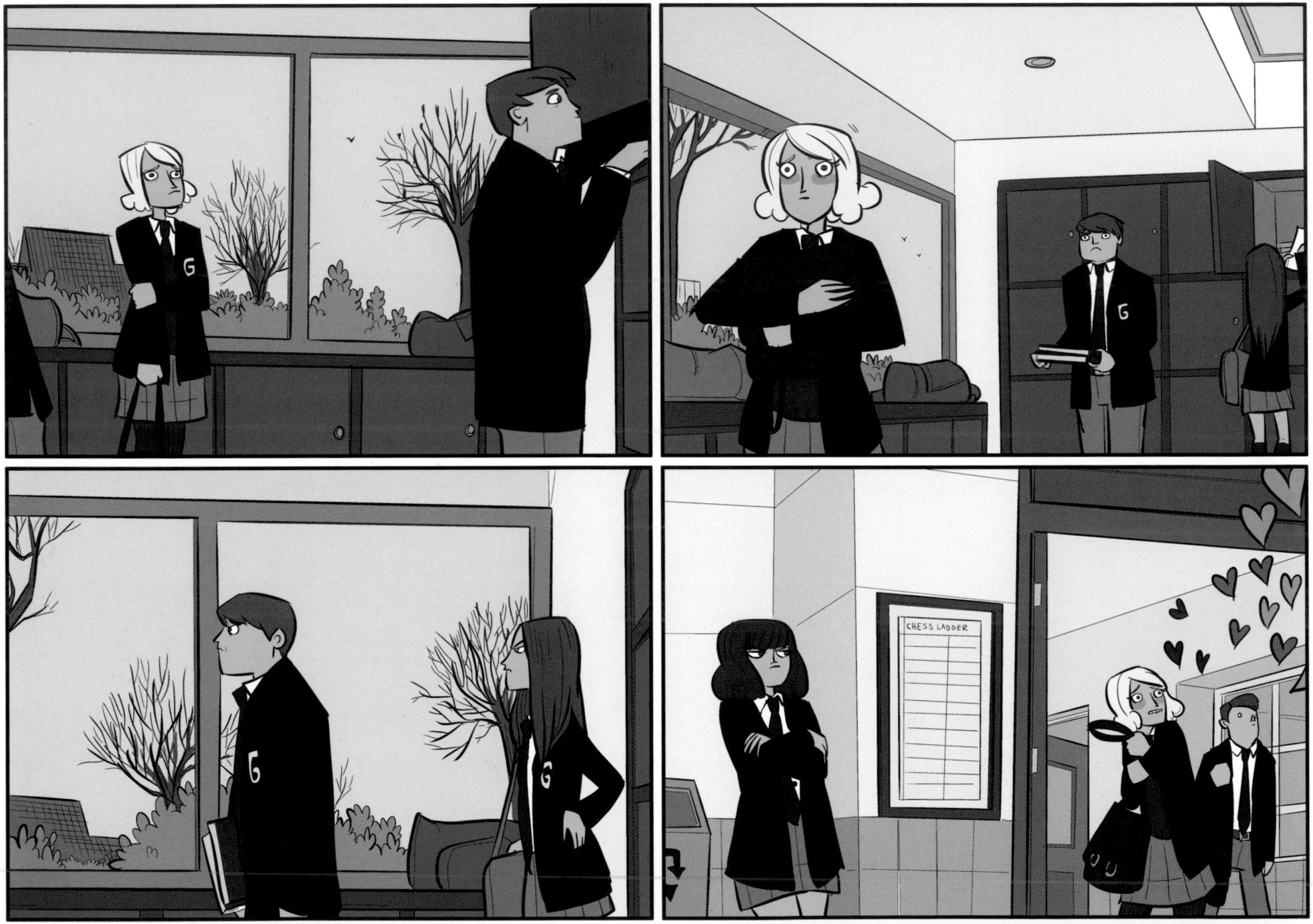
CHESS LADDER

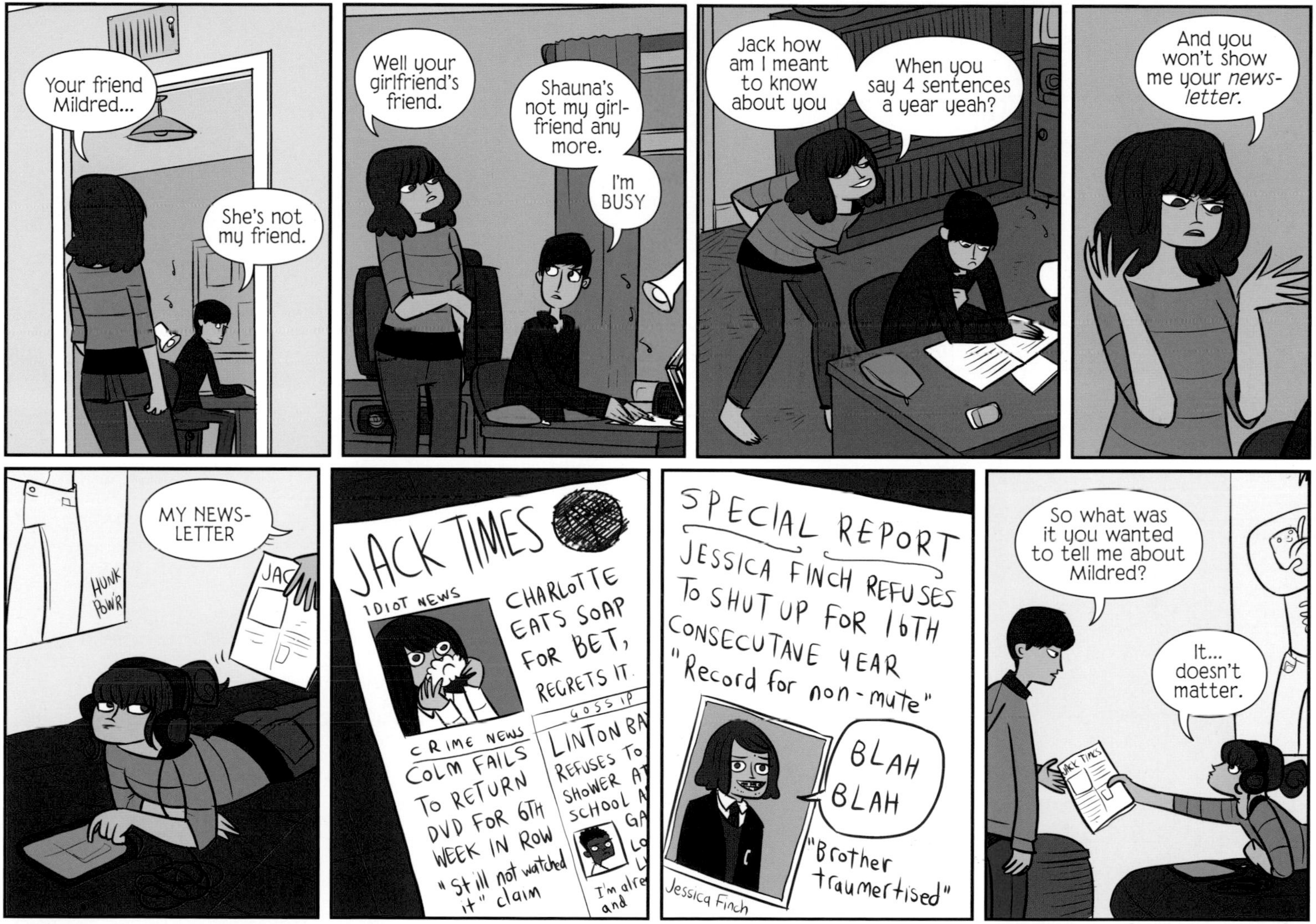

Your friend Mildred...
She's not my friend.
Well your girlfriend's friend.
Shauna's not my girl-friend any more.
I'm BUSY
Jack how am I meant to know about you
When you say 4 sentences a year yeah?
And you won't show me your *news-letter.*
HUNK POW'R
MY NEWS-LETTER
JACK TIMES
IDIOT NEWS
CHARLOTTE EATS SOAP FOR BET, REGRETS IT.
CRIME NEWS
COLM FAILS TO RETURN DVD FOR 6TH WEEK IN ROW
"Still not watched it" claim
GOSSIP
LINTON
REFUSES TO SHOWER
SCHOOL
SPECIAL REPORT
JESSICA FINCH REFUSES TO SHUT UP FOR 16TH CONSECUTAVE YEAR
"Record for non-mute"
BLAH BLAH
"Brother traumertised"
Jessica Finch
So what was it you wanted to tell me about Mildred?
It... doesn't matter.
JACK TIMES

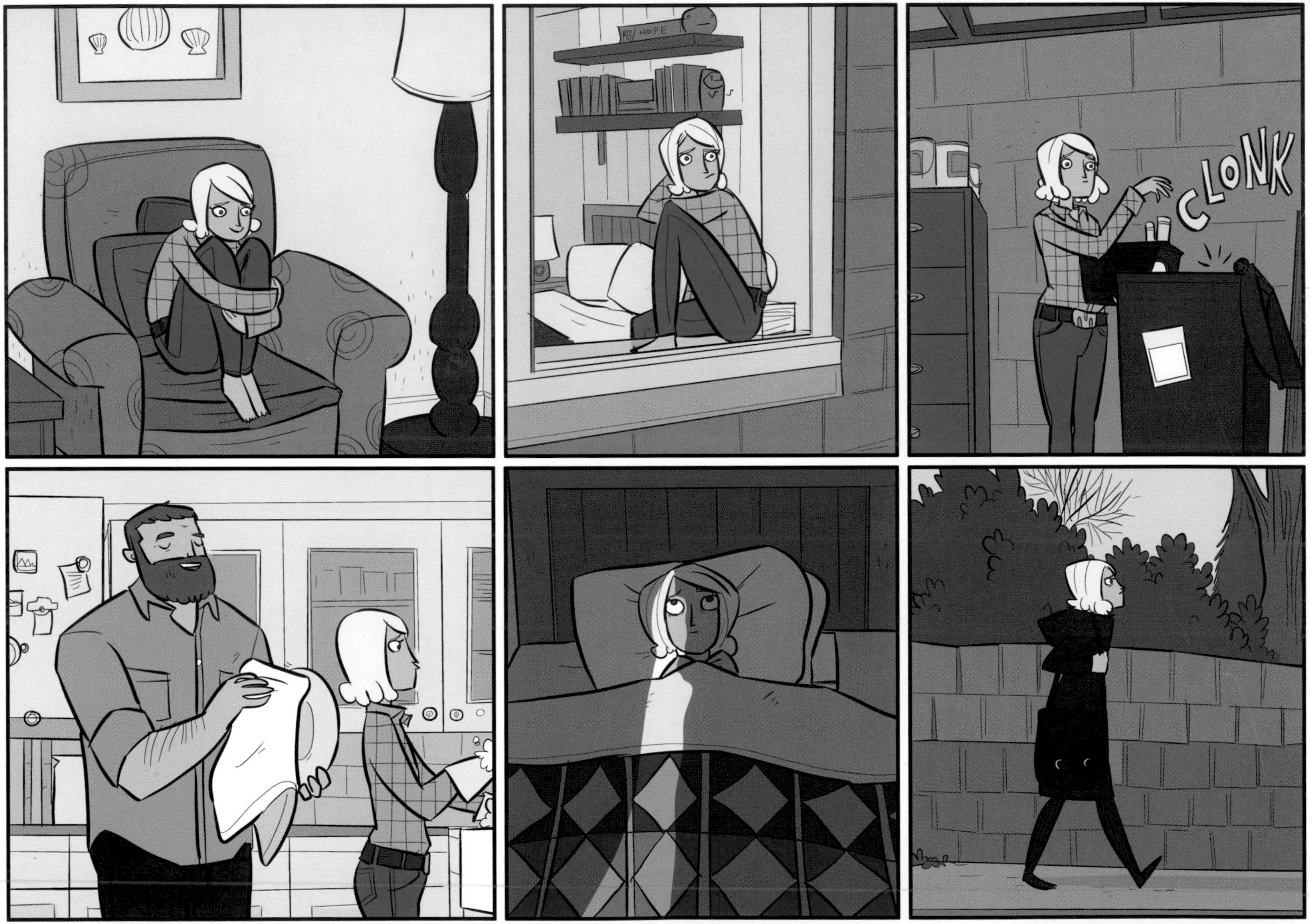
CLONK

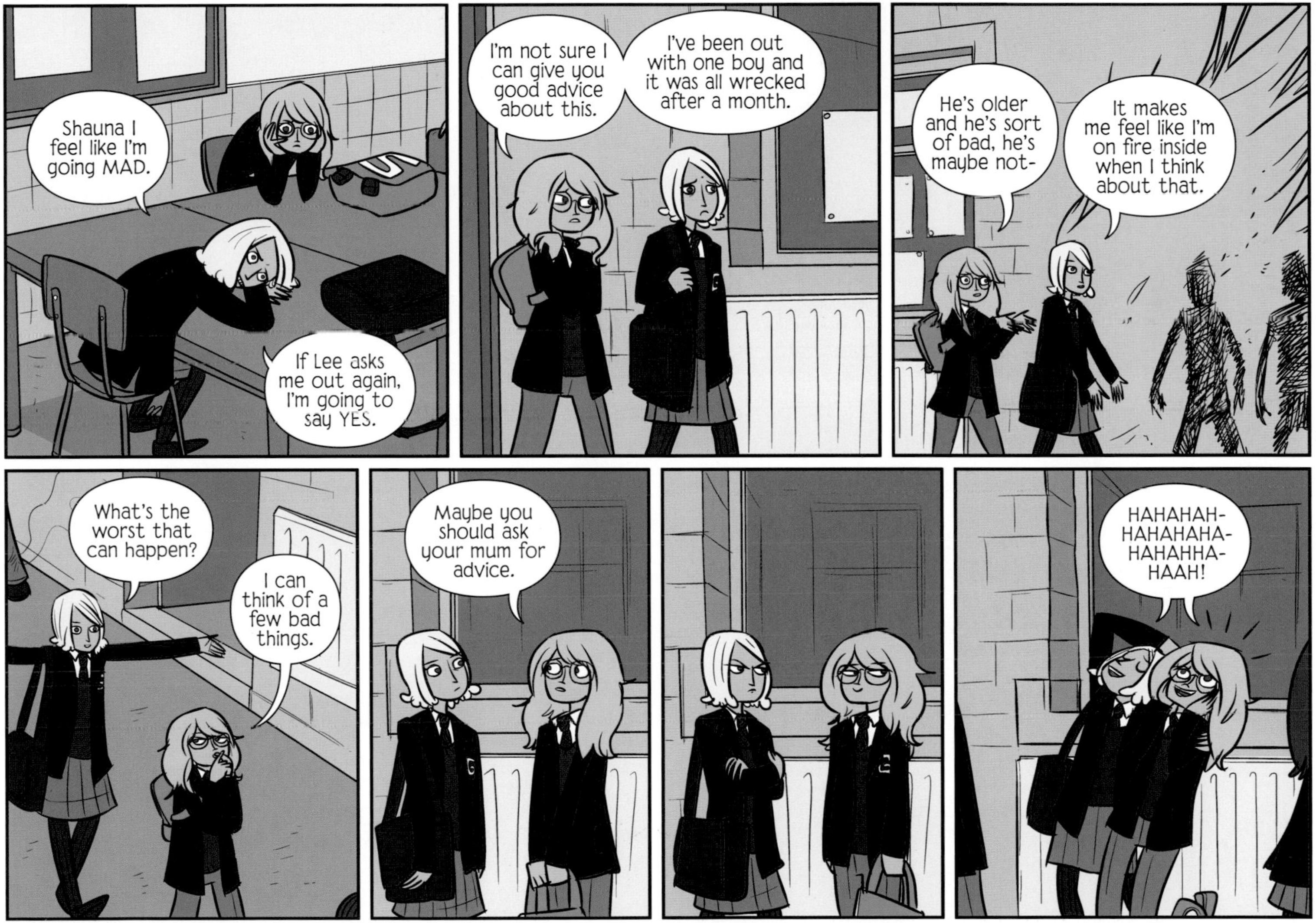
Shauna I feel like I'm going MAD.
If Lee asks me out again, I'm going to say YES.
I'm not sure I can give you good advice about this.
I've been out with one boy and it was all wrecked after a month.
He's older and he's sort of bad, he's maybe not-
It makes me feel like I'm on fire inside when I think about that.
What's the worst that can happen?
I can think of a few bad things.
Maybe you should ask your mum for advice.
HAHAHAH-HAHAHAHA-HAHAHHA-HAAH!

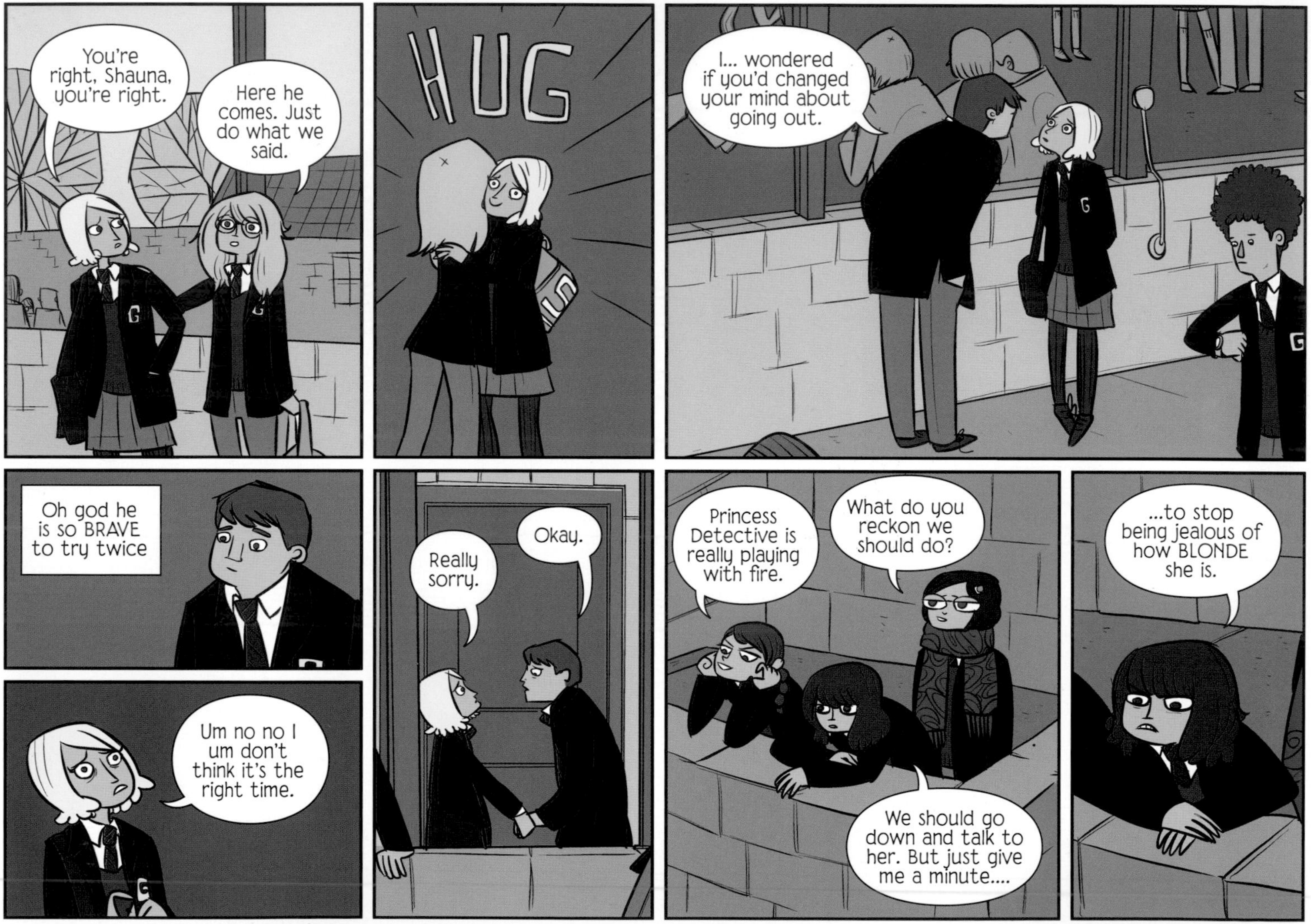
You're right, Shauna, you're right.
Here he comes. Just do what we said.
HUG
I... wondered if you'd changed your mind about going out.
Oh god he is so BRAVE to try twice
Um no no I um don't think it's the right time.
Really sorry.
Okay.
Princess Detective is really playing with fire.
What do you reckon we should do?
We should go down and talk to her. But just give me a minute....
...to stop being jealous of how BLONDE she is.

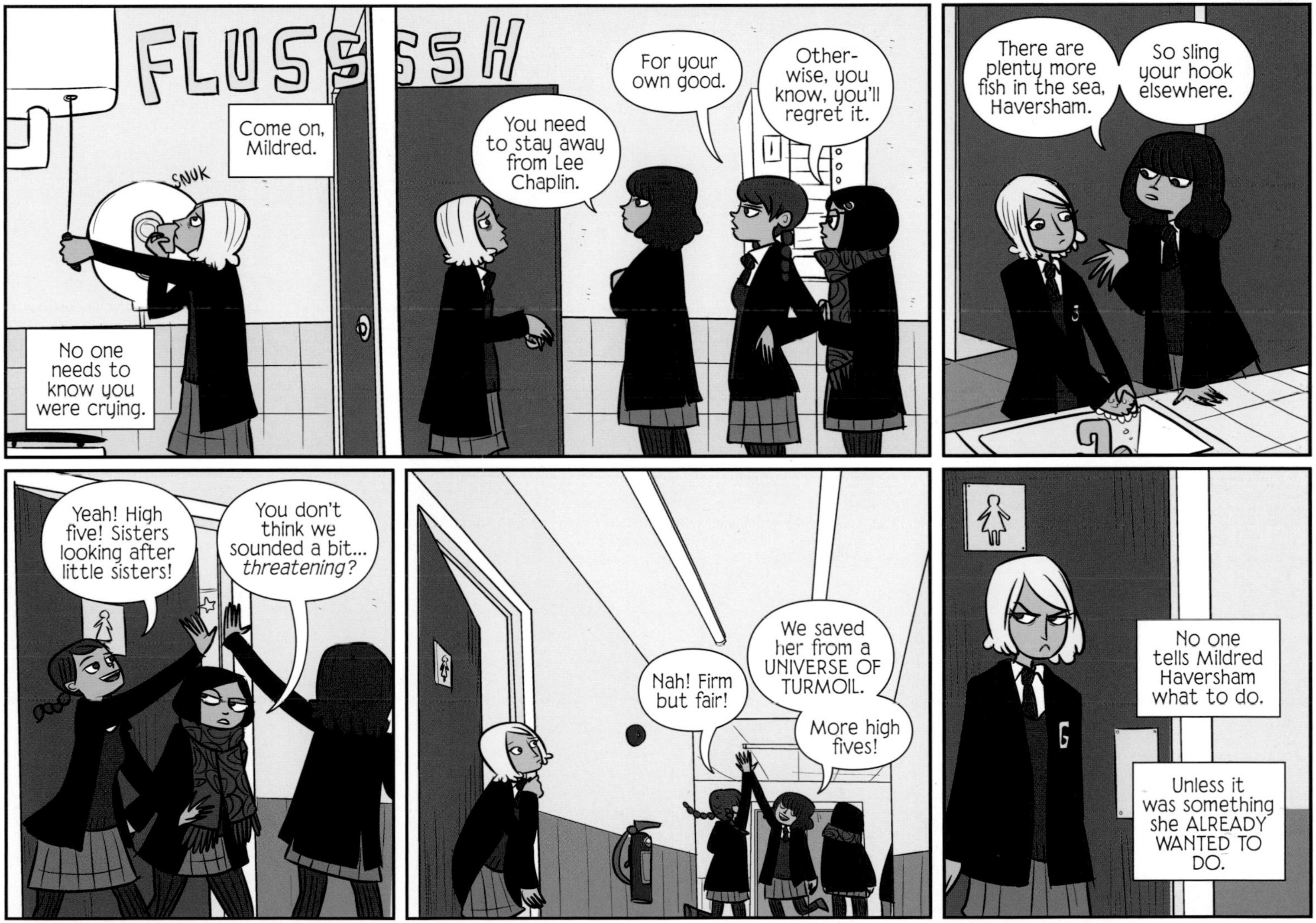
FLUSSSSH
Come on, Mildred.
SNUK
No one needs to know you were crying.
You need to stay away from Lee Chaplin.
For your own good.
Other-wise, you know, you'll regret it.
There are plenty more fish in the sea, Haversham.
So sling your hook elsewhere.
Yeah! High five! Sisters looking after little sisters!
You don't think we sounded a bit... *threatening?*
Nah! Firm but fair!
We saved her from a UNIVERSE OF TURMOIL.
More high fives!
No one tells Mildred Haversham what to do.
Unless it was something she ALREADY WANTED TO DO.

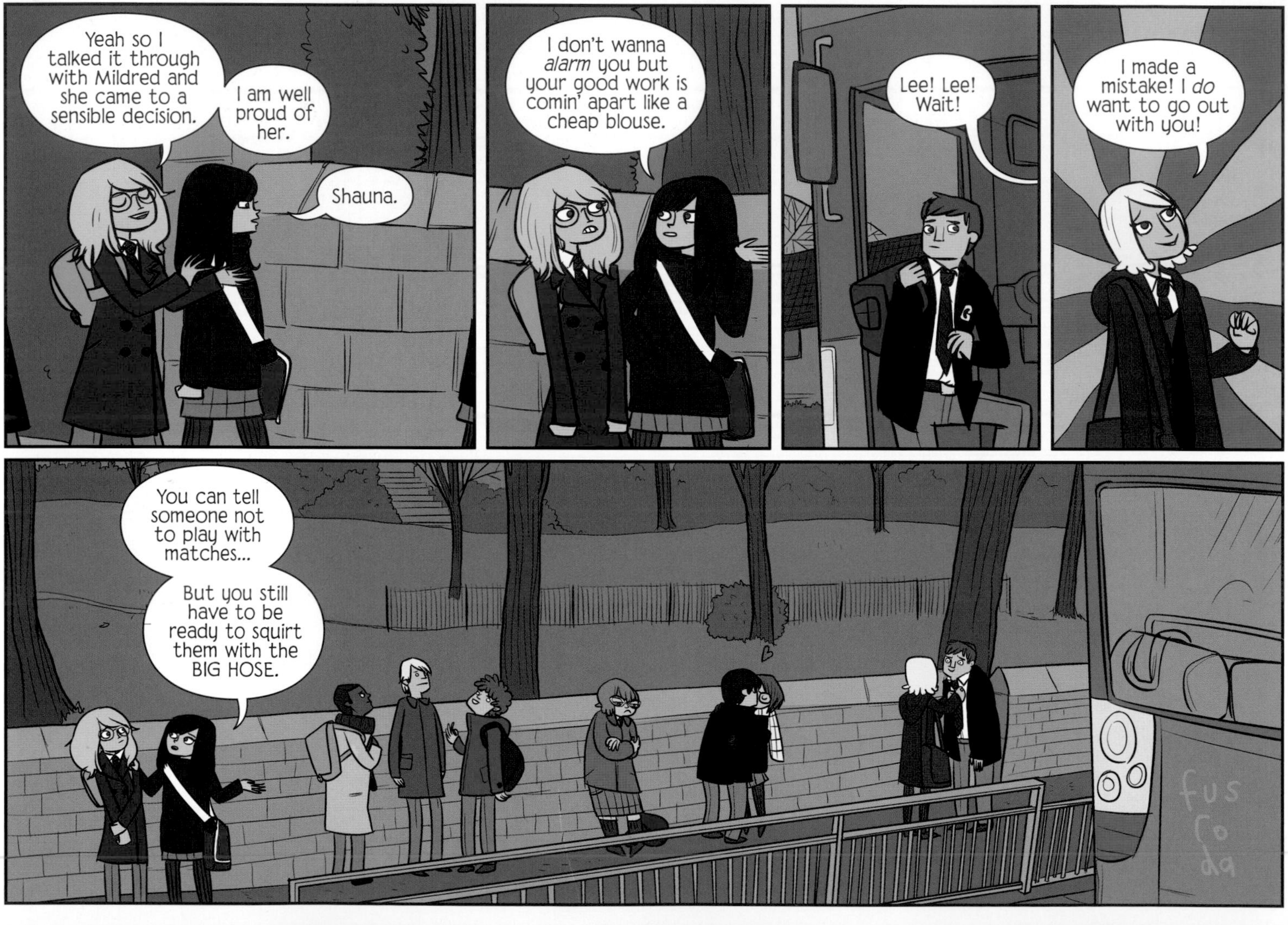
Yeah so I talked it through with Mildred and she came to a sensible decision.
I am well proud of her.
Shauna.
I don't wanna *alarm* you but your good work is comin' apart like a cheap blouse.
Lee! Lee! Wait!
I made a mistake! I *do* want to go out with you!
You can tell someone not to play with matches...
But you still have to be ready to squirt them with the BIG HOSE.
fus co da

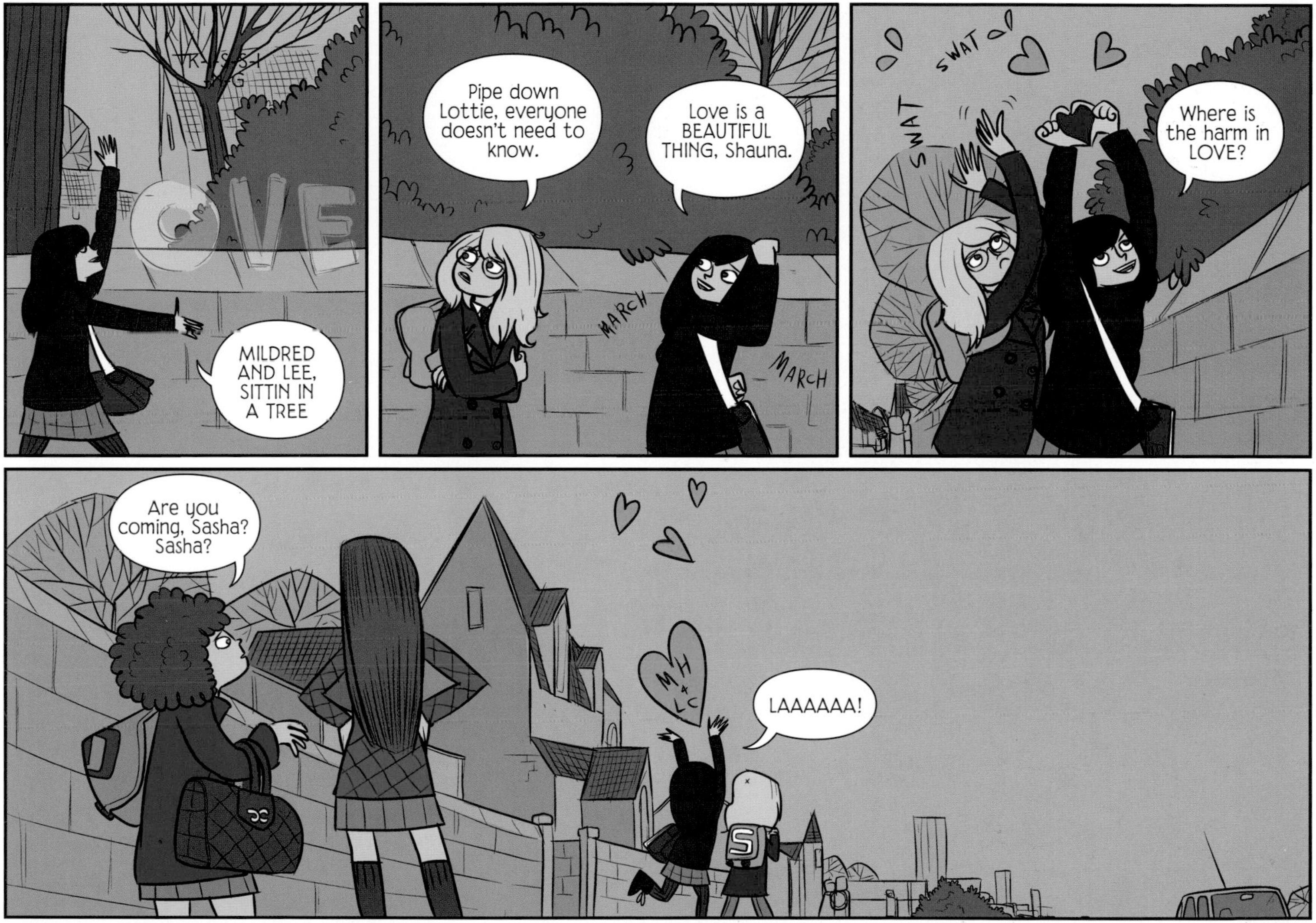
MILDRED AND LEE, SITTIN IN A TREE
Pipe down Lottie, everyone doesn't need to know.
MARCH
Love is a BEAUTIFUL THING, Shauna.
MARCH
SWAT
SWAT
Where is the harm in LOVE?
Are you coming, Sasha? Sasha?
LAAAAAA!

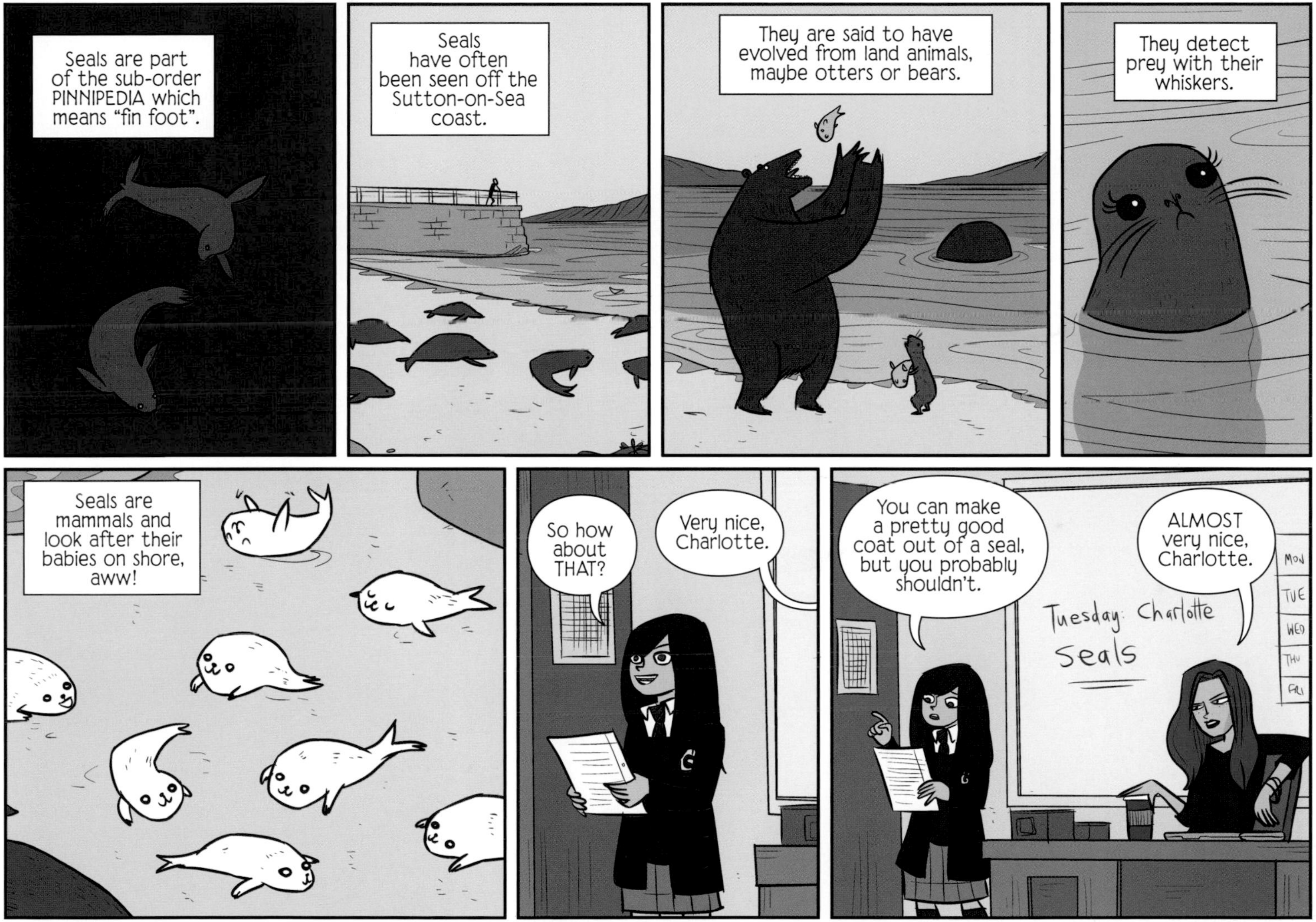
Seals are part of the sub-order PINNIPEDIA which means "fin foot".
Seals have often been seen off the Sutton-on-Sea coast.
They are said to have evolved from land animals, maybe otters or bears.
They detect prey with their whiskers.
Seals are mammals and look after their babies on shore, aww!
So how about THAT?
Very nice, Charlotte.
You can make a pretty good coat out of a seal, but you probably shouldn't.
ALMOST very nice, Charlotte.
Tuesday: Charlotte
Seals
MON
TUE
WED
THU
FRI

Bad Machinery, Volume Five

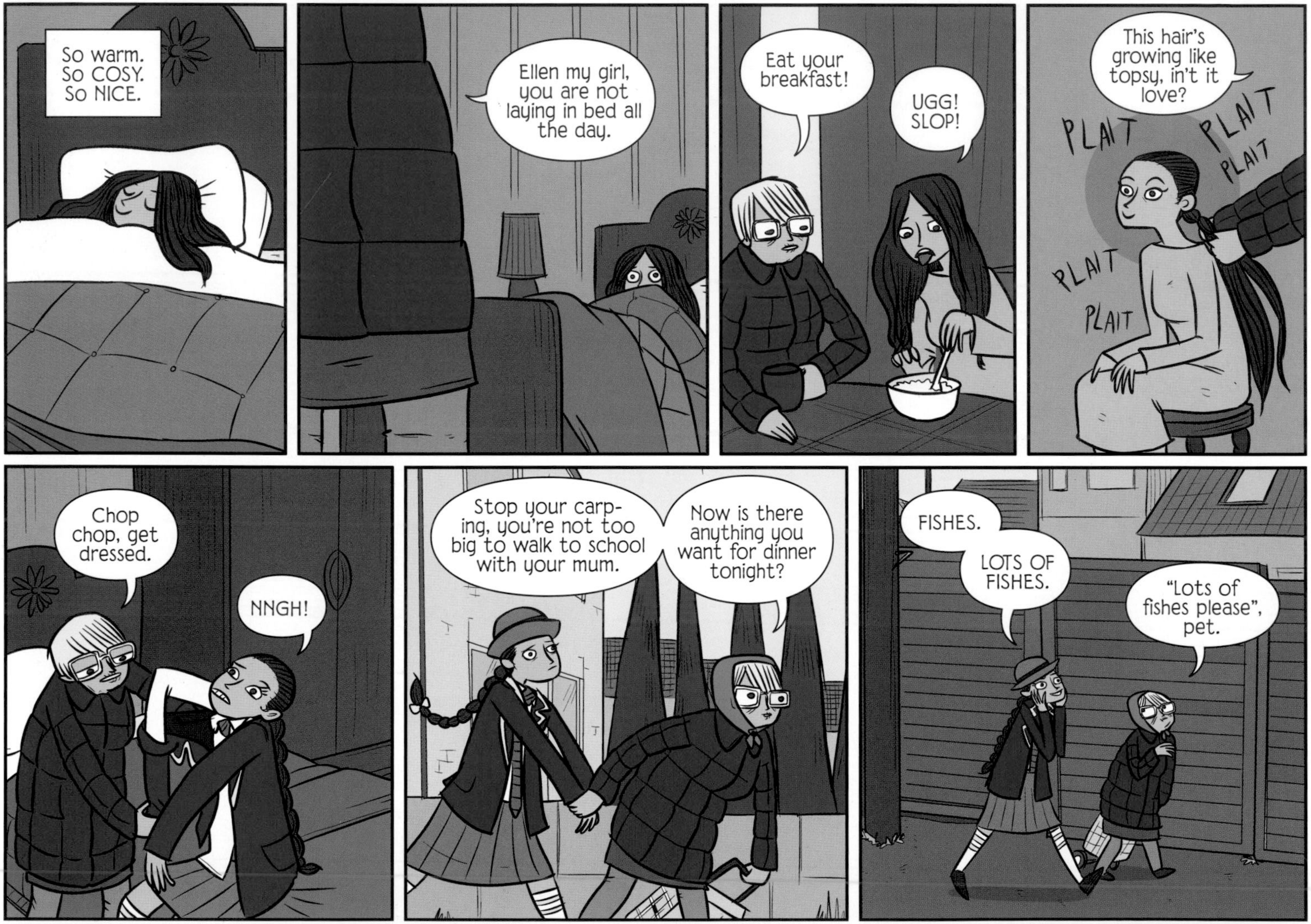
So warm. So COSY. So NICE.
Ellen my girl, you are not laying in bed all the day.
Eat your breakfast!
UGG! SLOP!
This hair's growing like topsy, in't it love?
PLAIT
PLAIT
PLAIT
PLAIT
PLAIT
PLAIT
Chop chop, get dressed.
NNGH!
Stop your carp-ing, you're not too big to walk to school with your mum.
Now is there anything you want for dinner tonight?
FISHES.
LOTS OF FISHES.
"Lots of fishes please", pet.

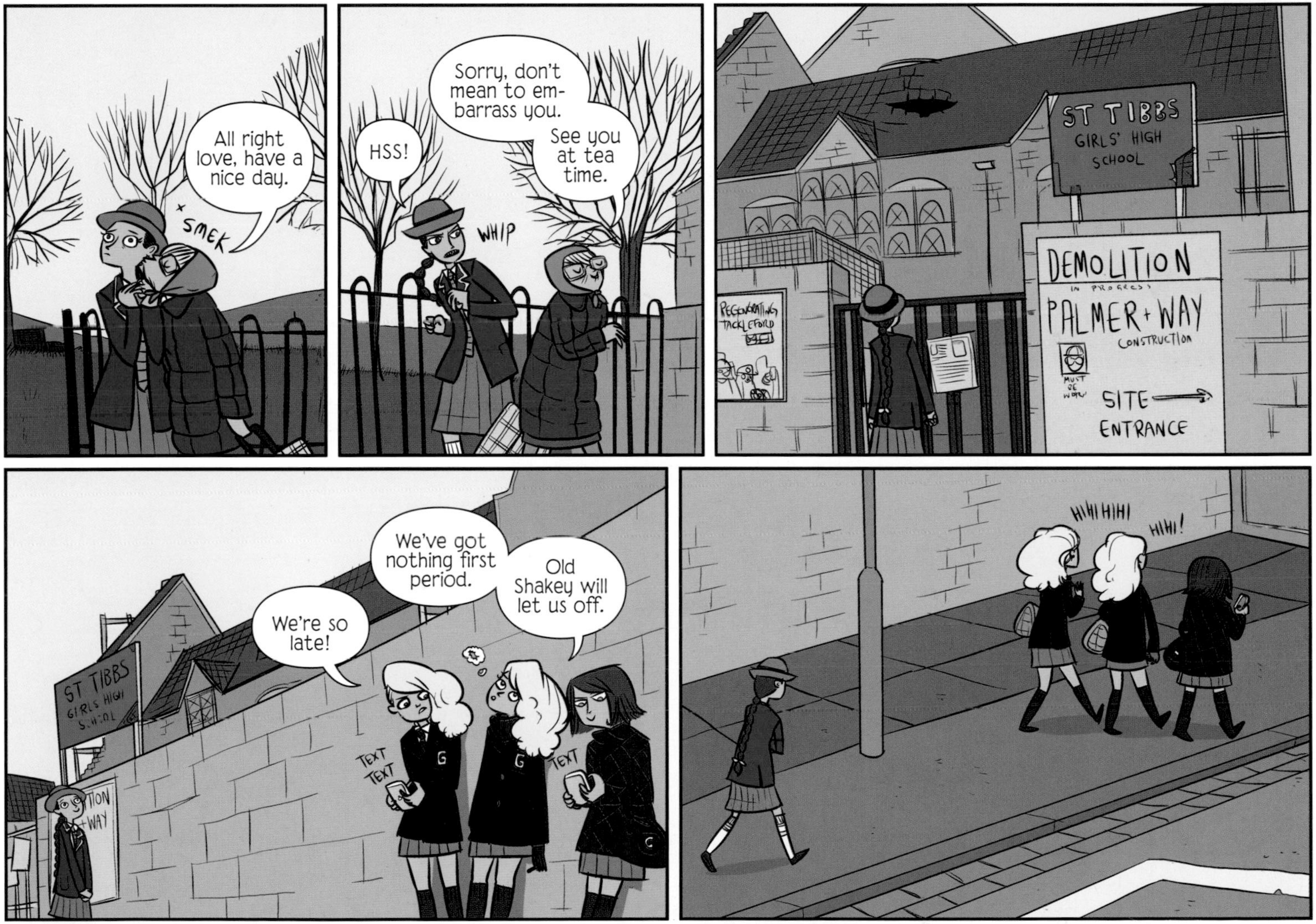
All right love, have a nice day.
SMEK
HSS!
Sorry, don't mean to embarrass you.
See you at tea time.
WHIP
ST TIBBS GIRLS' HIGH SCHOOL
REGENERATING TACKLEFORD
DEMOLITION IN PROGRESS
PALMER + WAY CONSTRUCTION
SITE ENTRANCE
We're so late!
We've got nothing first period.
Old Shakey will let us off.
TEXT TEXT
TEXT
ST TIBBS GIRLS HIGH SCHOOL
HIHI HIHI
HIHI!

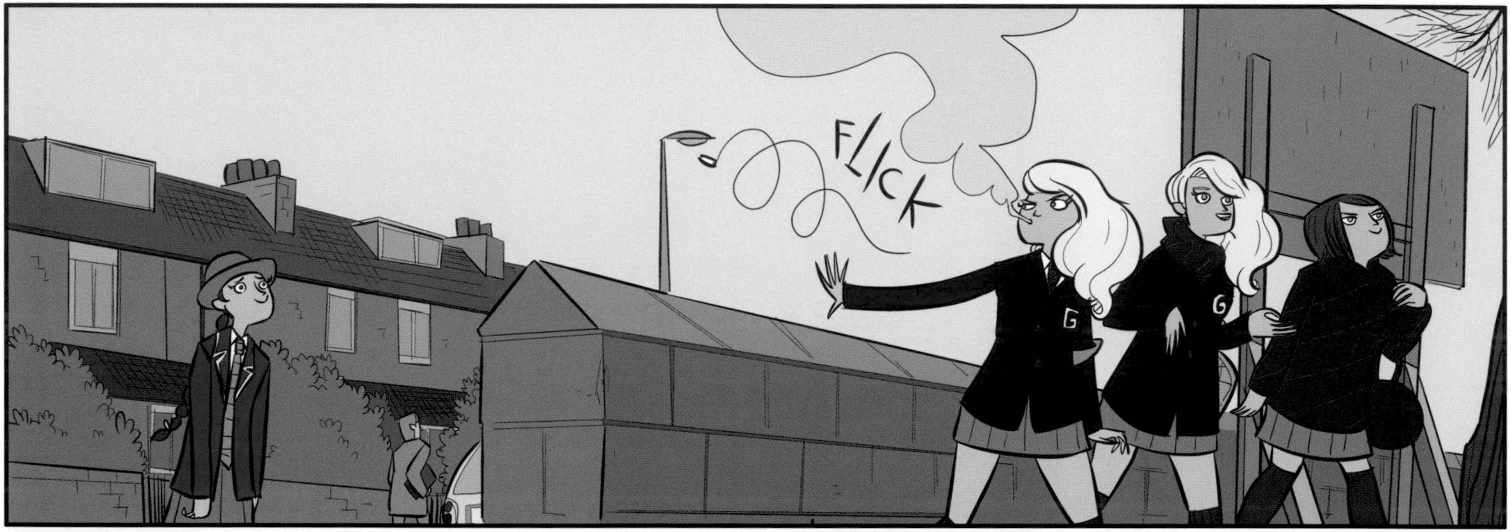
FLICK

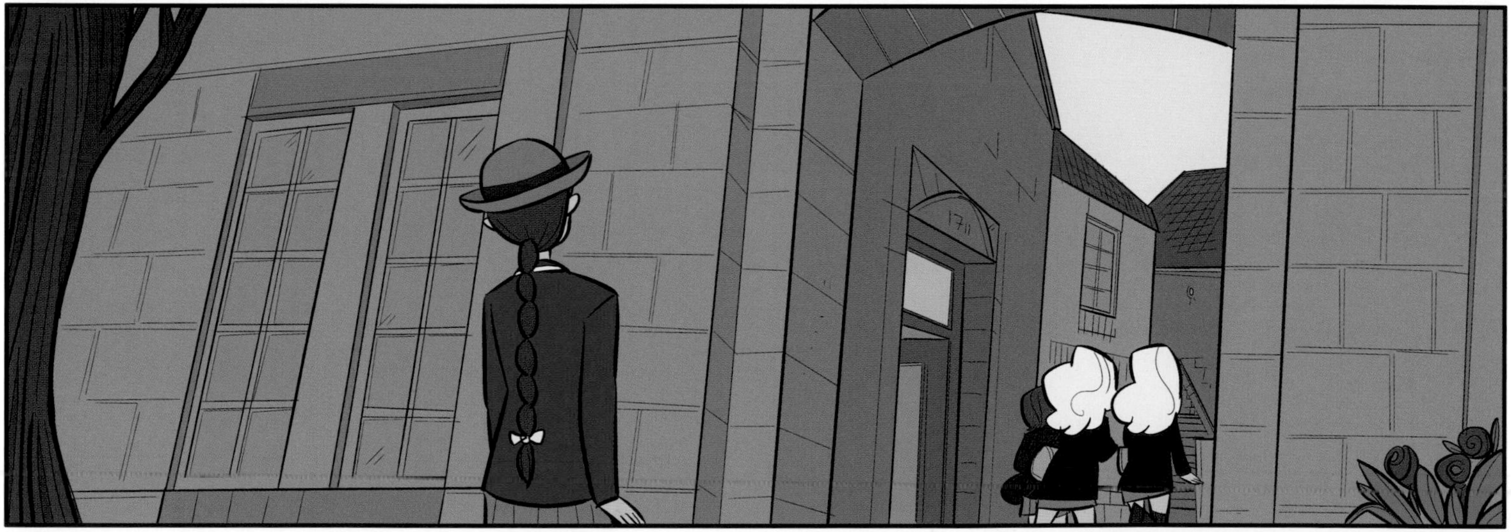
1711

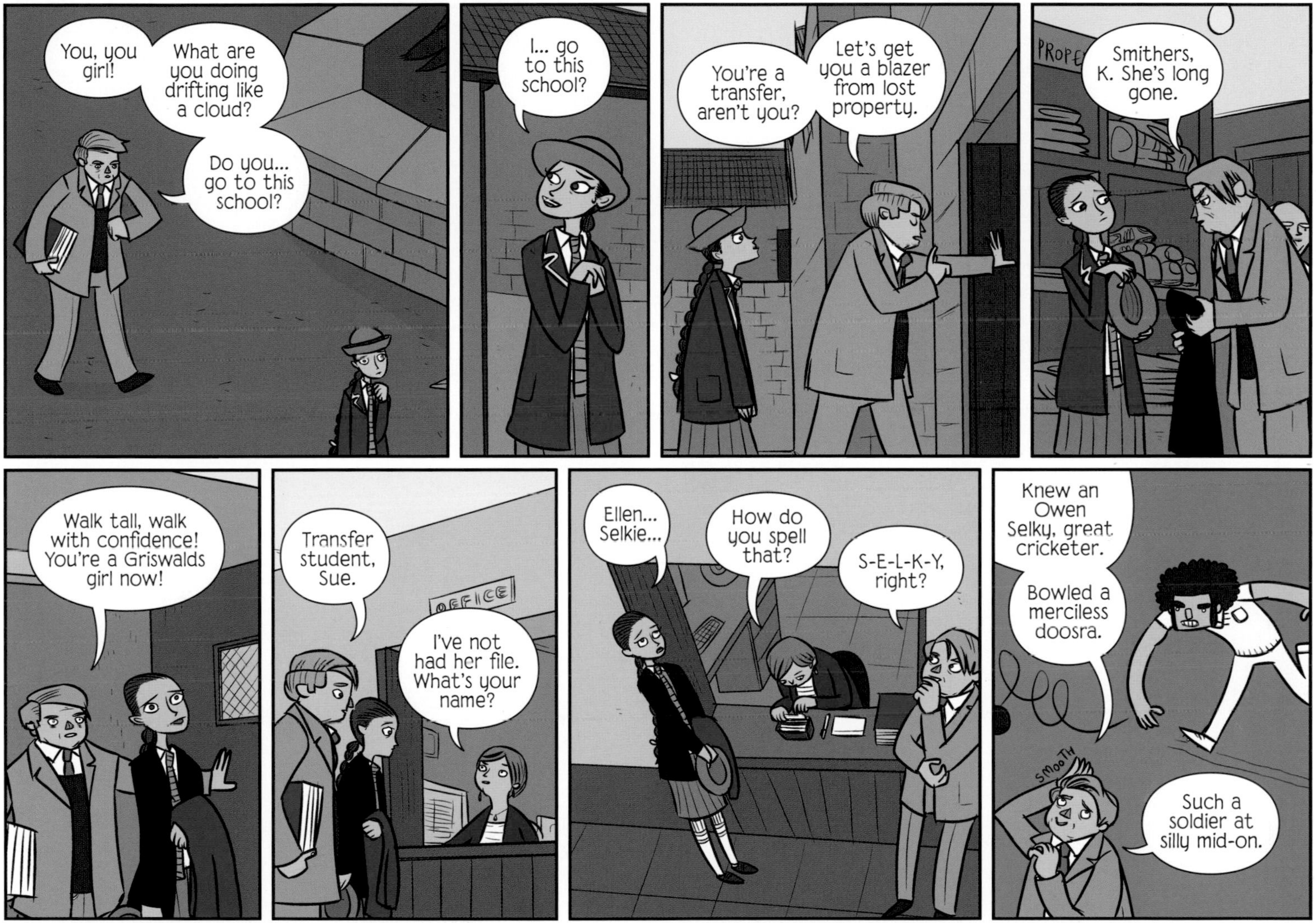
You, you girl!
What are you doing drifting like a cloud?
Do you... go to this school?
I... go to this school?
You're a transfer, aren't you?
Let's get you a blazer from lost property.
PROPE
Smithers, K. She's long gone.
Walk tall, walk with confidence! You're a Griswalds girl now!
Transfer student, Sue.
OFFICE
I've not had her file. What's your name?
Ellen... Selkie...
How do you spell that?
S-E-L-K-Y, right?
Knew an Owen Selky, great cricketer.
Bowled a merciless doosra.
SMOOTH
Such a soldier at silly mid-on.

Bad Machinery, Volume Five

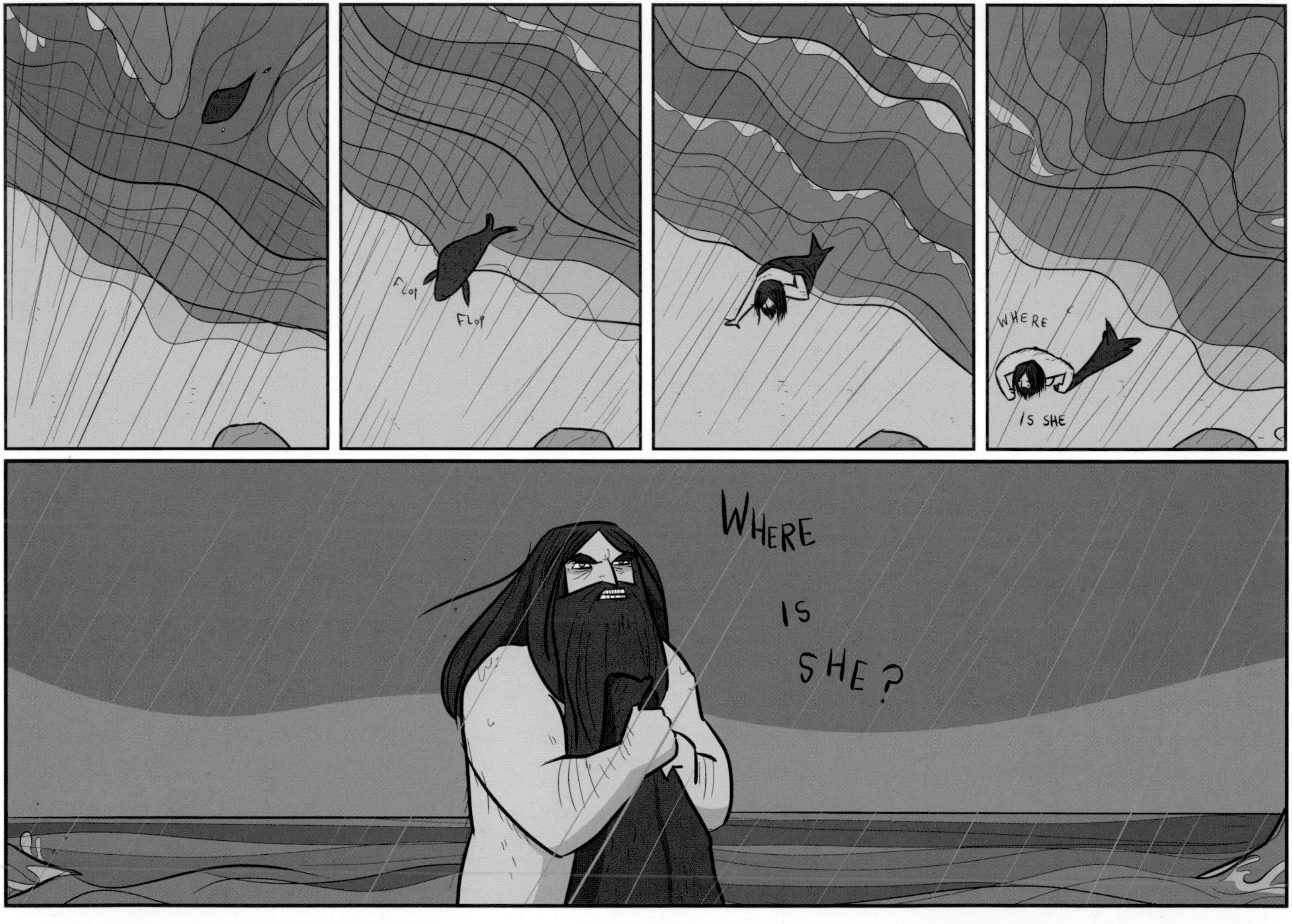
FLOP
FLOP
WHERE
IS SHE
WHERE
IS
SHE?

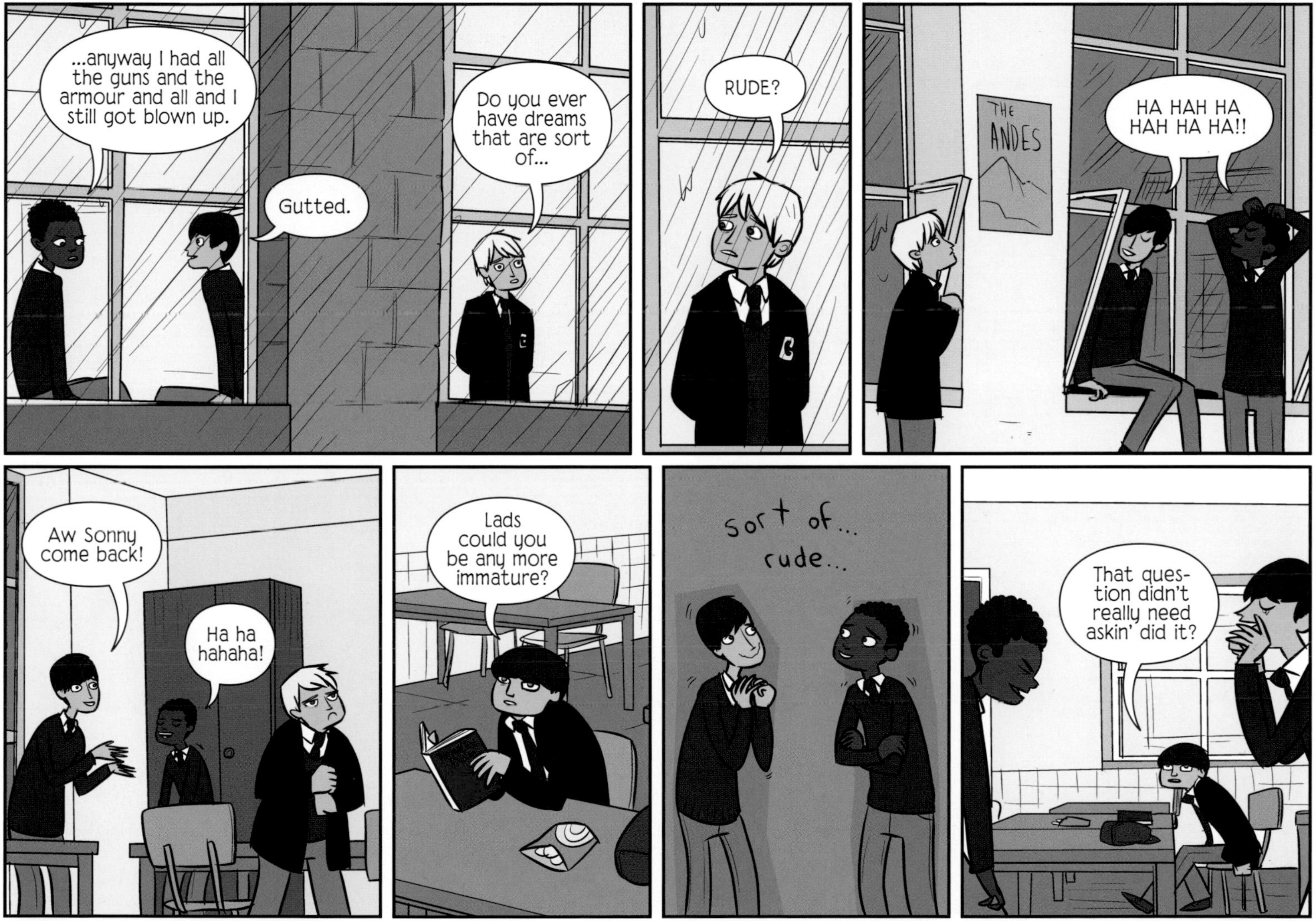
...anyway I had all the guns and the armour and all and I still got blown up.
Gutted.
Do you ever have dreams that are sort of...
RUDE?
THE ANDES
HA HAH HA HAH HA HA!!
Aw Sonny come back!
Ha ha hahaha!
Lads could you be any more immature?
sort of...
rude...
That ques-tion didn't really need askin' did it?

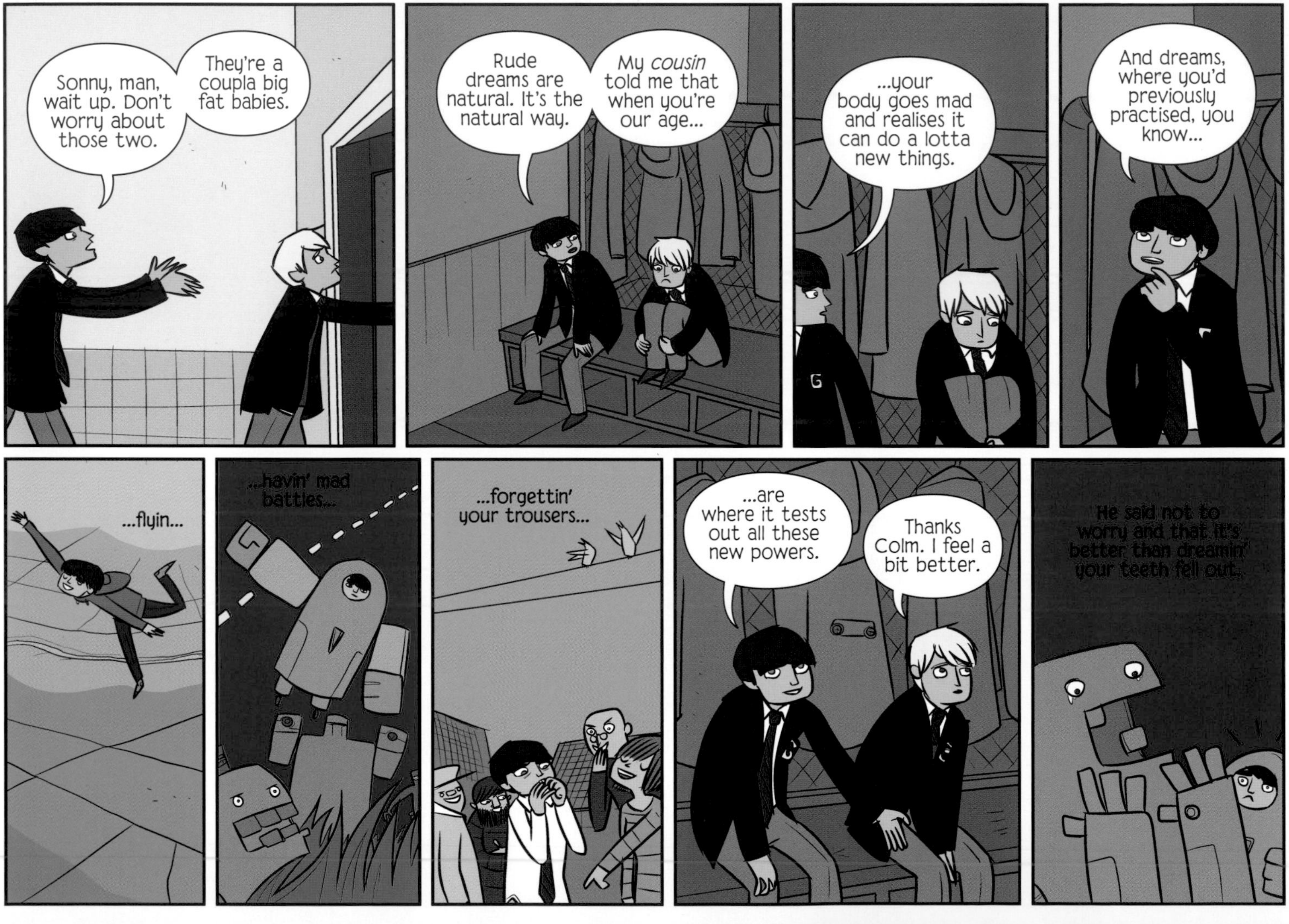
Sonny, man, wait up. Don't worry about those two.
They're a coupla big fat babies.
Rude dreams are natural. It's the natural way.
My *cousin* told me that when you're our age...
...your body goes mad and realises it can do a lotta new things.
And dreams, where you'd previously practised, you know...
...flyin...
...havin' mad battles...
...forgettin' your trousers...
...are where it tests out all these new powers.
Thanks Colm. I feel a bit better.
He said not to worry and that it's better than dreamin' your teeth fell out.

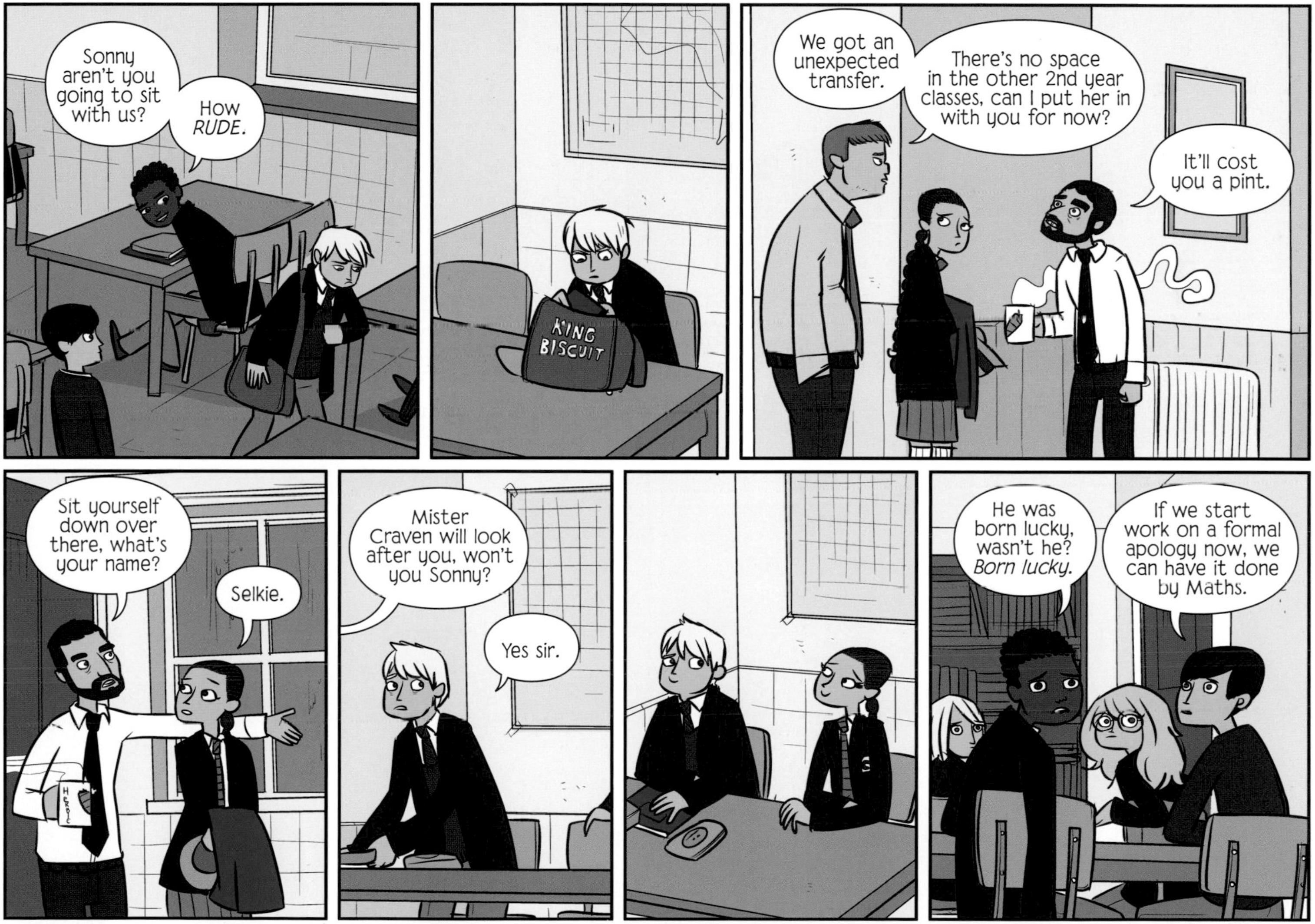
Sonny aren't you going to sit with us?
How *RUDE*.
KING BISCUIT
We got an unexpected transfer.
There's no space in the other 2nd year classes, can I put her in with you for now?
It'll cost you a pint.
Sit yourself down over there, what's your name?
Selkie.
Mister Craven will look after you, won't you Sonny?
Yes sir.
He was born lucky, wasn't he? *Born lucky.*
If we start work on a formal apology now, we can have it done by Maths.

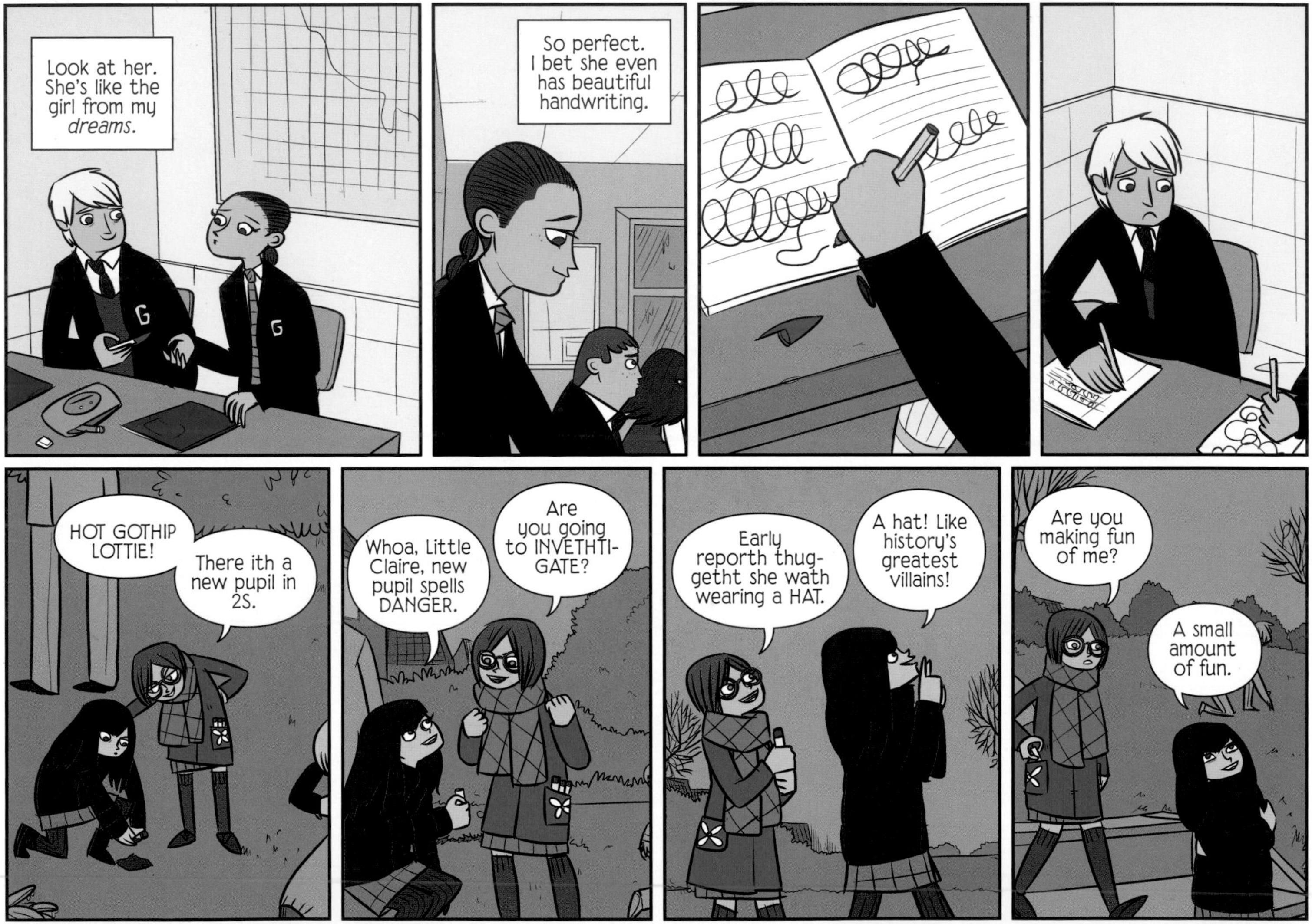

Look at her. She's like the girl from my *dreams*.
So perfect. I bet she even has beautiful handwriting.
HOT GOTHIP LOTTIE!
There ith a new pupil in 2S.
Whoa, Little Claire, new pupil spells DANGER.
Are you going to INVETHTI-GATE?
Early reporth thug-getht she wath wearing a HAT.
A hat! Like history's greatest villains!
Are you making fun of me?
A small amount of fun.

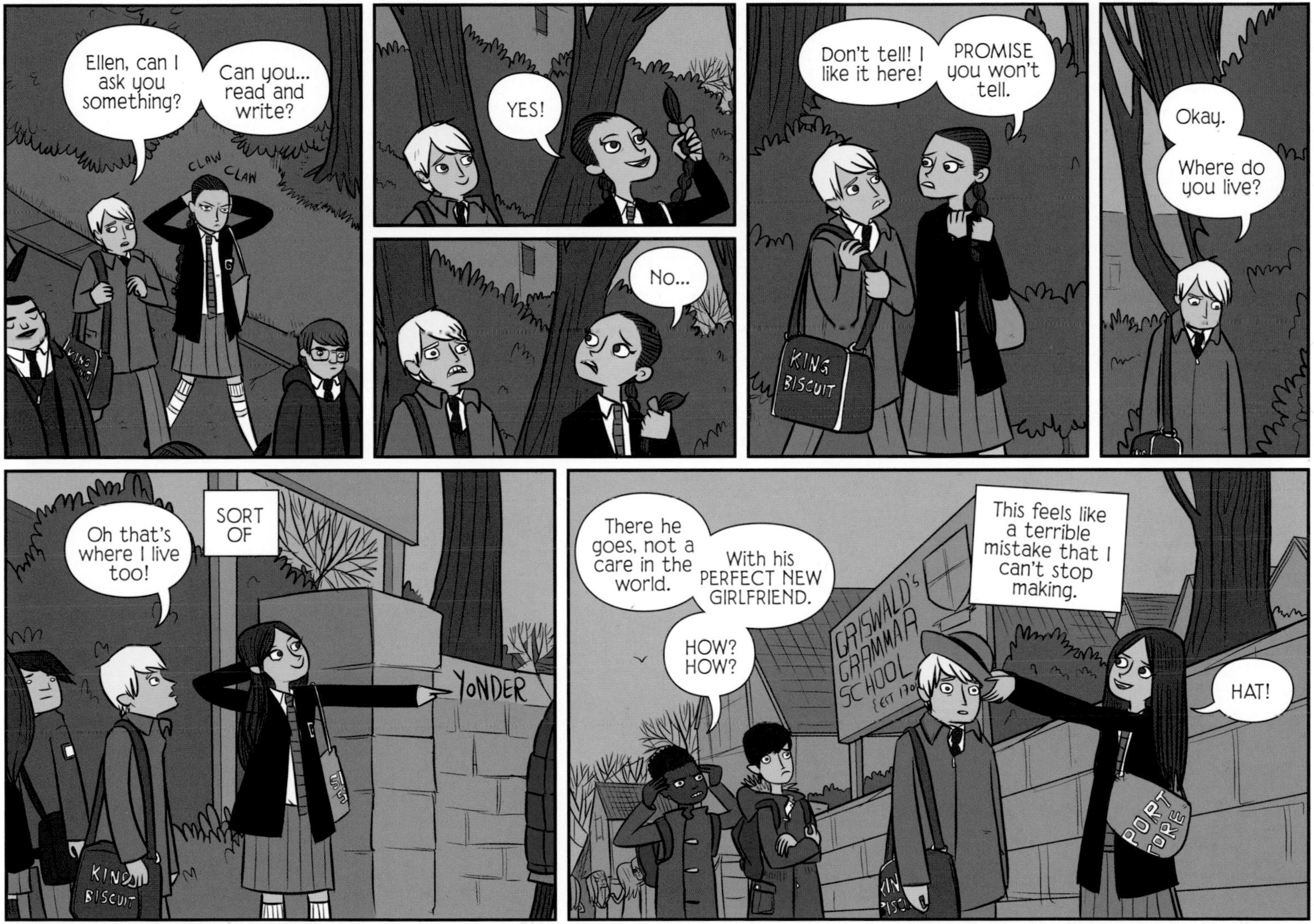
Ellen, can I ask you something?
Can you... read and write?
CLAW
CLAW
YES!
No...
Don't tell! I like it here!
PROMISE you won't tell.
KING BISCUIT
Okay.
Where do you live?
Oh that's where I live too!
SORT OF
YONDER
KING BISCUIT
There he goes, not a care in the world.
With his PERFECT NEW GIRLFRIEND.
HOW? HOW?
This feels like a terrible mistake that I can't stop making.
GRISWALD'S GRAMMAR SCHOOL
HAT!

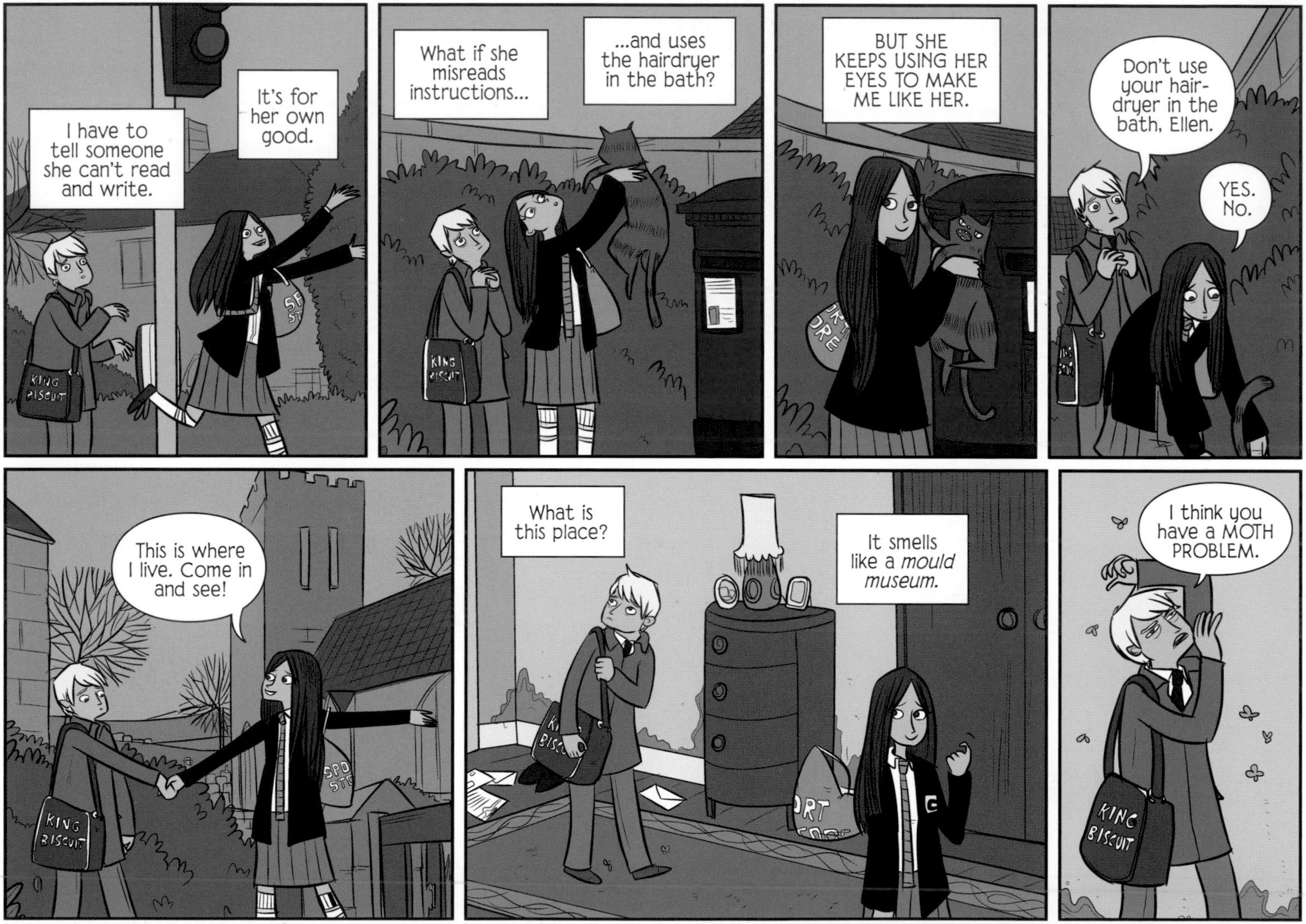
I have to tell someone she can't read and write.
It's for her own good.
What if she misreads instructions...
...and uses the hairdryer in the bath?
BUT SHE KEEPS USING HER EYES TO MAKE ME LIKE HER.
Don't use your hair-dryer in the bath, Ellen.
YES. No.
This is where I live. Come in and see!
What is this place?
It smells like a *mould museum.*
I think you have a MOTH PROBLEM.

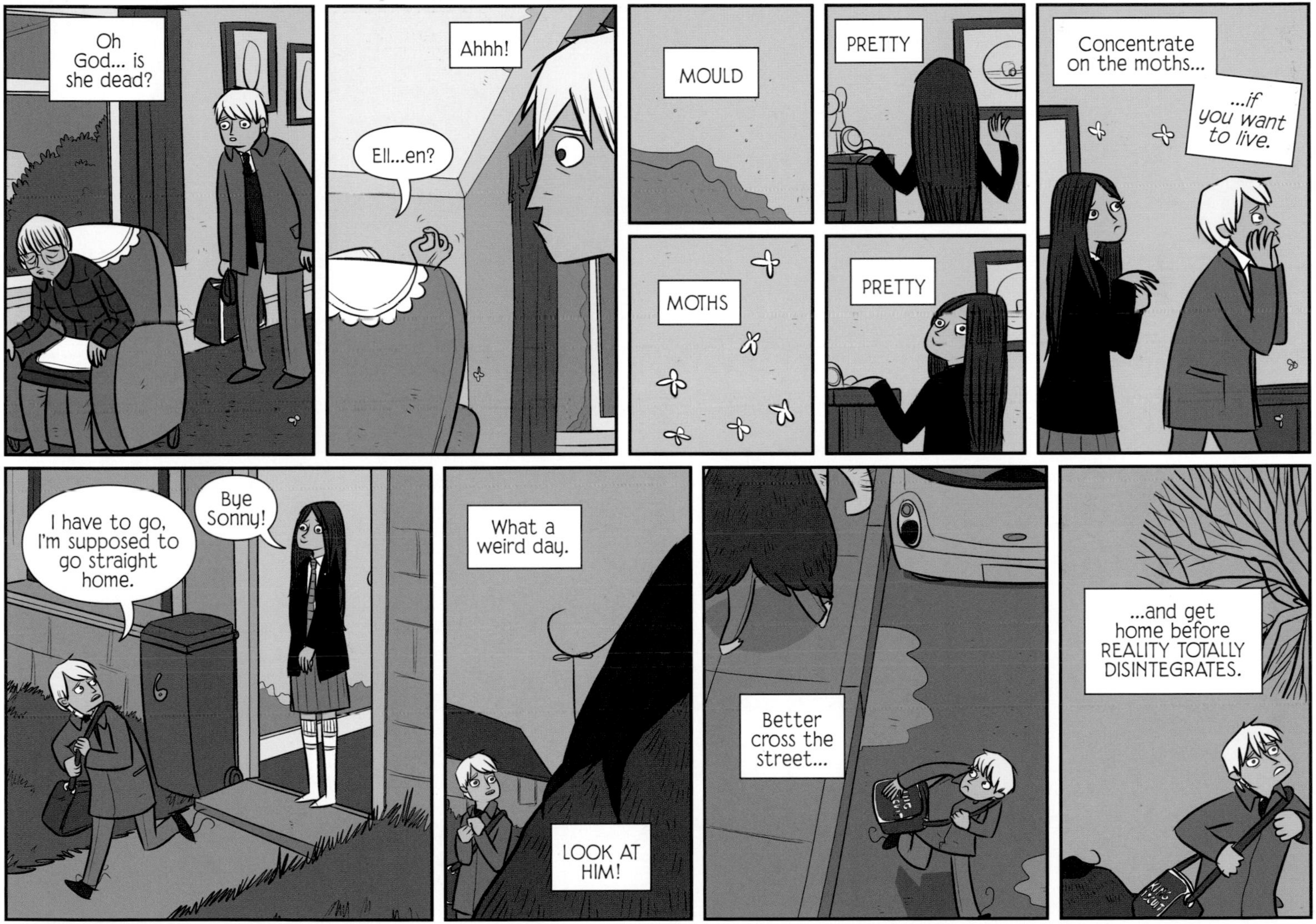

Oh God... is she dead?
Ahhh!
Ell...en?
MOULD
PRETTY
Concentrate on the moths...
...if you want to live.
MOTHS
PRETTY
I have to go, I'm supposed to go straight home.
Bye Sonny!
What a weird day.
LOOK AT HIM!
Better cross the street...
...and get home before REALITY TOTALLY DISINTEGRATES.

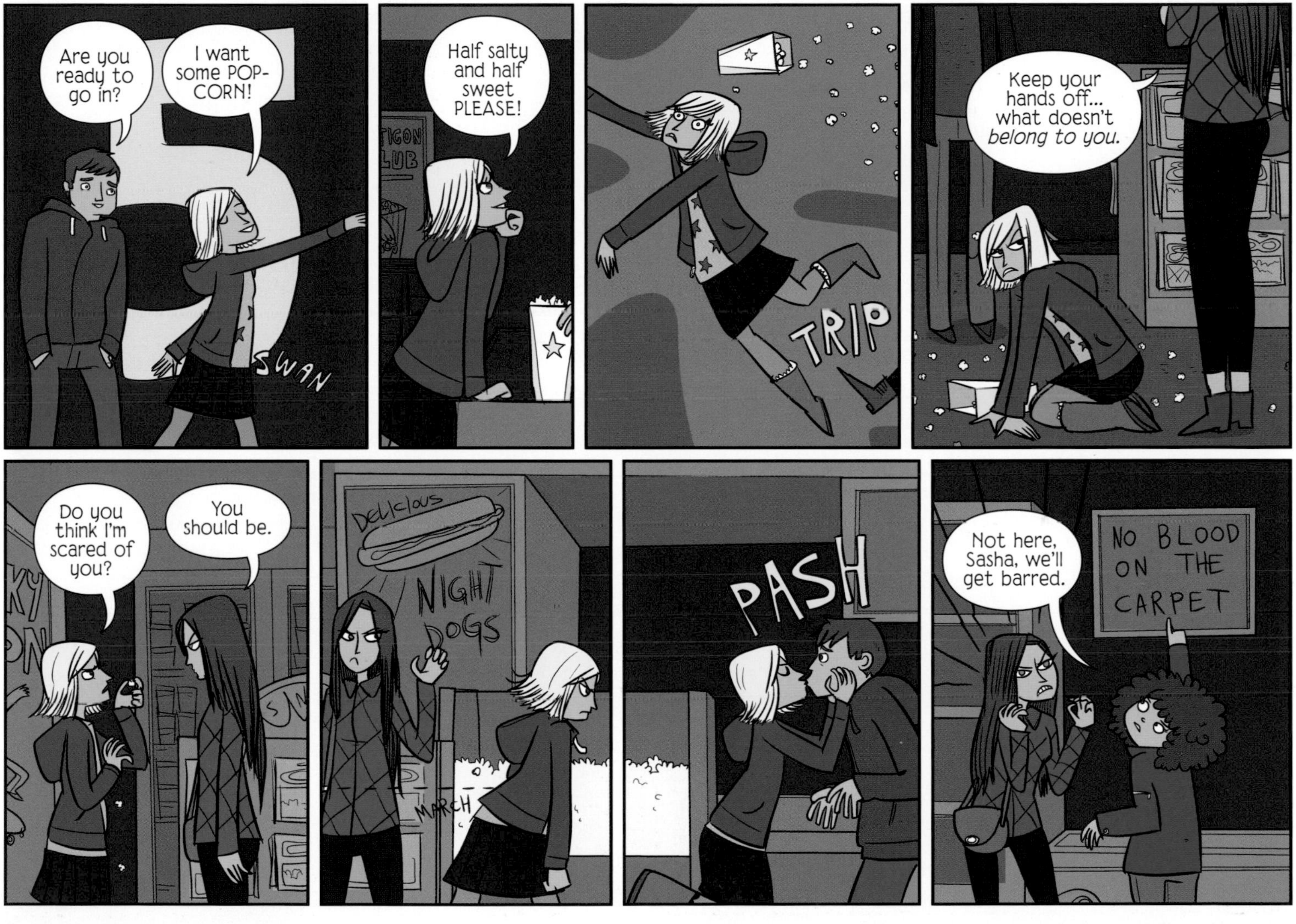
Are you ready to go in?
I want some POP-CORN!
SWAN
Half salty and half sweet PLEASE!
TRIP
Keep your hands off... what doesn't *belong to you.*
Do you think I'm scared of you?
You should be.
DELICIOUS
NIGHT DOGS
MARCH
PASH
Not here, Sasha, we'll get barred.
NO BLOOD ON THE CARPET

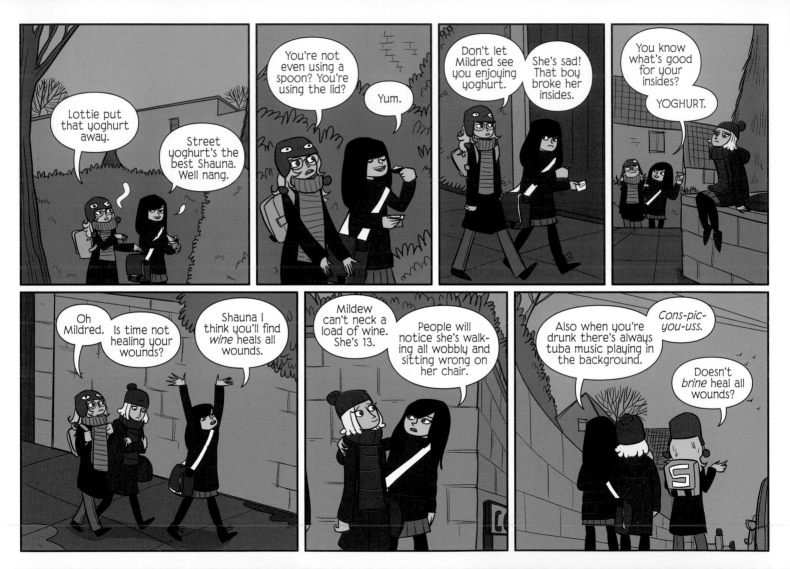

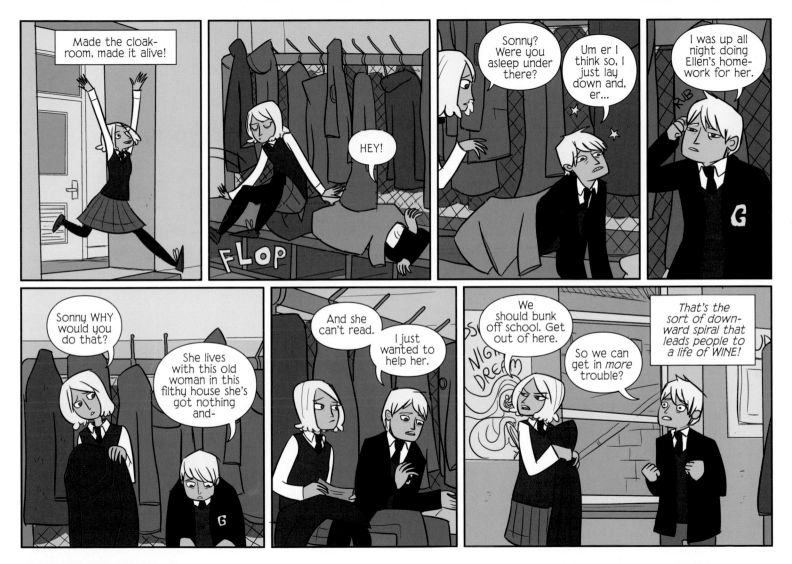

The Case of the Fire Inside

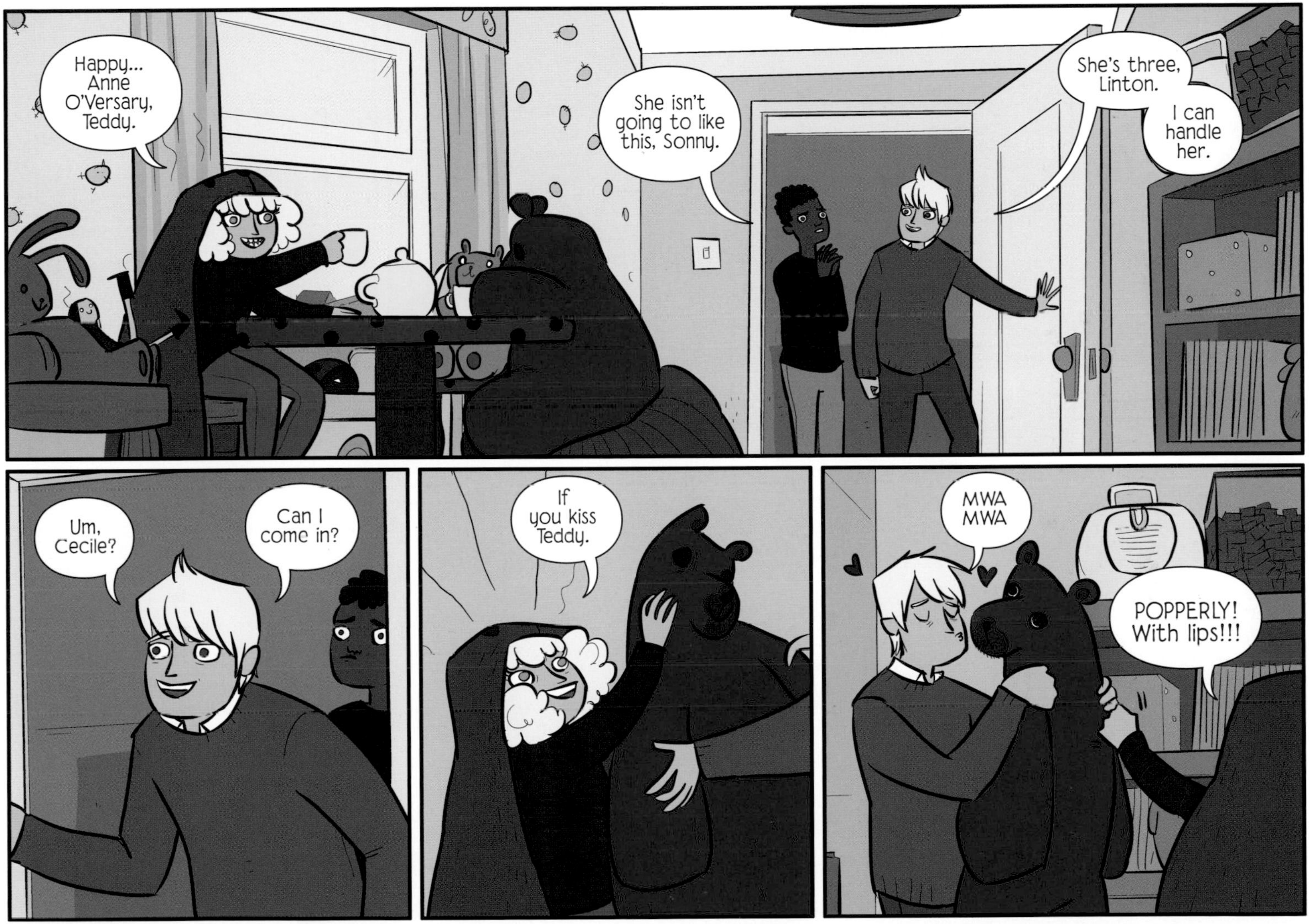
Happy... Anne O'Versary, Teddy.
She isn't going to like this, Sonny.
She's three, Linton.
I can handle her.
Um, Cecile?
Can I come in?
If you kiss Teddy.
MWA MWA
POPPERLY! With lips!!!

The Case of the Fire Inside

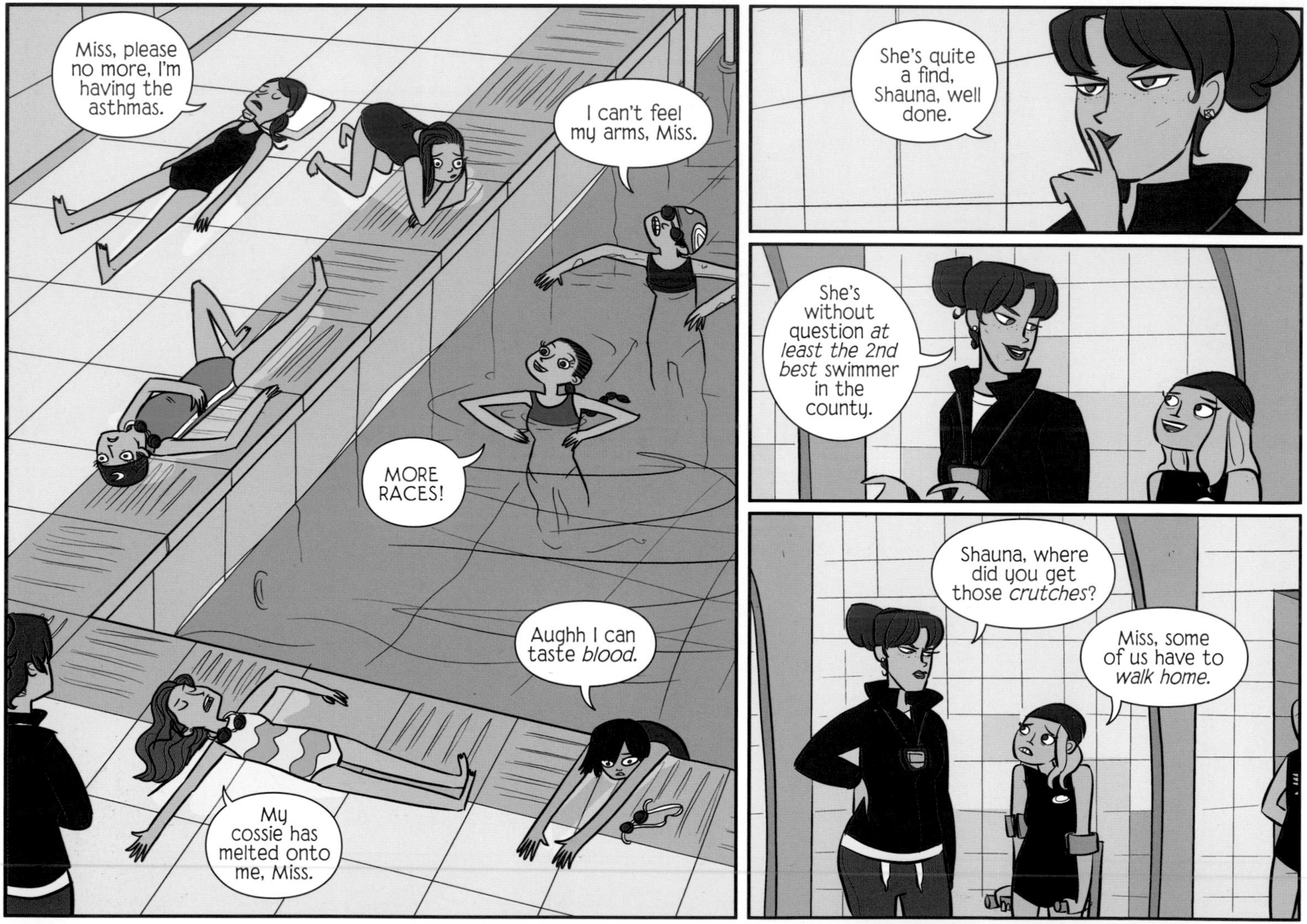
Miss, please no more, I'm having the asthmas.
I can't feel my arms, Miss.
MORE RACES!
Aughh I can taste *blood.*
My cossie has melted onto me, Miss.
She's quite a find, Shauna, well done.
She's without question *at least the 2nd best* swimmer in the county.
Shauna, where did you get those *crutches*?
Miss, some of us have to *walk home.*

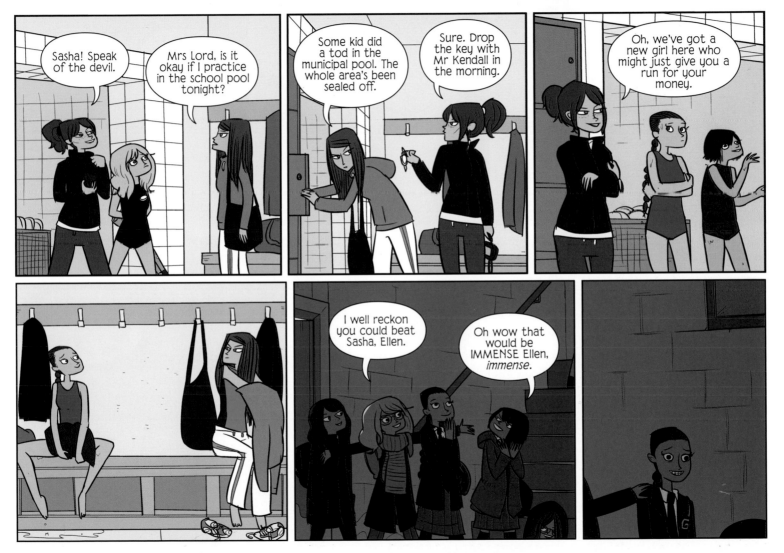

The Case of the Fire Inside

The Case of the Fire Inside

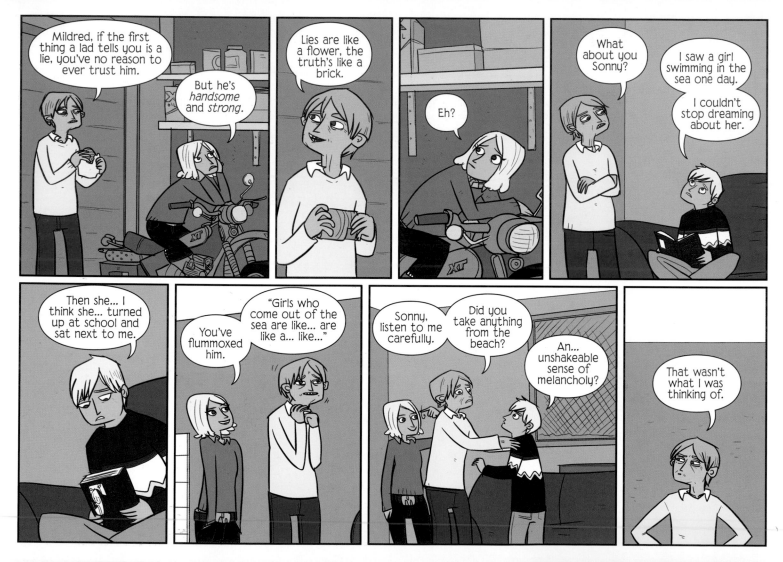

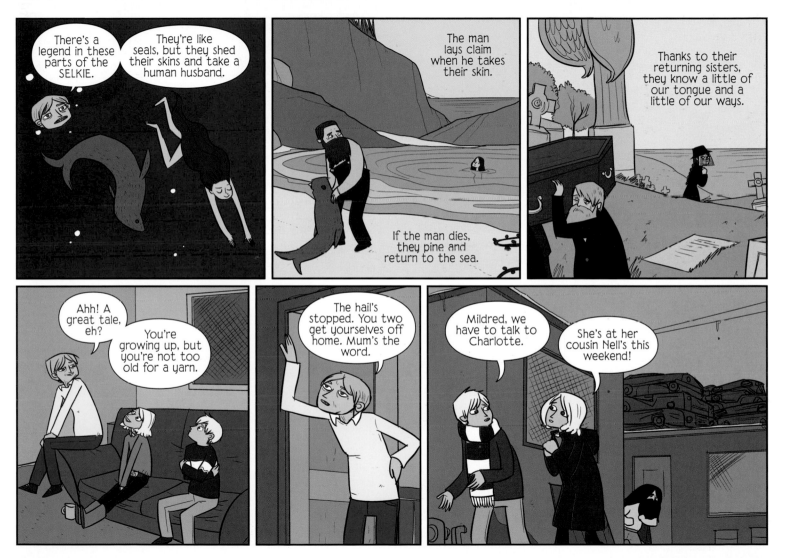

# 3

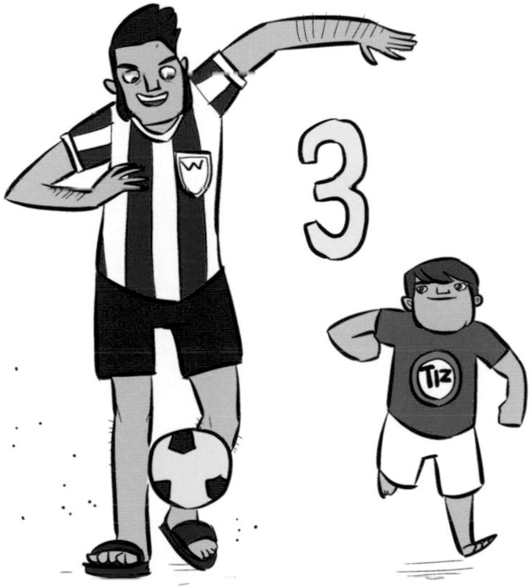
TIZ

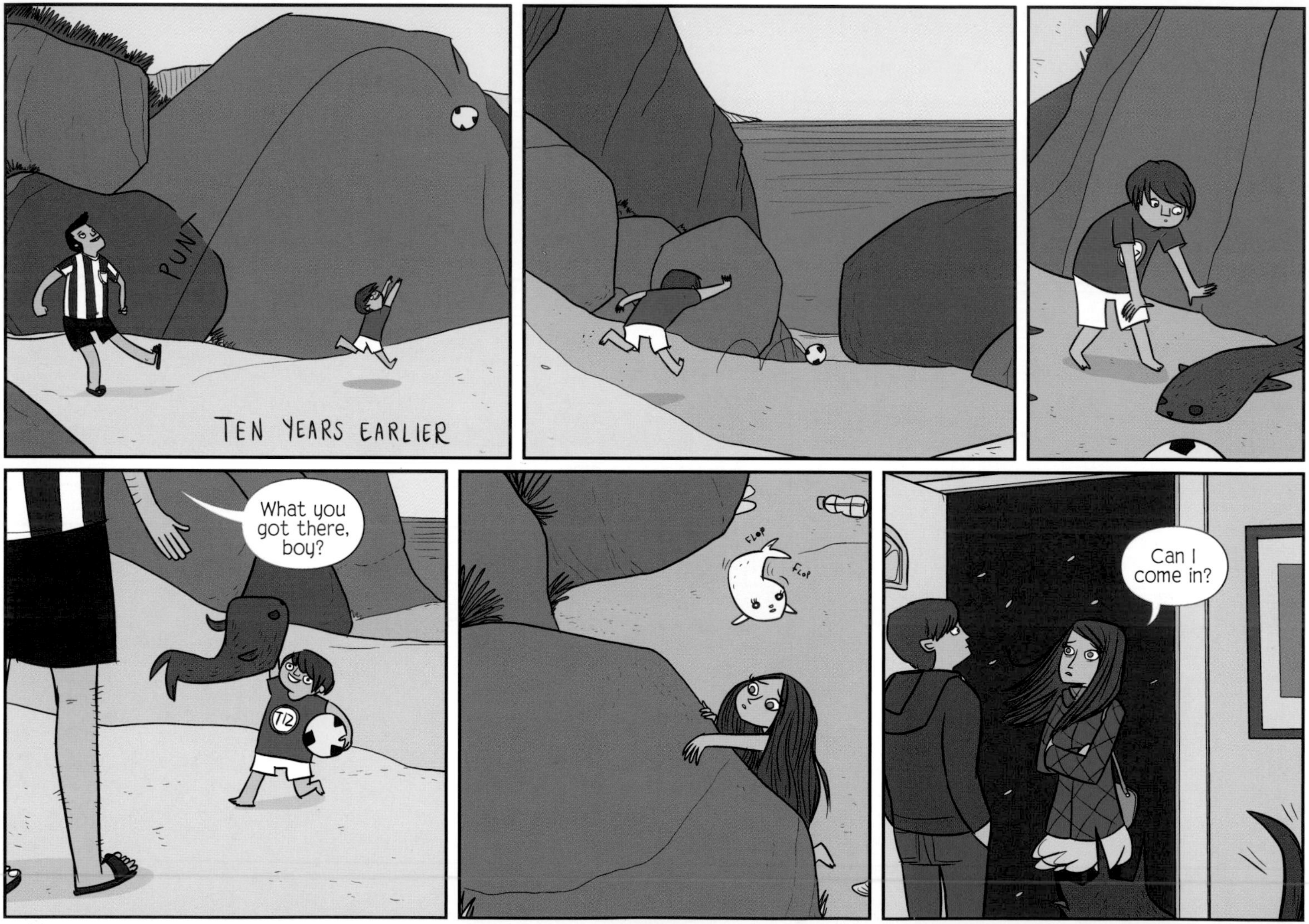
PUNT
TEN YEARS EARLIER
What you got there, boy?
FLOP
FLOP
Can I come in?

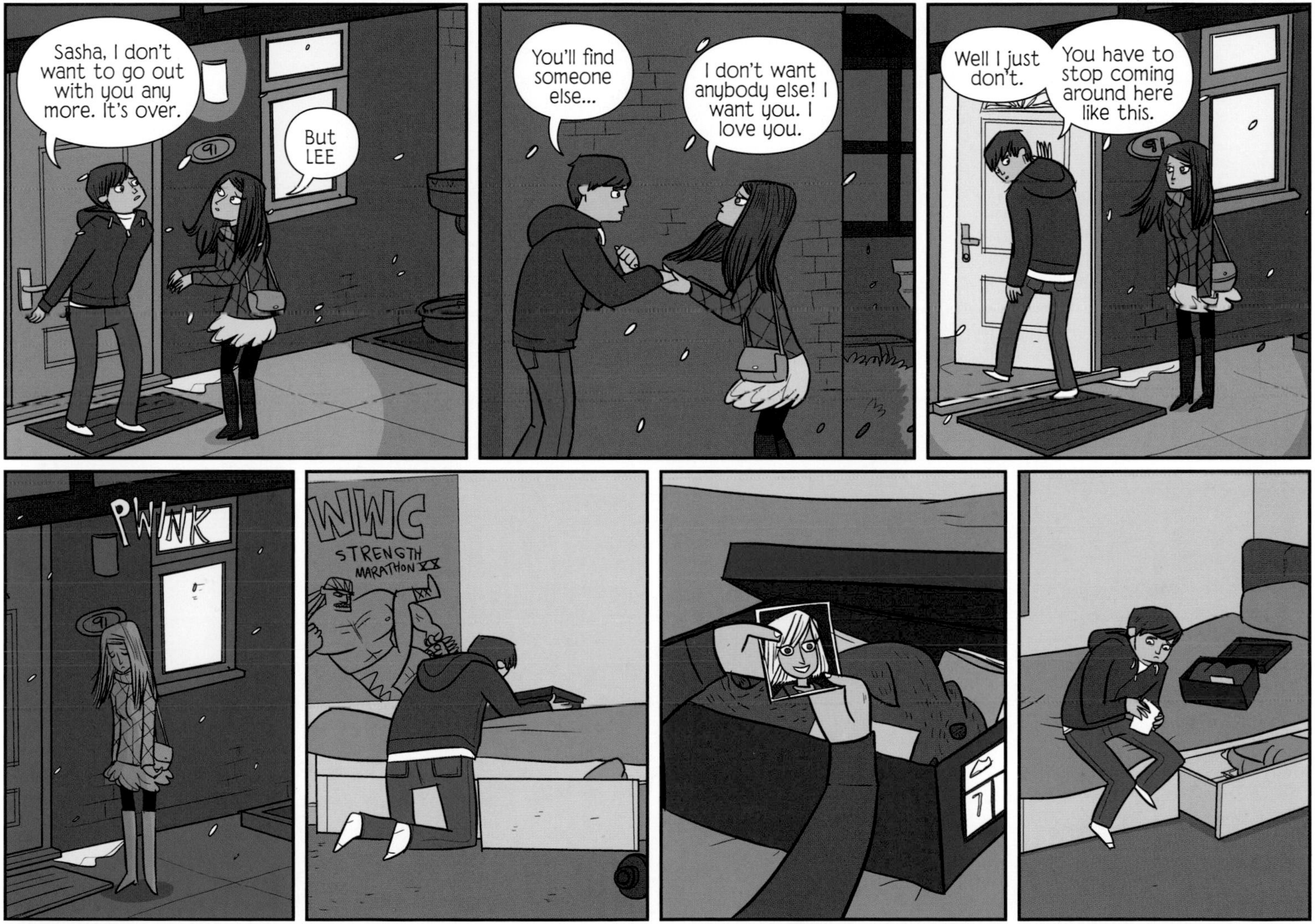

Sasha, I don't want to go out with you any more. It's over.
But LEE
You'll find someone else...
I don't want anybody else! I want you. I love you.
Well I just don't.
You have to stop coming around here like this.
PWINK
WWC
STRENGTH MARATHON XX

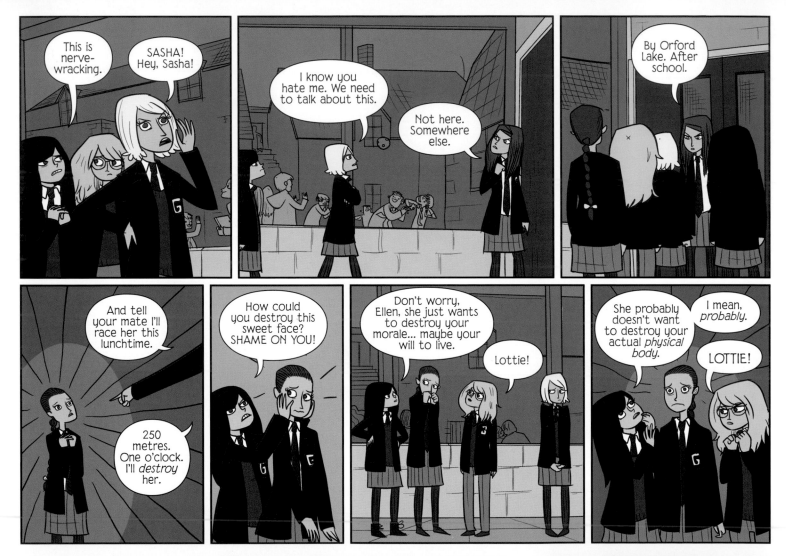

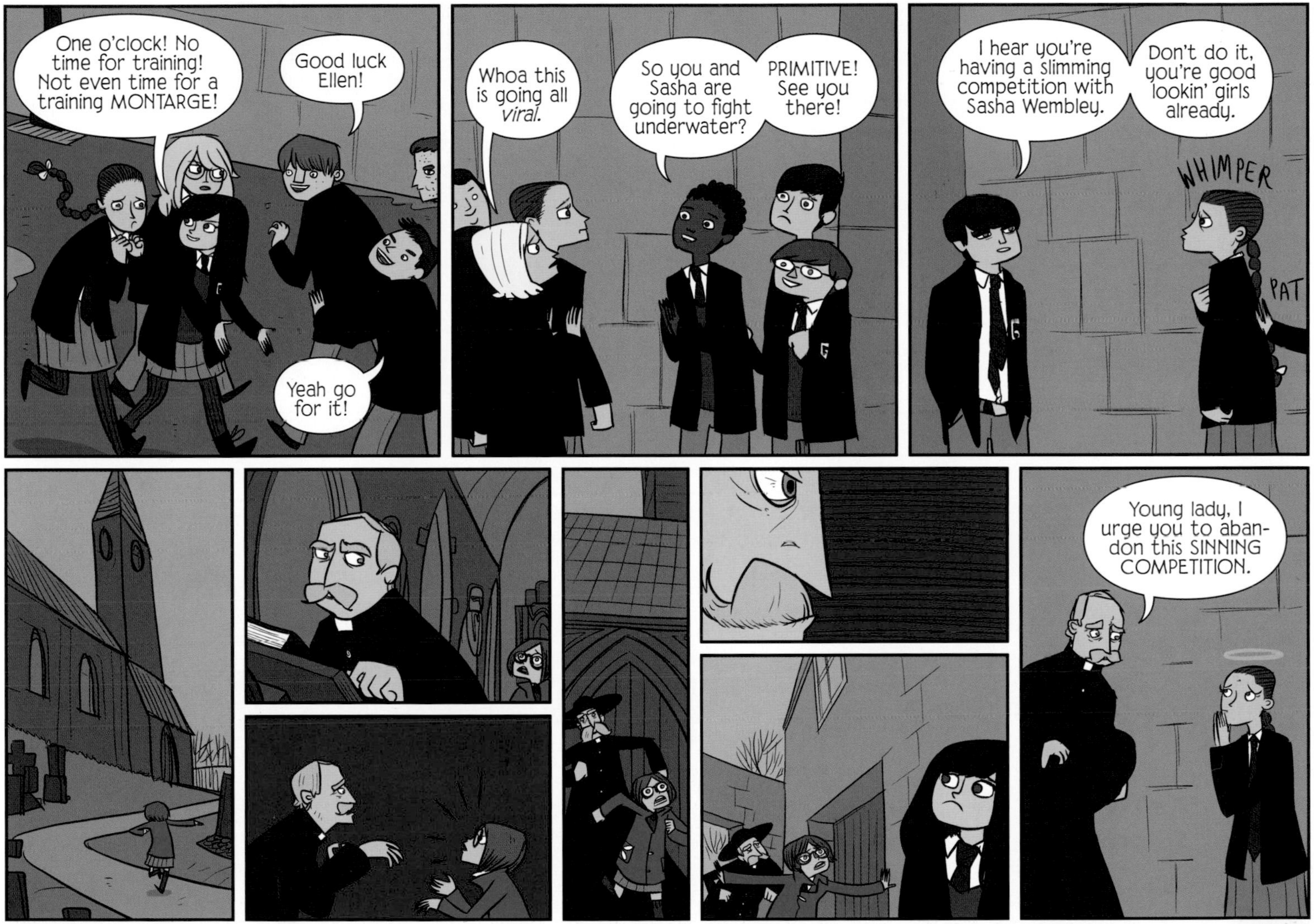
One o'clock! No time for training! Not even time for a training MONTARGE!
Good luck Ellen!
Yeah go for it!
Whoa this is going all *viral*.
So you and Sasha are going to fight underwater?
PRIMITIVE! See you there!
I hear you're having a slimming competition with Sasha Wembley.
Don't do it, you're good lookin' girls already.
WHIMPER
PAT
Young lady, I urge you to abandon this SINNING COMPETITION.

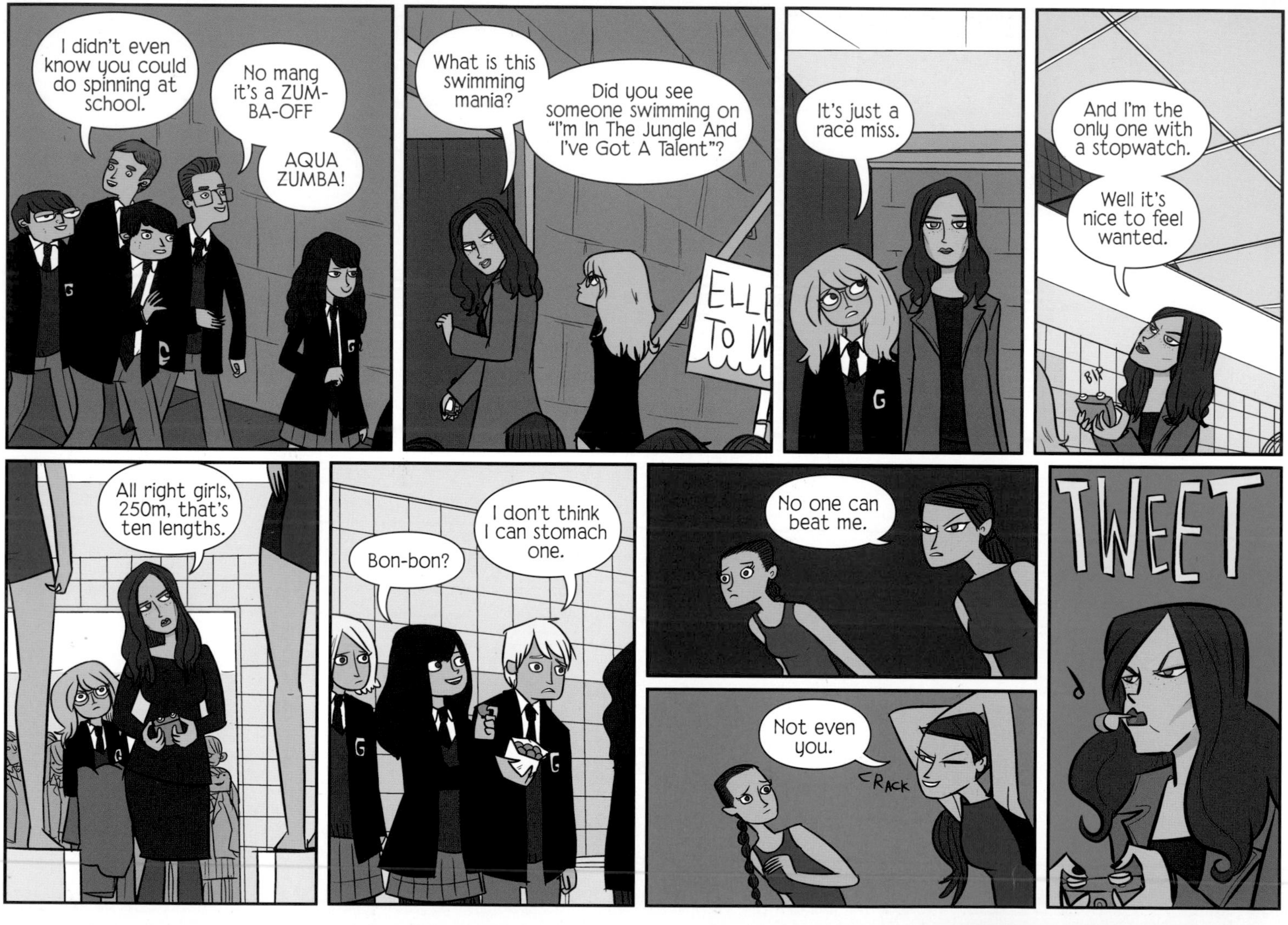
I didn't even know you could do spinning at school.
No mang it's a ZUM-BA-OFF
AQUA ZUMBA!
What is this swimming mania?
Did you see someone swimming on "I'm In The Jungle And I've Got A Talent"?
ELL
TO W
It's just a race miss.
And I'm the only one with a stopwatch.
Well it's nice to feel wanted.
BIP
All right girls, 250m, that's ten lengths.
Bon-bon?
I don't think I can stomach one.
No one can beat me.
Not even you.
CRACK
TWEET

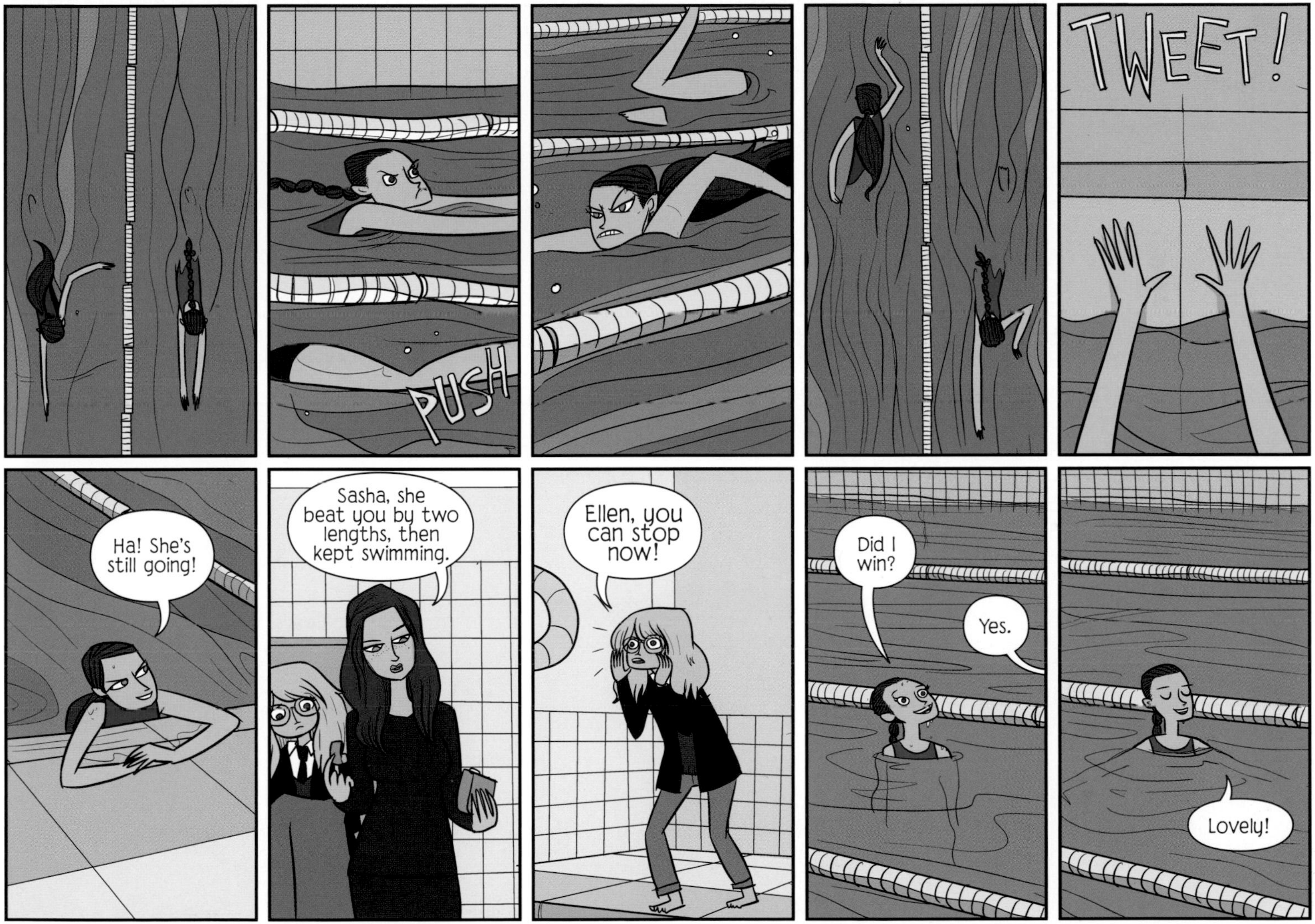
PUSH
TWEET!
Ha! She's still going!
Sasha, she beat you by two lengths, then kept swimming.
Ellen, you can stop now!
Did I win?
Yes.
Lovely!

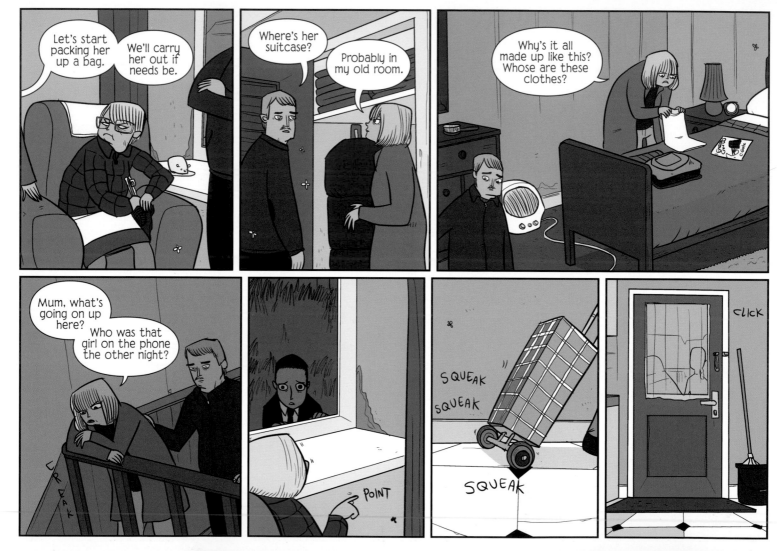

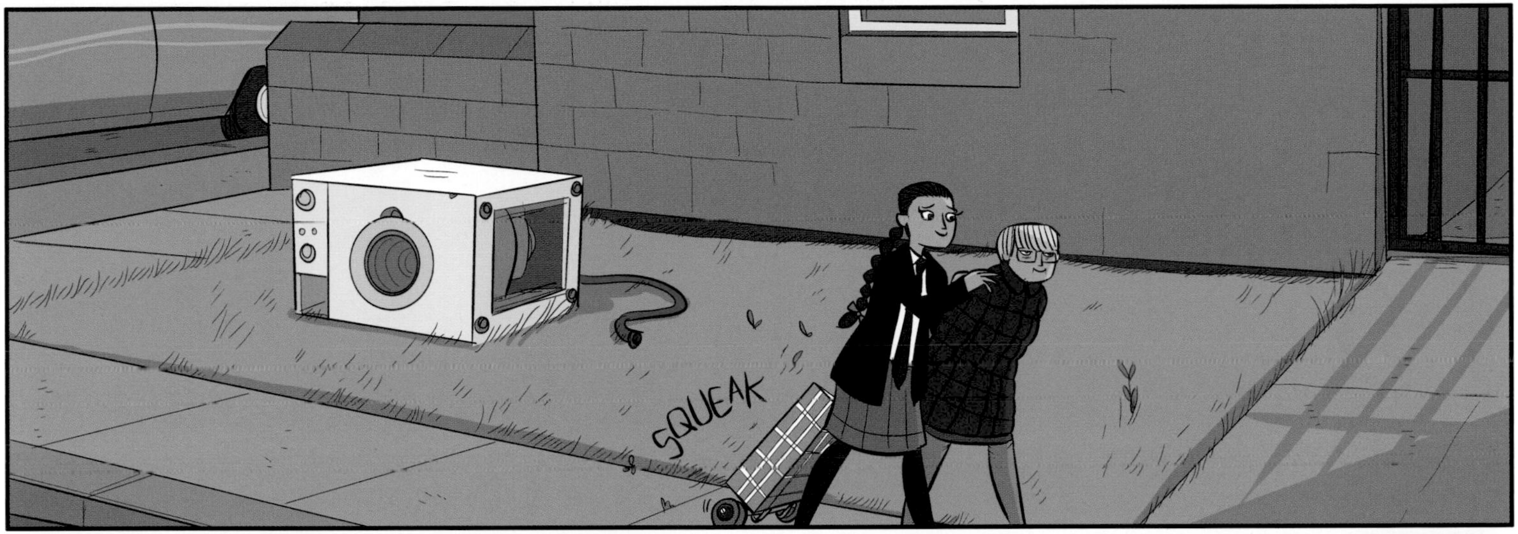
SQUEAK

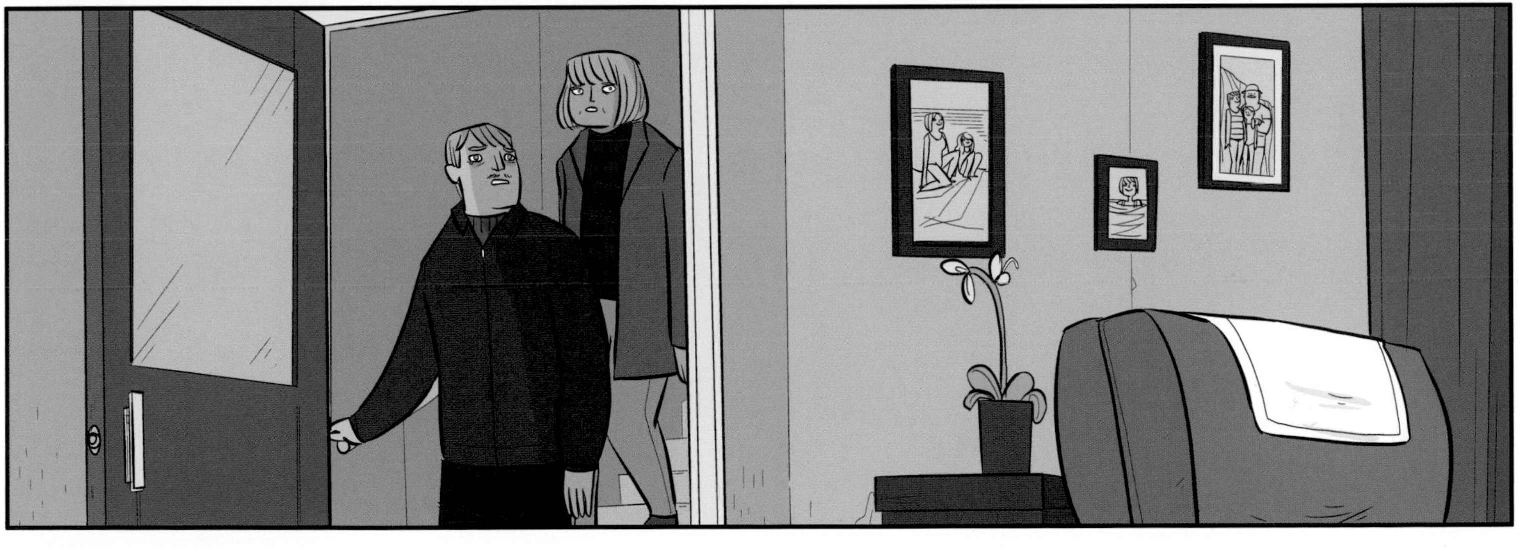

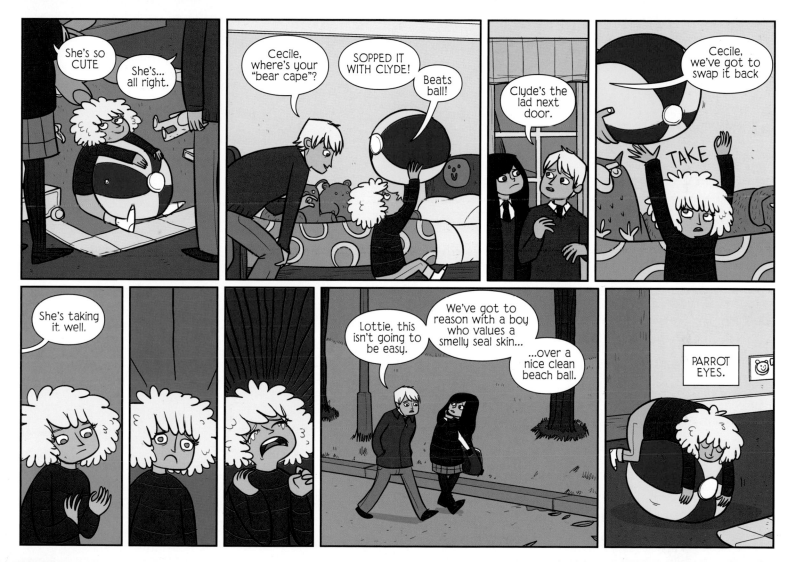

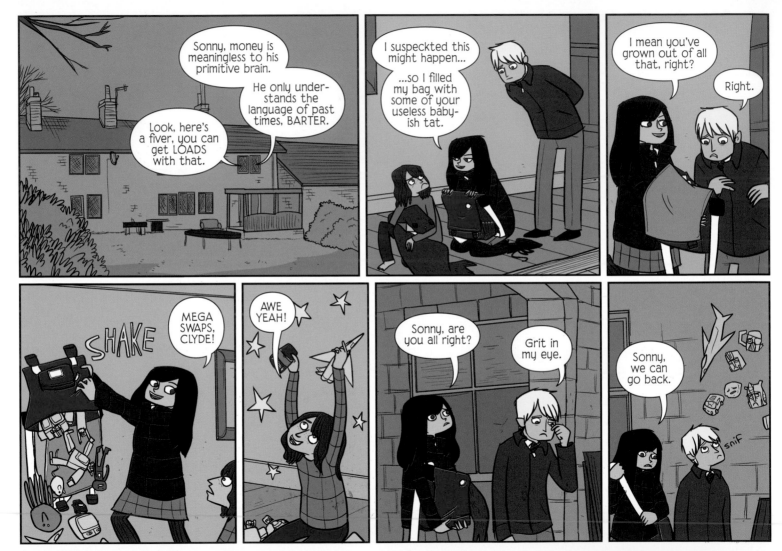

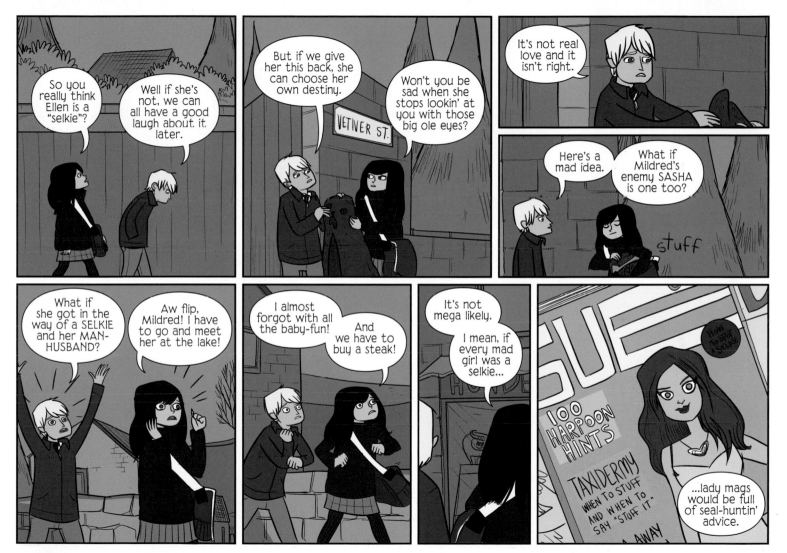

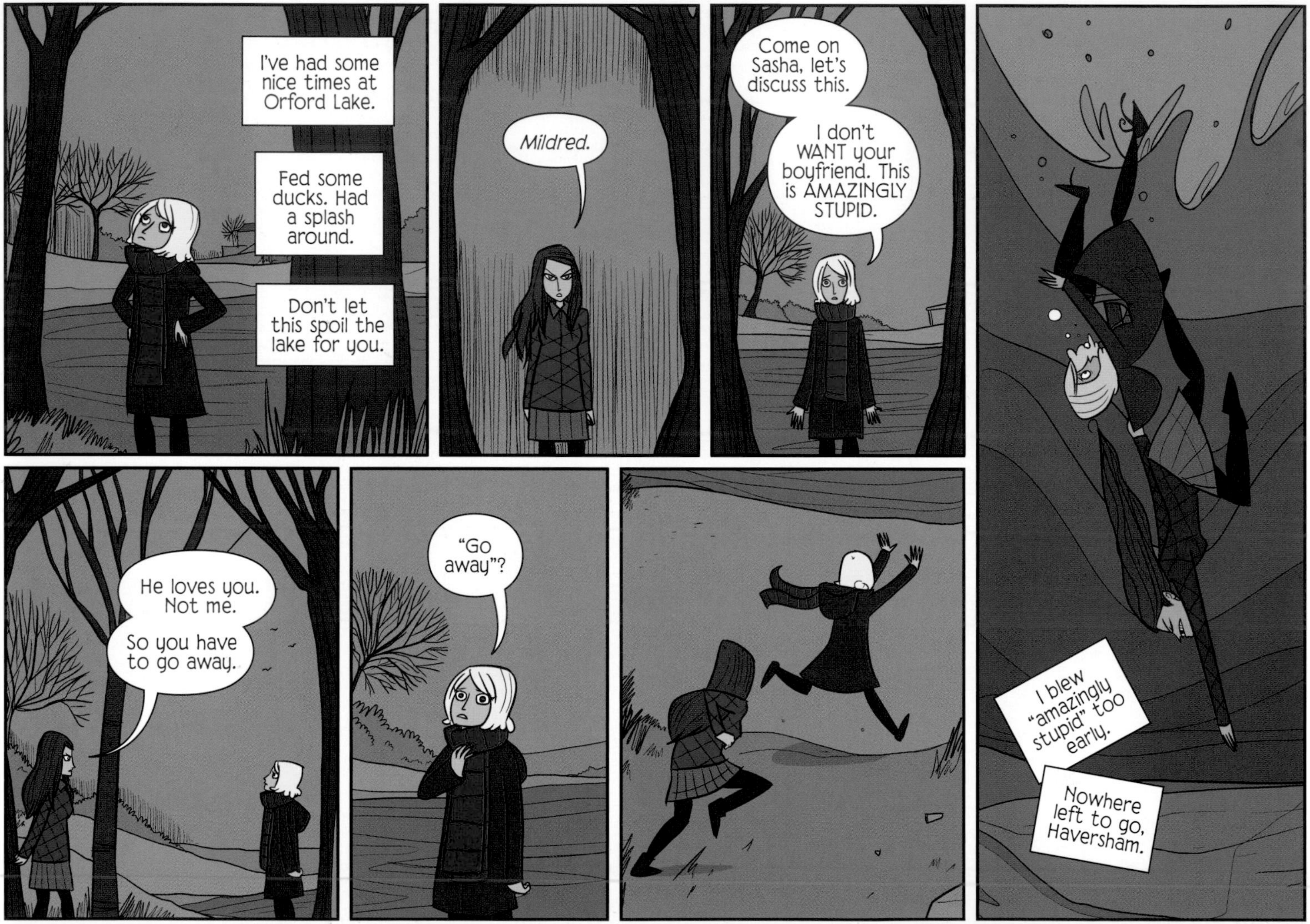
I've had some nice times at Orford Lake.
Fed some ducks. Had a splash around.
Don't let this spoil the lake for you.
*Mildred.*
Come on Sasha, let's discuss this.
I don't WANT your boyfriend. This is AMAZINGLY STUPID.
I blew "amazingly stupid" too early.
Nowhere left to go, Haversham.
He loves you. Not me.
So you have to go away.
"Go away"?

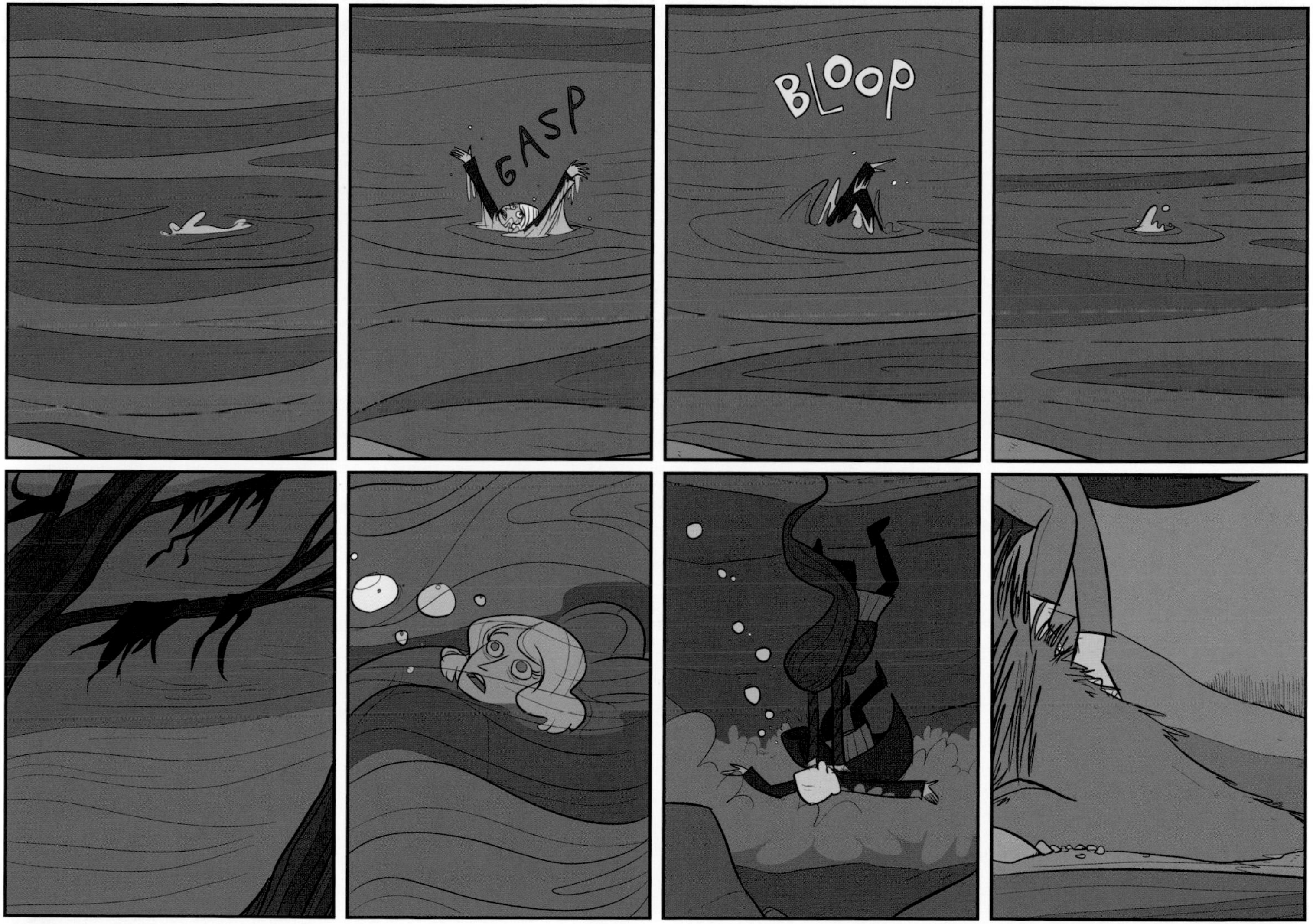
GASP
BLOOP

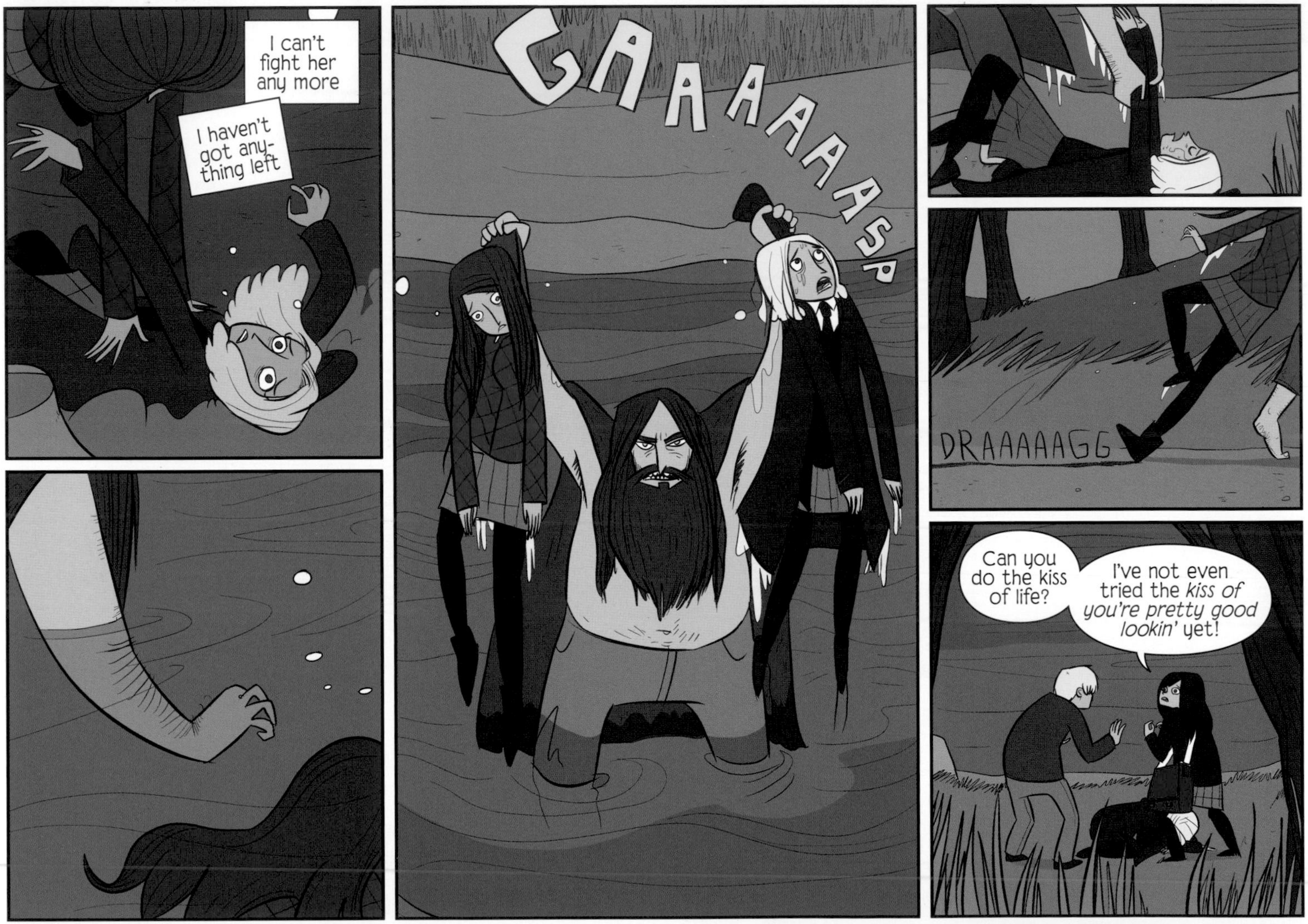
I can't fight her any more
I haven't got any-thing left
GAAAAAASP
DRAAAAAGG
Can you do the kiss of life?
I've not even tried the *kiss of you're pretty good lookin'* yet!

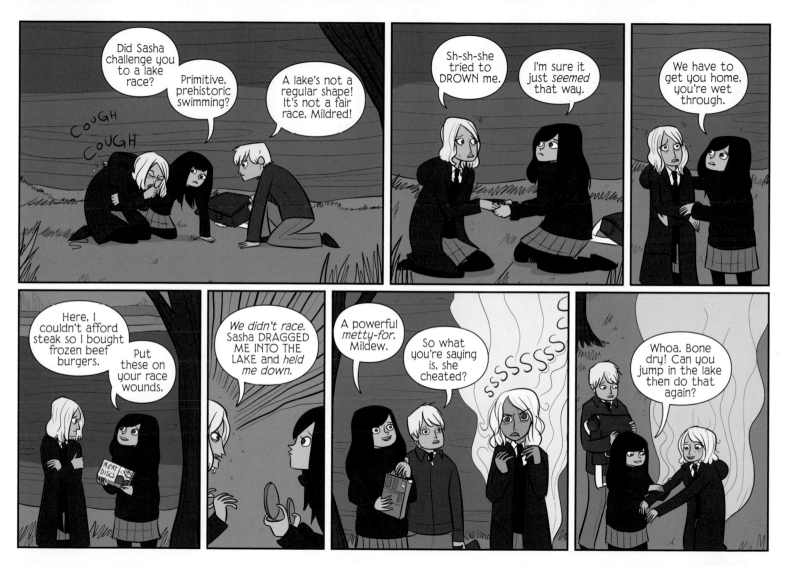

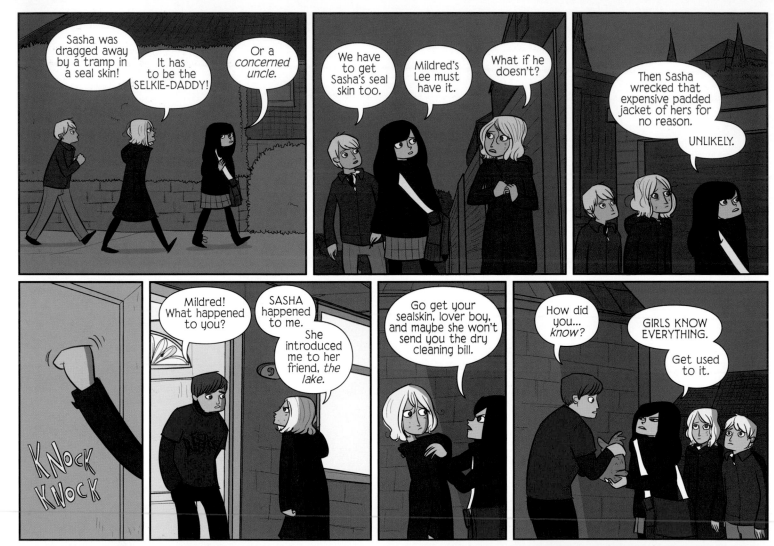

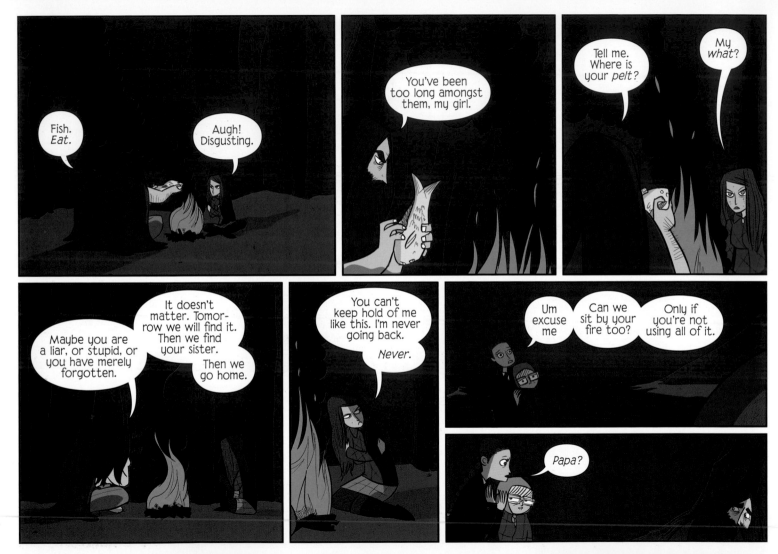

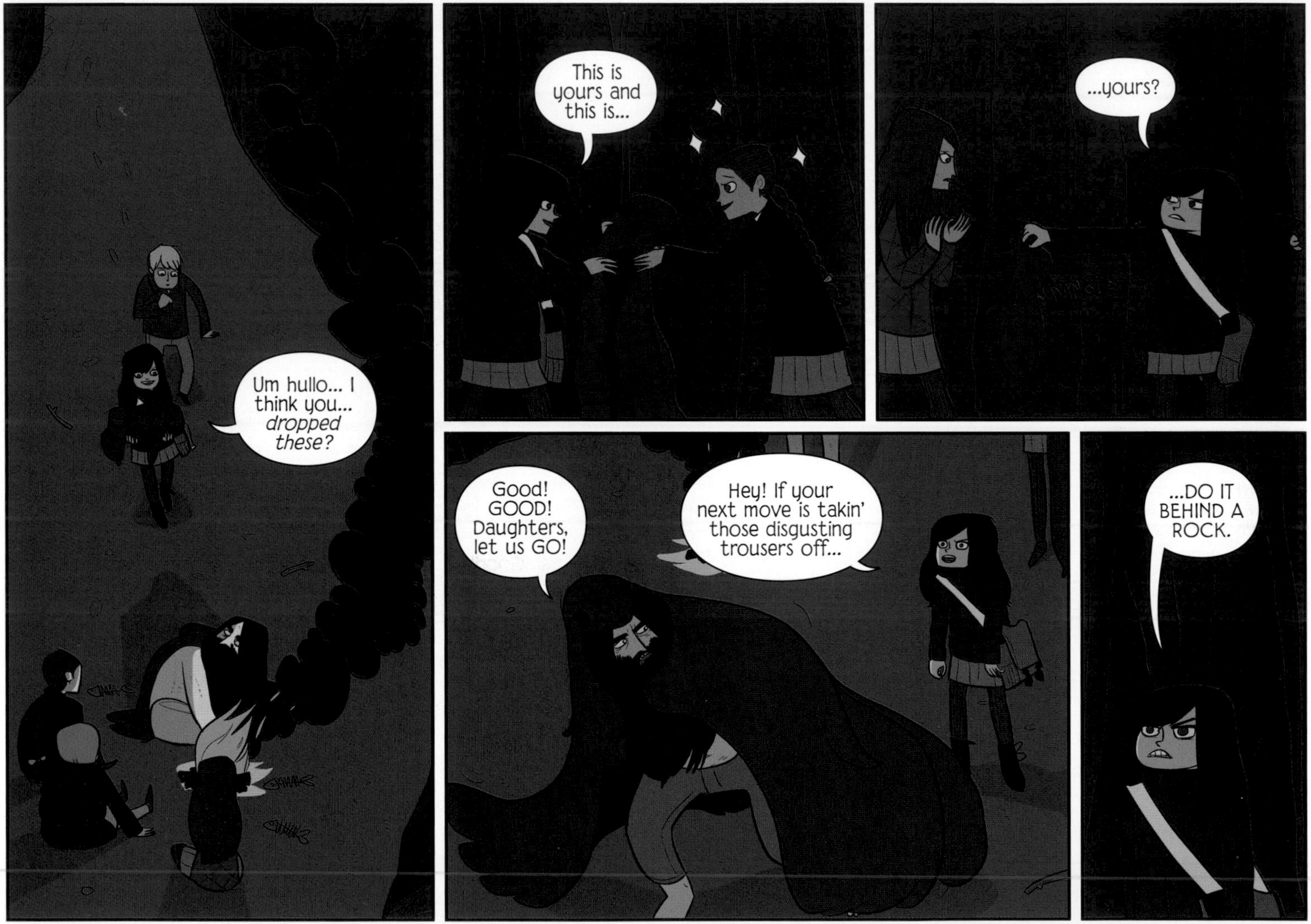
Um hullo... I think you... *dropped these?*
This is yours and this is...
...yours?
Good! GOOD! Daughters, let us GO!
Hey! If your next move is takin' those disgusting trousers off...
...DO IT BEHIND A ROCK.

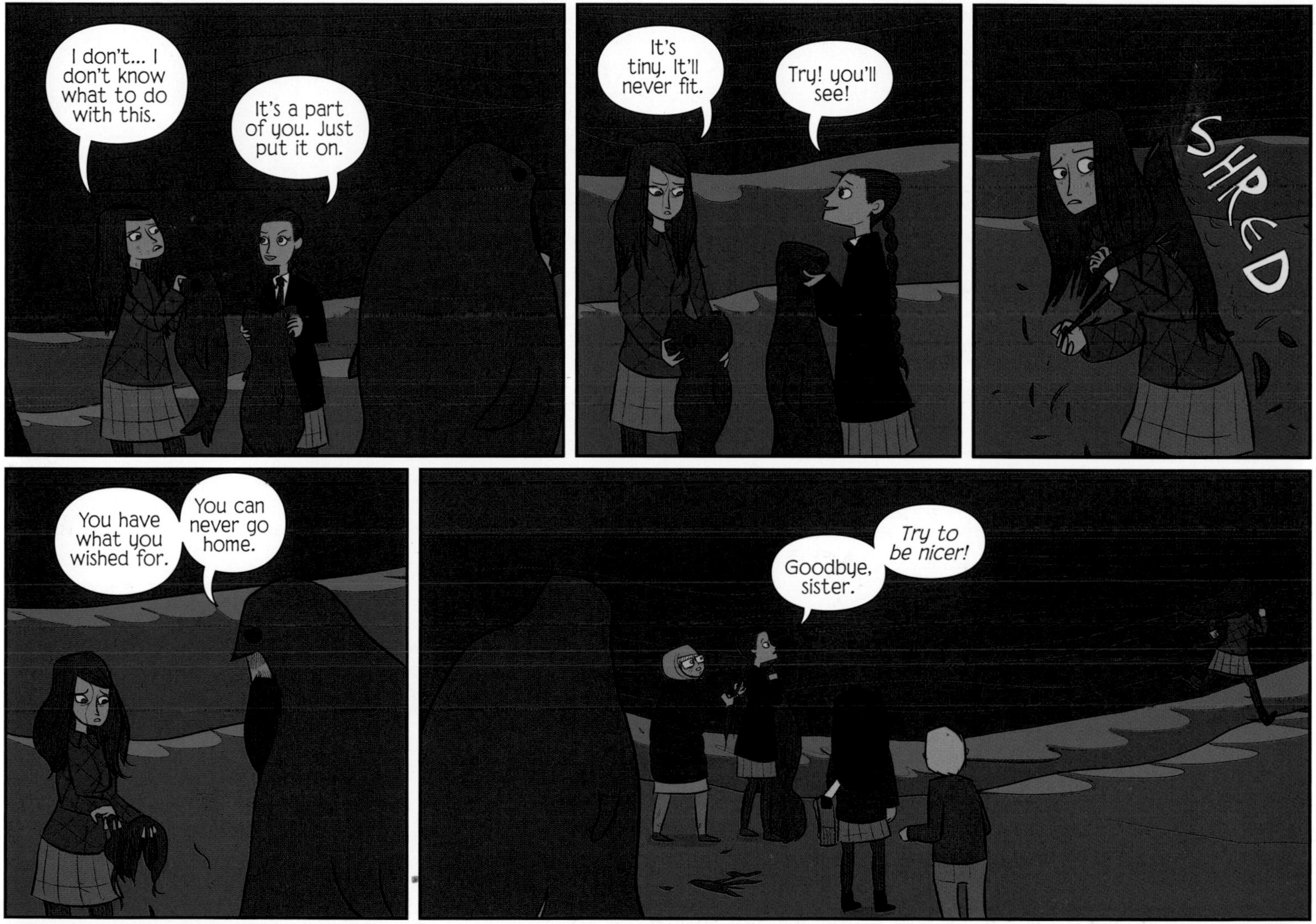
I don't... I don't know what to do with this.
It's a part of you. Just put it on.
It's tiny. It'll never fit.
Try! you'll see!
SHRED
You have what you wished for.
You can never go home.
Goodbye, sister.
*Try to be nicer!*

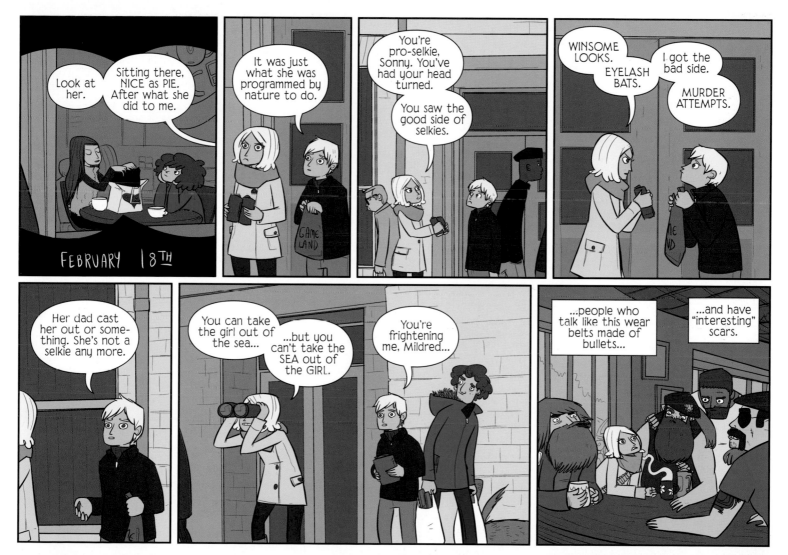

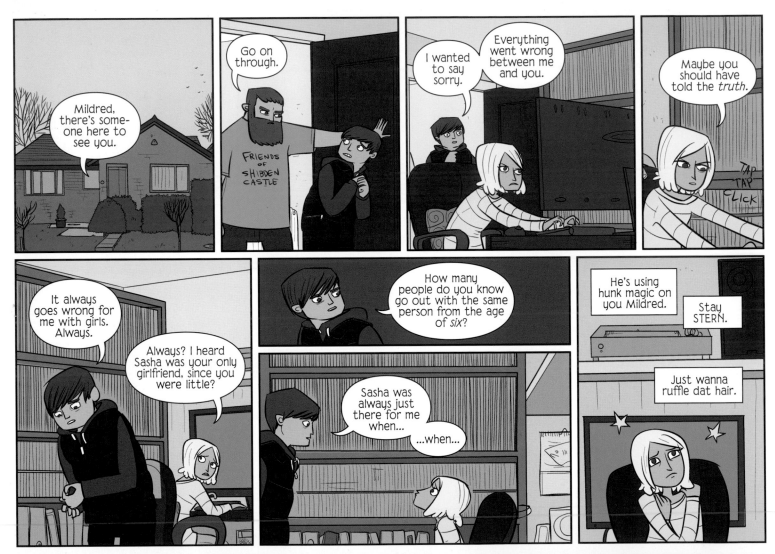

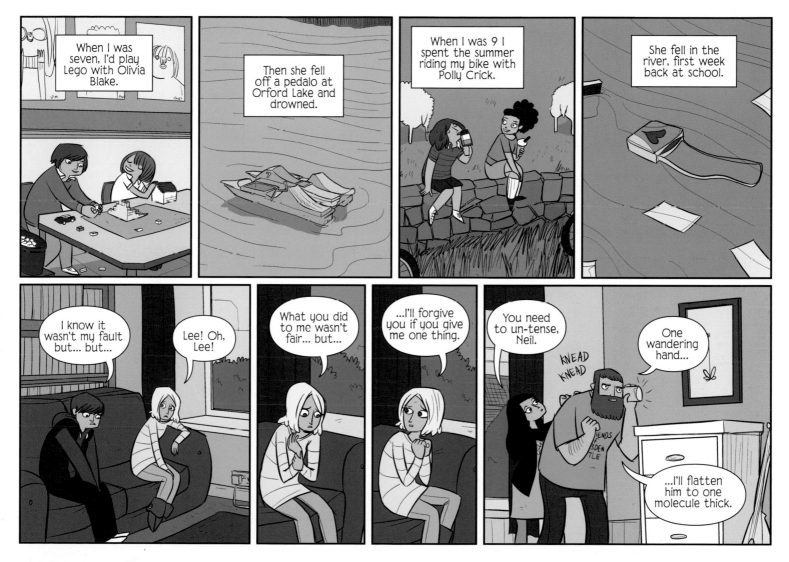

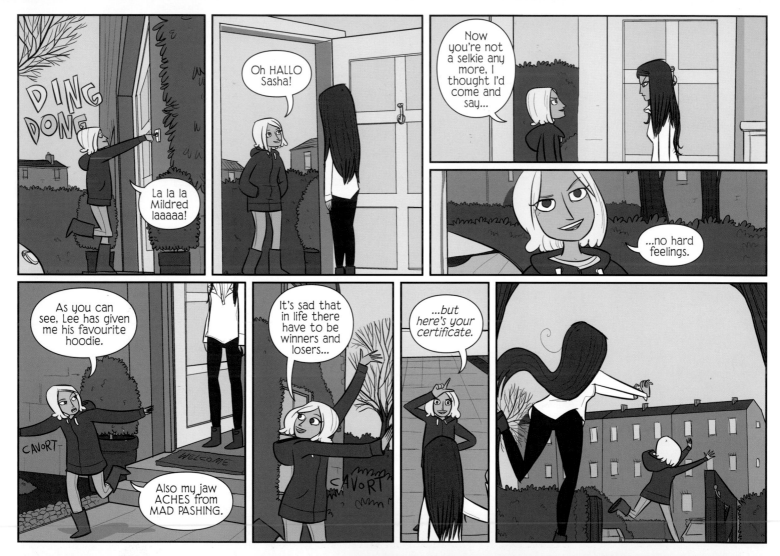

The Case of the Fire Inside

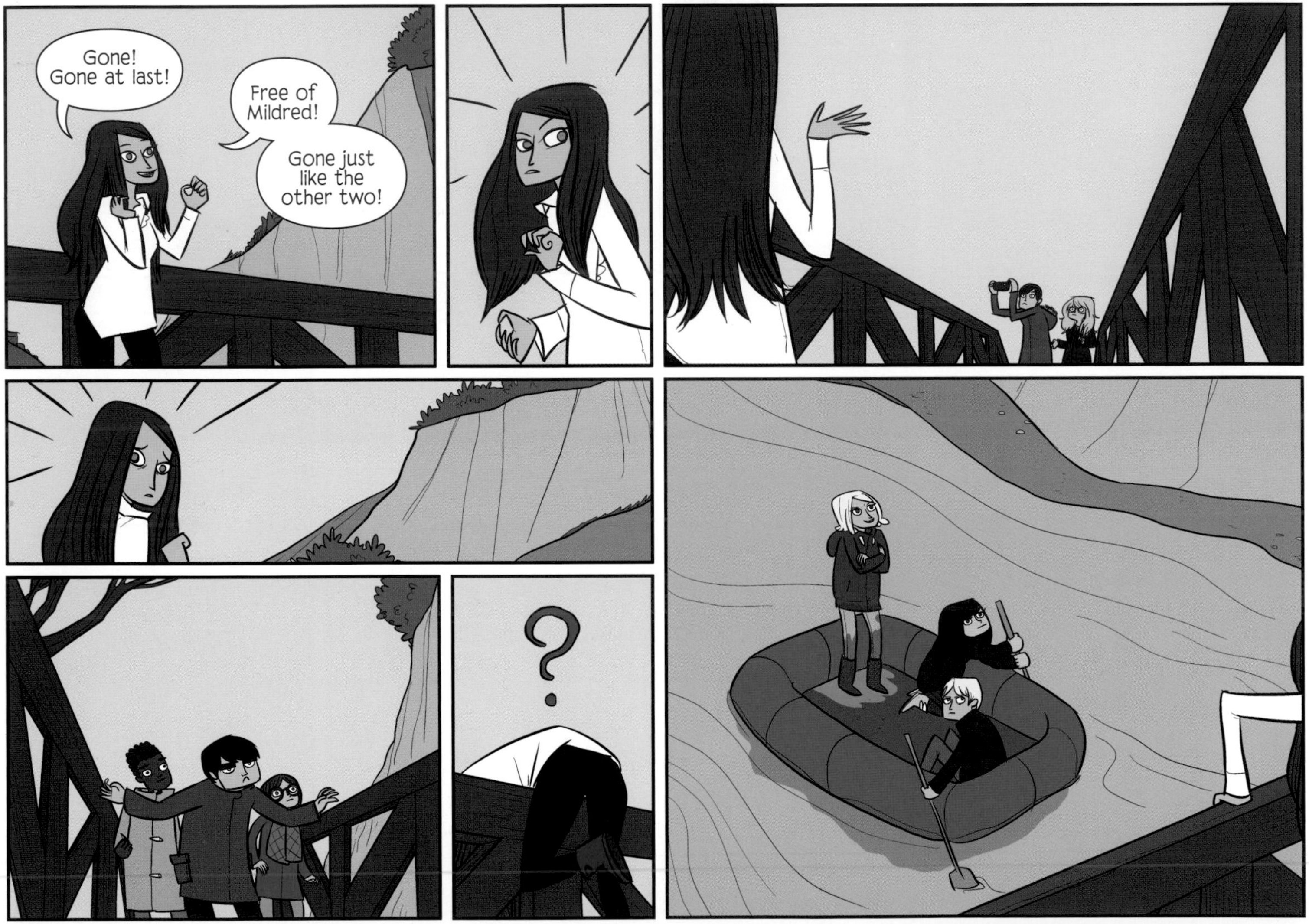
Gone! Gone at last!
Free of Mildred!
Gone just like the other two!
?

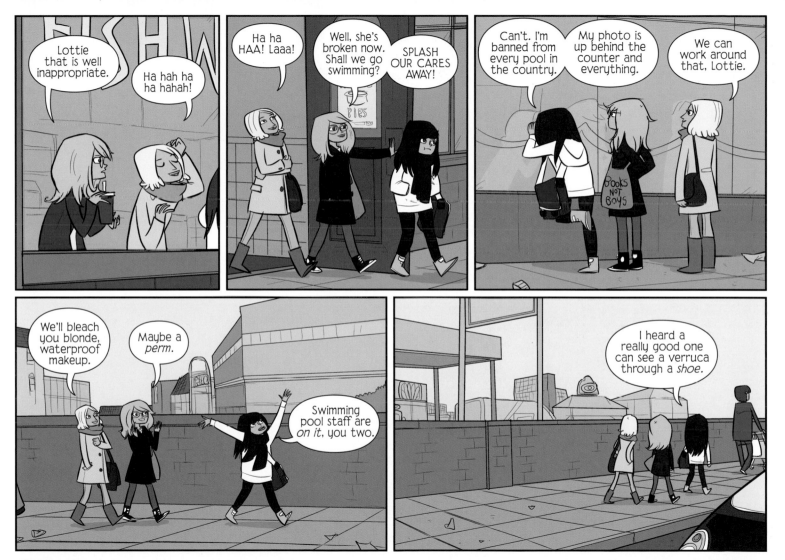

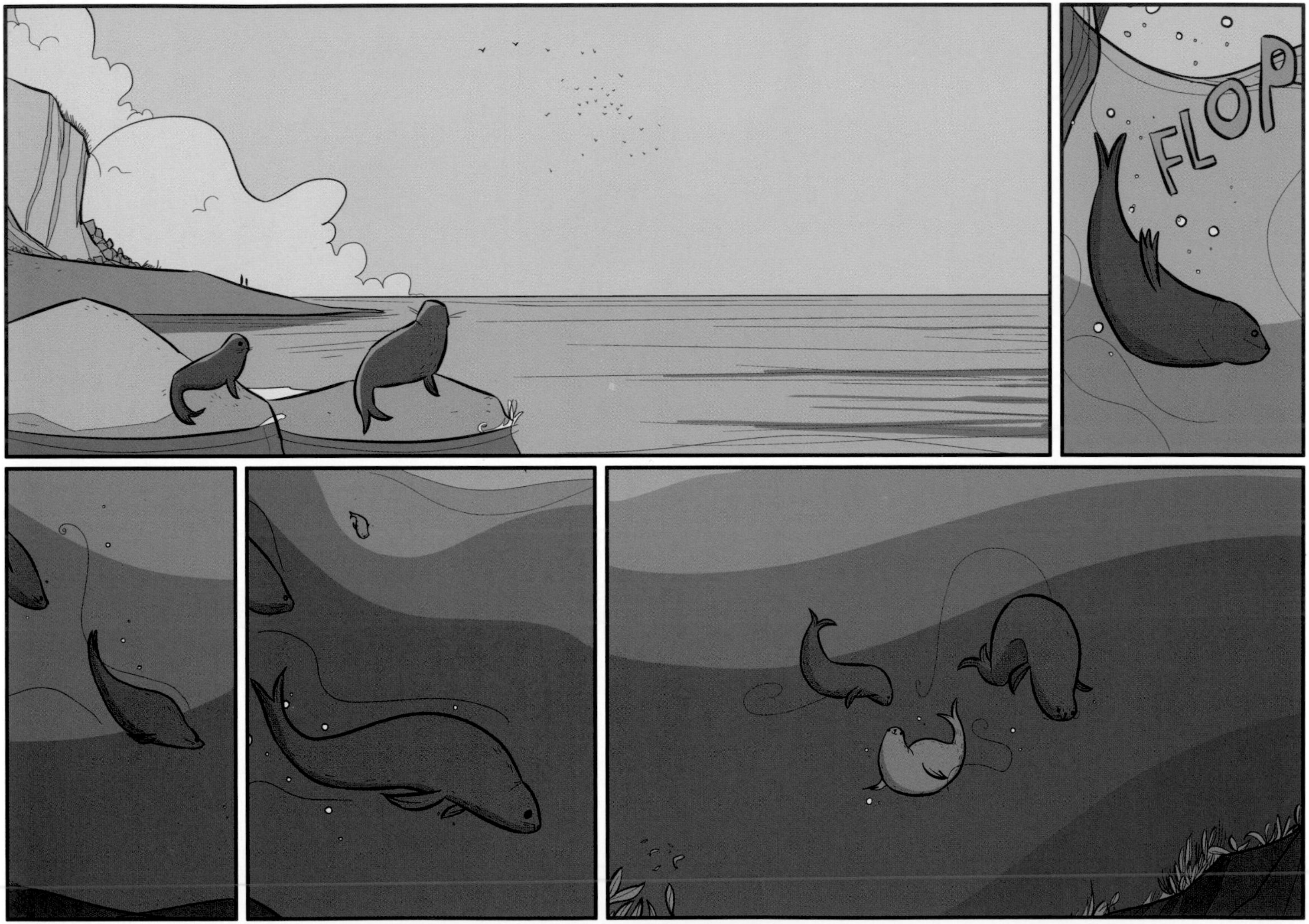
FLOP

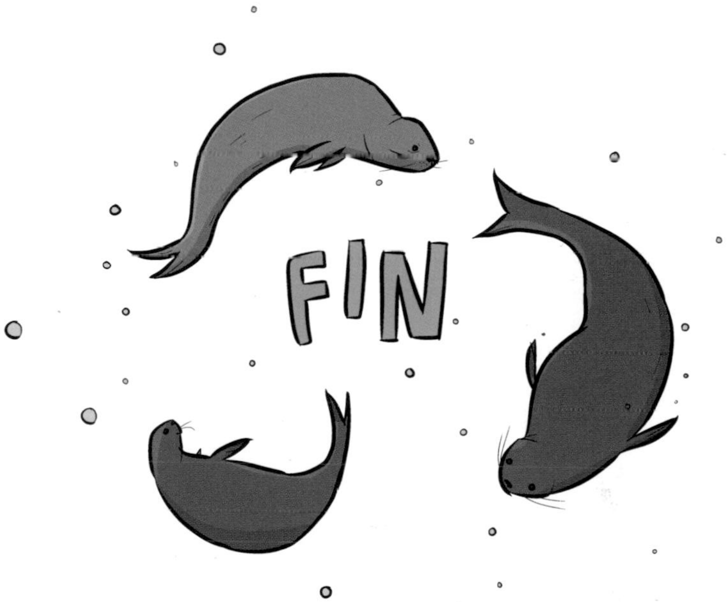
FIN

# ELLEN
## (THE SELKIE)

LONG HAIR DEFENDS MODESTY

Where is it?

WASHING LINE THIEF

GHOSTLY AT WINDOWS

BIG, SEAL-LIKE EYES

GNAM GNAM GNAM

FERAL EATING STYLE

Selkies are alluring mythological seal-people who emerge from the sea and make lovers of the men or women who find their sealskins. There are lots of variations on the myth, probably because at the time folklorists cooked up these tales, there was no Wikipedia to check your facts against. At best you had to get the Microsoft Encarta CD-ROM, and only rich kids had that.

Ellen the selkie is sweet-natured and kind, as you imagine a seal would be as you stare into its big liquid eyes. Sasha is more vindictive, as a seal probably actually is as it whacks you over the head with its big muscular tail after you looked sideways at half-eaten fish it was "saving for later". I don't claim to be an expert on seals any more than I am an expert on any other animal, but I do know that they are excellent players of the "arrayed honking horn", making them the only animal with musical talent apart from the praying mantis*.

*Note to self: check this on Wikipedia/Encarta '98.

SCHOOL UNIFORMS STRAW BOATER

SKINNY TIE

LONG PONY TAIL WITH A BOW

SKIRT ALWAYS BELOW THE KNEE

WHITE SOCKS

GRISWALDS

ST TIBBS

READY TO SWIM 100% OF THE TIME

SWIMMING COSTUME

# SASHA
## (ALSO THE SELKIE)

PADDED JACKETS, SHARP HAIR, EXPENSIVE BAGS

HISSSSSS

BASICALLY MURDEROUS

ALSO ALLURING

SHE IS "OF MONEY"

One question this story never really answers about Sasha is, how did she manage to to find a family who buys her sweet padded jackets and nice bags and all that? My feeling was that she was adopted as a foundling by a rich family.

I don't think that family is to blame for the trail of drowned little girls Sasha has left in her wake, but at the same time, they should perhaps have noticed that the roll-call at their little angel's birthday parties was starting to look a bit sparse. Also, Lee must have spent a long time in denial. Either that, or he's not very bright. (He's not very bright.)

SACHA'S FRIEND
- ALWAYS WEARS SAME COLOURS
- PROBABLY GOOD AT TURNING A "BLIND EYE"

# THE SELKIE-DADDY

FAMILY HAIRCUT

HE'S BIG

MUCH BLUBBER

While Ellen and Sasha have no problem blending in on land (apart from the illiteracy and the drownings), their father resembles the kind of wild figure one would cross the road to avoid. While it is only fair to take each person on their personal merits, there is something about the combination of massive shirtless bulk, untamed beard and stinking, oily seal-cape that quickens the pulse in a primal way.

Your donation of seventy-five cents could buy this man a comb.

GET HIM IN TROUSERS A.S.A.P

PROBABLY SHOULDN'T BE LIVING ON HER OWN ANY MORE

CLASSIC TARTAN SHOPPING TROLLEY

PADDED JACKET AT 45° TO THE YOUNGSTERS

A LOST FIGURE

THICK GLASSES, SELF-CUT HAIR

REVITALISED BY LOOKING AFTER "ELLEN"

THANK YOU, MUM!

A MUTUALLY BENEFICIAL ARRANGEMENT

MARCHES WITH PURPOSE

SOLID.

GOES INTO THE SEA

# ENERGY CROW

I've written you a book, Barry! With COMPLIMENTS!

Energy Crow
by C. Grote

Between *The Case Of The Lonely One* and this book, I wrote a short story called "Murder She Writes", where Lottie is taken on a writers' retreat by the author Shelley Winters, and has to solve a murder. Having successfully foiled the killers, she pens her own book designed to expand young minds. That book is called *Energy Crow*.

Under no circumstances should any young minds be allowed to read the full manuscript of *Energy Crow*, which may be a the most degenerate publication ever aimed at under-5s.

I well reckon this book is "educational" heh heh

Energy Crow

# ELLEN'S "MUM"

"Mum" is a sad figure. I felt very protective of her when I was writing this story. Her life isn't great until Ellen arrives, but somehow two people in quite dire circumstances make the best of things. When the story originally ran on the web, people asked me after Mum walked into the sea, "did she end her own life?" I made things a little bit ambiguous, which was mean, because a lot of people liked her and felt protective of her the way I did.

My feeling was that she was a selkie too, whose land-born husband had died, but stayed around for her children long after they had needed her, slowly becoming vague and disconnected. Ellen wakes something up in her, and she leaves with her own seal-skin in her tartan shopping trolley and returns to the sea.

So this version of *The Case Of The Fire Inside* has a happier ending than it did when I first made the pages. It's the same ending I always saw in my head, but I feel better for having finally put it on the page. That's assuming that the grey seal is Mum. It might not be. But I like to think that it is.

# LEE

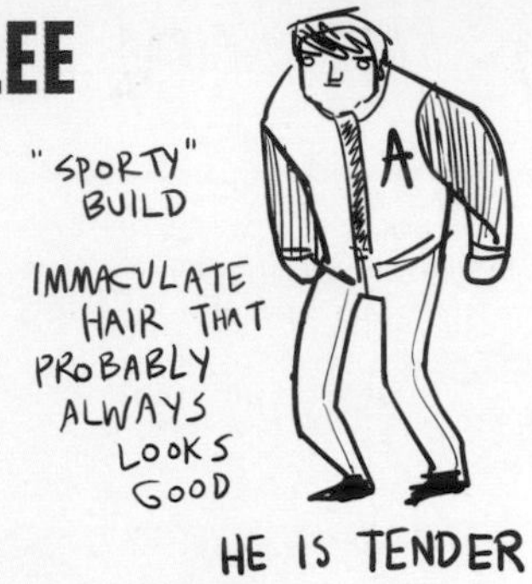
"SPORTY" BUILD
IMMACULATE HAIR THAT PROBABLY ALWAYS LOOKS GOOD
HE IS TENDER

Lee was first seen in *The Case Of The Lonely One* as one of the "bad kids" Mildred joins in detention. "Bad" is probably the wrong word, but one imagines that he is the sort of boy who would begin throwing a tennis ball around in class the second the teacher leaves the classroom to do a bit of photocopying. This isn't his fault, it's a medical condition suffered by many youths who were exposed at a young age to sporting goods stores.

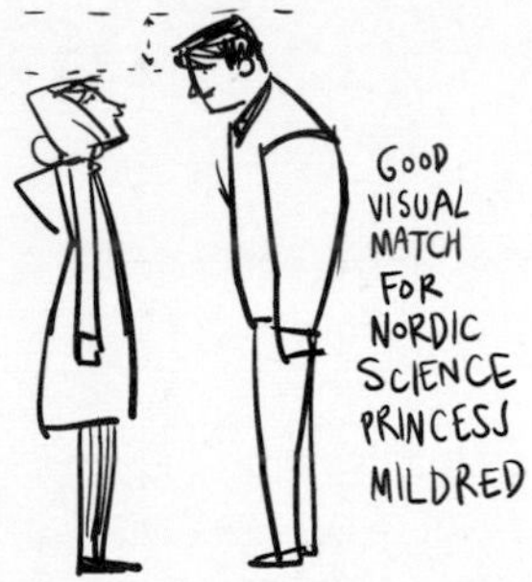
GOOD VISUAL MATCH FOR NORDIC SCIENCE PRINCESS MILDRED

# CECILE

Cecile Craven isn't quite four in this story, but already she is beginning to develop a powerful agency. With just three summers under her belt, she's able to intimidate her mild-mannered brother Sonny. There's little telling what kind of person Cecile will grow up into, but I've long felt that she represents a "clear and present danger" to good order in Tackleford.

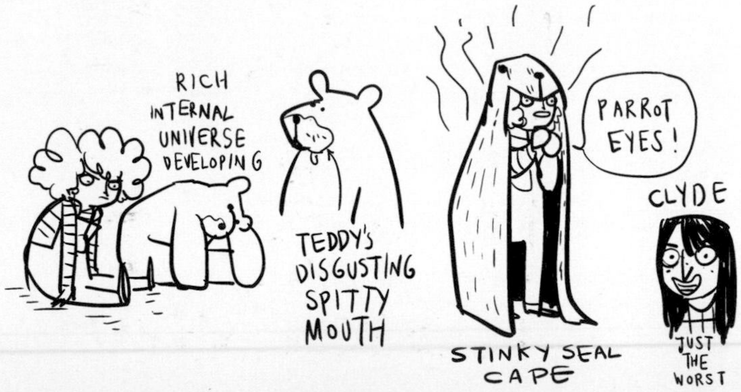
RICH INTERNAL UNIVERSE DEVELOPING
TEDDY'S DISGUSTING SPITTY MOUTH
PARROT EYES!
STINKY SEAL CAPE
CLYDE
JUST THE WORST

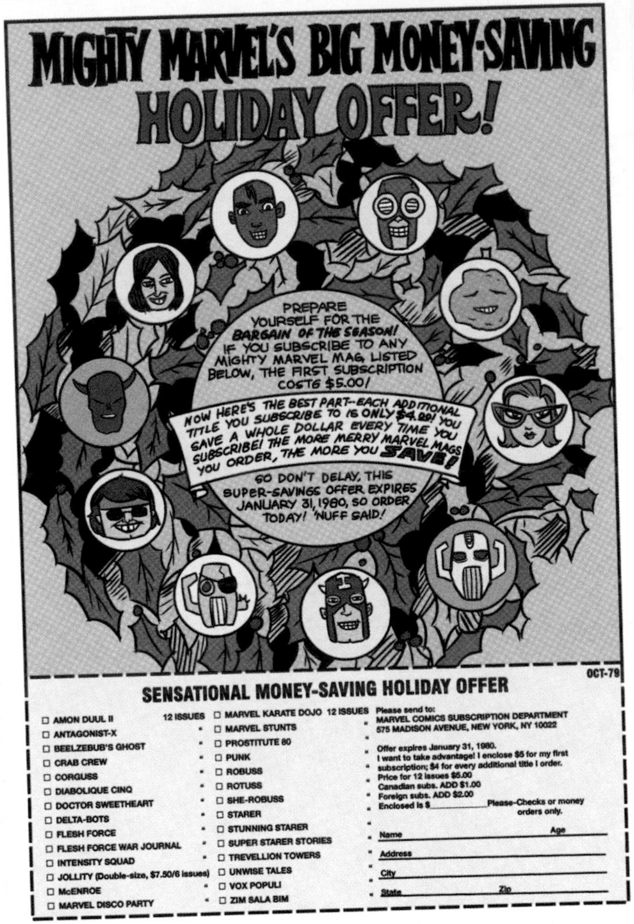
MIGHTY MARVEL'S BIG MONEY-SAVING HOLIDAY OFFER!
PREPARE YOURSELF FOR THE BARGAIN OF THE SEASON! IF YOU SUBSCRIBE TO ANY MIGHTY MARVEL MAG LISTED BELOW, THE FIRST SUBSCRIPTION COSTS $5.00!
NOW HERE'S THE BEST PART--EACH ADDITIONAL TITLE YOU SUBSCRIBE TO IS ONLY $4.00! YOU SAVE A WHOLE DOLLAR EVERY TIME YOU SUBSCRIBE! THE MORE MERRY MARVEL MAGS YOU ORDER, THE MORE YOU SAVE!
SO DON'T DELAY, THIS SUPER-SAVINGS OFFER EXPIRES JANUARY 31, 1980, SO ORDER TODAY! 'NUFF SAID!
OCT-79
SENSATIONAL MONEY-SAVING HOLIDAY OFFER
☐ AMON DUUL II 12 ISSUES
☐ ANTAGONIST-X "
☐ BEELZEBUB'S GHOST "
☐ CRAB CREW "
☐ CORGUSS "
☐ DIABOLIQUE CINQ "
☐ DOCTOR SWEETHEART "
☐ DELTA-BOTS "
☐ FLESH FORCE "
☐ FLESH FORCE WAR JOURNAL "
☐ INTENSITY SQUAD "
☐ JOLLITY (Double-size, $7.50/6 issues)
☐ McENROE "
☐ MARVEL DISCO PARTY "
☐ MARVEL KARATE DOJO 12 ISSUES
☐ MARVEL STUNTS "
☐ PROSTITUTE 80 "
☐ PUNK "
☐ ROBUSS "
☐ ROTUSS "
☐ SHE-ROBUSS "
☐ STARER "
☐ STUNNING STARER "
☐ SUPER STARER STORIES "
☐ TREVELLION TOWERS "
☐ UNWISE TALES "
☐ VOX POPULI "
☐ ZIM SALA BIM "
Please send to:
MARVEL COMICS SUBSCRIPTION DEPARTMENT
575 MADISON AVENUE, NEW YORK, NY 10022
Offer expires January 31, 1980.
I want to take advantage! I enclose $5 for my first subscription; $4 for every additional title I order.
Price for 12 issues $5.00
Canadian subs. ADD $1.00
Foreign subs. ADD $2.00
Enclosed is $ ______ Please-Checks or money orders only.
Name ______ Age ______
Address ______
City ______
State ______ Zip ______

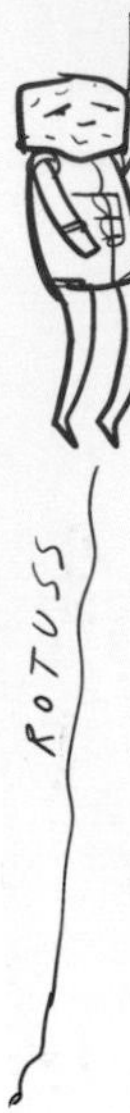
ROTUSS

# SONNY'S TOYS

I have an irresponsible attitude to character creation, as the fake subscription ad above confirms. Stop me before I do it again.

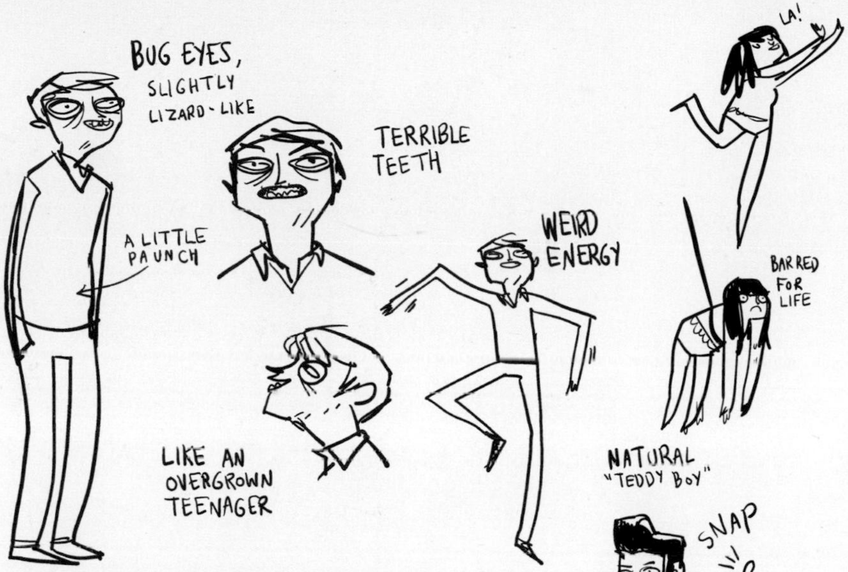
BUG EYES,
SLIGHTLY
LIZARD-LIKE
TERRIBLE
TEETH
A LITTLE
PAUNCH
WEIRD
ENERGY
LA!
BARRED
FOR
LIFE
LIKE AN
OVERGROWN
TEENAGER

# GRANPA JOE

Granpa (short for "Grandpa", which is short for "Grandfather", which is itself short for "Lord Prince Grandfather, Patriarch and Duke") Joe is a scallywag. His marriage to Grandma Josephine probably didn't last very long. It's likely that he never really connected with such concepts as "responsibility" or "being around". I imagine that the last straw was when he stripped down a motorcycle engine on the dinner table, while the best tablecloth was on it, and his mother-in-law was visiting. But the things that made Joe a terrible husband and a dangerous father make him a great grandparent. Freed of the need to do anything so quotidien as provide for his brood, he can concentrate on the important things—inappropriate anecdotes, forbidden treats, trips to not entirely on-the-level tradesmen with his descendents in tow. Not in toe, though. That mortoned monster needs to be kept firmly under wraps.

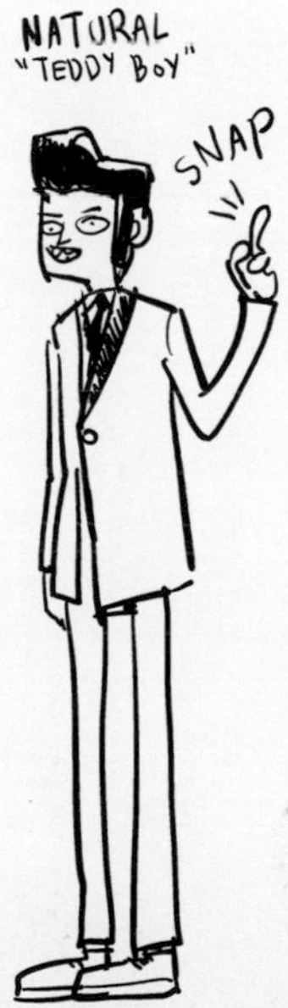
NATURAL
"TEDDY BOY"
SNAP

# THE RULES OF THE POOL

The "Rules Of The Pool" poster is a British design classic, which is to say that the government didn't bother to update it for thirty years, and when they finally did, the person who did the new one did a terrible job of it. Generations of British teenagers were introduced to the word "petting" this way, long after it passed out of common use.

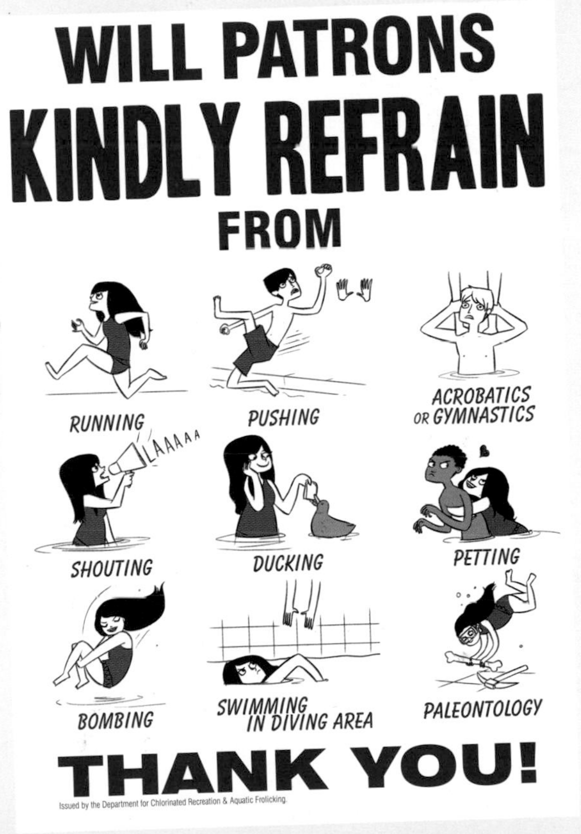
WILL PATRONS
KINDLY REFRAIN
FROM
RUNNING
PUSHING
ACROBATICS
OR GYMNASTICS
LAAAAAA
SHOUTING
DUCKING
PETTING
BOMBING
SWIMMING
IN DIVING AREA
PALEONTOLOGY
THANK YOU!
Issued by the Department for Chlorinated Recreation & Aquatic Frolicking.

# JOHN ALLISON

Born in a hidden village deep within the British Alps, John Allison came into this world a respectable baby with style and taste. Having been exposed to American comics at an early age, he spent decades honing his keen mind and his massive body in order to burn out this colonial cultural infection.

One of the longest continuously publishing independent web-based cartoonists, John has plied his trade since the late nineties moving from *Bobbins* to *Scary Go Round* to *Bad Machinery*, developing the deeply weird world of Tackleford long after many of his fellow artists were ground into dust and bones by Time Itself.

He has only once shed a single tear, but you only meet Sergio Aragonés for the first time once.

John resides in Letchworth Garden City, England and is known to his fellow villagers only as He Who Has Conquered.

—Contributed by Richard Stevens III

**ALSO BY JOHN ALLISON!**

bad machinery
The Case Of The Team Spirit
1
JOHN ALLISON

**BAD MACHINERY, VOLUME 1:**
**THE CASE OF THE TEAM SPIRIT**
By John Allison
ISBN 978-1-62010-387-6
**Pocket Edition In Stores Now!**

bad machinery
The Case Of The Good Boy
2
JOHN ALLISON

**BAD MACHINERY, VOLUME 2:**
**THE CASE OF THE GOOD BOY**
By John Allison
ISBN 978-1-62010-421-7
**Pocket Edition In Stores Now!**

bad machinery
The Case Of The Simple Soul
3
JOHN ALLISON

**BAD MACHINERY, VOLUME 3:**
**THE CASE OF THE SIMPLE SOUL**
By John Allison
ISBN 978-1-62010-443-9
**Pocket Edition In Stores Now!**

bad machinery
The Case Of The Lonely One
BOOKS NOT BOYS
4
JOHN ALLISON

**BAD MACHINERY, VOL. 4:**
**THE CASE OF THE LONELY ONE**
By John Allison
ISBN 978-1-62010-457-6
**Pocket Edition In Stores Now!**

bad machinery
The Case Of The Unwelcome Visitor
6
JOHN ALLISON

**BAD MACHINERY, VOL. 6: THE CASE OF THE UNWELCOME VISITOR**
By John Allison
ISBN 978-1-62010-543-6
**Pocket Edition Coming September 2018!**

bad machinery
THE CASE OF THE FORKED ROAD
JOHN ALLISON

**BAD MACHINERY, VOL. 7:**
**THE CASE OF THE FORKED ROAD**
By John Allison
ISBN 978-1-62010-390-6
**Pocket Edition Coming December 201**

ONI PRESS
www.onipress.com

bad machinery
**THE CASE OF THE MODERN MEN**

Coming Soon!

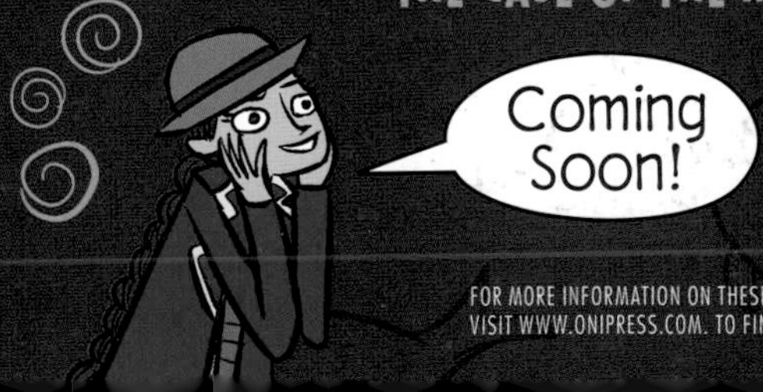

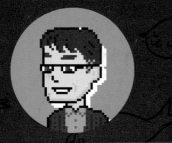

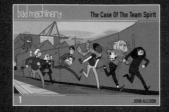

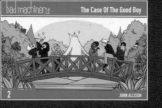

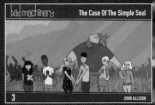

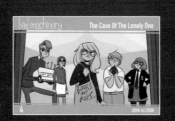

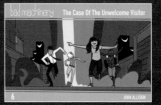

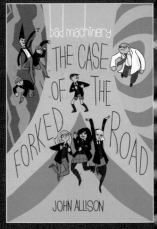

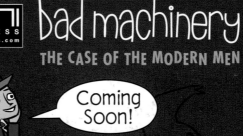